MAD GOD

"The Green Priests are not an order of suicides," Granny said calmly. "If they were, they'd all be dead. They are an order of people who *plan* to commit suicide, which is an entirely different thing. I should think that was obvious."

"Nissy's done more than plan," Jehane said bitterly. "She's gotten her luck bound into that cat of hers, so when the cat dies, she will, too. And I used to like Floradazul."

Granny shook her head. "You Benedictis! Don't any of you ever think things through? Floradazul was a spanking-new cat when I gave her to Nerissa; she's got at least eight lives to go. Even if she wastes a few more getting kicked by camels, she has a good chance of lasting another seventy or eighty years. Nerissa will probably die of old age long before the cat does. Drink your tea."

—From "Mad God"
by PATRICIA C. WREDE

Ace books edited by Will Shetterly and Emma Bull

LIAVEK
LIAVEK: THE PLAYERS OF LUCK
LIAVEK: WIZARD'S ROW
LIAVEK: SPELLS OF BINDING

Ace books by Will Shetterly

CATS HAVE NO LORD
WITCH BLOOD

Ace books by Emma Bull

WAR FOR THE OAKS

SPELLS OF BINDING

edited by
Will Shetterly
and Emma Bull

ACE BOOKS, NEW YORK

This book is an Ace original edition, and has never been previously published.

LIAVEK:
SPELLS OF BINDING

An Ace Book / published by arrangement with the editors

PRINTING HISTORY
Ace edition/November 1988

Cover art by Darrell Sweet.
Maps by Jack Wickwire.

For information address: The Berkley Publishing Group, 200 Madison Avenue, New York, New York 10016.

ISBN: 0-441-48191-4

Ace Books are published by The Berkley Publishing Group, 200 Madison Avenue, New York, New York 10016.

PRINTED IN THE UNITED STATES OF AMERICA

10 9 8 7 6 5 4 3 2 1

To Liz, who moved Liavek to Ontario;
and to Lynda, Heather, Jean, and Dot,
who plug Liavek in Pennsylvania.

CONTENTS

Tichen
EMPIRE OF TICHEN
THE GREAT WASTE
Trader's Town
SILVERSPINE
Liavek
Saltigos
Ombaya City
Hrothvek
Crab Island
Gold Harbor
THE SEA OF LUCK
Ka Thow
Ka Zhir
N

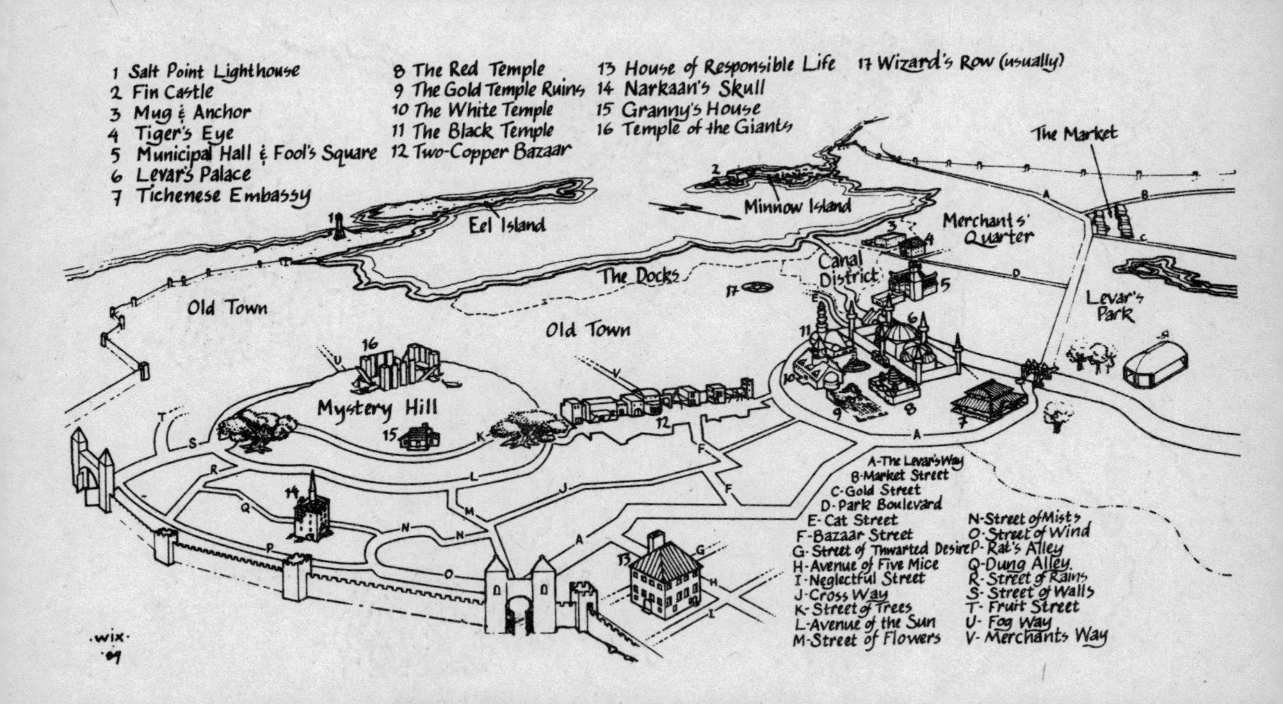
1 Salt Point Lighthouse
2 Fin Castle
3 Mug & Anchor
4 Tiger's Eye
5 Municipal Hall & Fool's Square
6 Levar's Palace
7 Tichenese Embassy
8 The Red Temple
9 The Gold Temple Ruins
10 The White Temple
11 The Black Temple
12 Two-Copper Bazaar
13 House of Responsible Life
14 Narkaan's Skull
15 Granny's House
16 Temple of the Giants
17 Wizard's Row (usually)
The Market
Eel Island
Minnow Island
Merchants' Quarter
Canal District
The Docks
Old Town
Old Town
Levar's Park
Mystery Hill
A-The Levar's Way
B-Market Street
C-Gold Street
D-Park Boulevard
E-Cat Street
F-Bazaar Street
G-Street of Thwarted Desire
H-Avenue of Five Mice
I-Neglectful Street
J-Cross Way
K-Street of Trees
L-Avenue of the Sun
M-Street of Flowers
N-Street of Mists
O-Street of Wind
P-Rat's Alley
Q-Dung Alley
R-Street of Rains
S-Street of Walls
T-Fruit Street
U-Fog Way
V-Merchants Way
.wix.
'89

Riding the Hammer

by John M. Ford

COPPER HAD A lantern in his hand, a clock on his mind, and murder in his heart. It was the second week of Wind, and cold by night; Copper wore a jacket and trousers of black leather, high black boots, and felt the chill clear as the moon in the sky.

He stepped over a few loose spikes, shone the light past the barrels of tieplates, the stacks of ties and rail, the wall of the construction shack. Beyond it, Saltigos was sleeping, flat roofs silvered by the nearly full moon. It was less than a quarter hour to midnight. Copper didn't have long to find Deno and put him on the road— "Deno!" he shouted. There wasn't any reply.

"Copper, hey, Copper," someone sang out. It was Peysin, the track foreman, a woollen cloak tossed over her work coverall. She had a lantern out, and a mallet and wrench hung from her belt, looking oddly like weapons. "Lookin' for Deno, right?"

"Of course I'm looking for him," Copper snapped, then in a softer voice, "Sorry, Peyse. Not your fault. You know where he is?"

"This way. But you're not gonna like it."

"Oh, I know that," Copper said, and followed Peysin back to the track gang's house. The lights were low—blue damn, Copper thought, the lights ought to be *out* at this hour—and three men were on the porch, not quite sitting, more dropped untidily. Two were tracklayers. The middle one was Deno.

Copper kicked the sole of Deno's boot, hard. The driver didn't stir. "What was it?"

Peysin said "Gold Harbor rum. The fella that brought it in came whinin' to me that these three took it from him, or I'd never have found any o'the lot." She shuttered her lantern, crossed her arms. "They won't be movin' 'til morning."

"Gold Harbor rum, only one part'll be moving in the morning," Copper said, "and that'll gallop. All right," he said, no longer really angry; there wasn't anything else to be done here. He pulled a gold ten-levar piece from his leather jacket, shoved it into Deno's breast pocket. The man didn't even stir. "When he's sensible again, tell him to celebrate as long as he can on that: it's his severance."

"He's a good driver," Peysin said mildly.

"But not for me. You want to take him on the track crew, that's your job and your business. I'm done with him."

"Your department. Where are you going?"

"Someone's got to drive the midnight." He glanced once more sharply at Deno, then turned away. "And all honest men are sleeping now." He headed for the railway tracks.

The Lucksea Coastal & Northerly Railway stopped here, half a mile from the Saltigos town limit, on the landward side. There was still a political war going on with the wagoners as to when, if ever, tracks would run to the docks. There was one track complete to Liavek, sixty miles down the coast; there, the glass roof of the Main Station was already up, though the Railway would not officially open until the Levar's Birthday celebrations next year. Here there was only a temporary station, a wooden box with an all-purpose office and a mostly purposeless freight room. Just past the station, spur tracks switched out to the engine shed and the tracklayers' buildings.

By the time Copper reached the tracks, the hostler was unhooking the two-horse hitch that had pulled *Brazen Venture* from the shed; the little steam engine sat silent on her six coupled wheels while one engine tender bailed water into her tank and another shoveled wood chips into the fuel bunker. *Venture* was the smallest functional engine the line had, her bronze boiler and pipes lagged in raw wool and cased in oak, the wood further sheathed in sheet brass: in the light of lanterns and the fat moon, she looked like a great shiny beetle.

Zelle, the station supervisor, was locking up four iron-bound dispatch boxes with keys on an enormous ring. She looked up as Copper approached. "Deno?"

"No Deno, and no more Deno, either."

"Oh, Copper, you didn't kill him."

"Knew I'd forgotten something." He looked at the engine, at the sky. "How long 'til midnight?"

Zelle snapped the last lock. "Spitting distance."

"I'll need a hot start then. Is Omalfi awake?"

"He is now," Omalfi said, stepping onto the station platform, sashing a black velvet gown over his red nightshirt. He stretched out his arms and went dancing barefoot down the platform steps, singing "There's no rest for the wicked, no, and the wizard isn't born who can sleep when the moon turns full—*ah!*" He snapped his fingers, shooting sparks. "Figured you'd need me."

"Just warm her up, Omalfi," Copper said, but he was smiling.

Omalfi bowed elaborately and skipped off to *Brazen Venture*'s side. Copper picked up the dispatch cases; Zelle said, "I'll get your clock." Copper nodded and followed the wizard.

Omalfi was standing in the little cabin of the engine, feet and arms spread, sleeves pushed back. The moonlight caught a sheen of sweat on his forehead and neck; there was a dull red glow around his splayed fingers, and another coming to life in the engine's firebox. Copper shoved the cases into a corner of the cabin, vaulted up, and spun the stoker crank. A steel auger, like those that raised grain from underground storage, ground woodchips into the open firebox, and they flared.

Omalfi leaned forward, bracing his hands on the boiler above the fire. Red-gold light rippled over his shoulders, through his hands, and the engine shuddered slightly; a valve spat steam, and there was a rumble as the water bubbled in the boiler tubes. Copper stoked the fire, checked it for even burn, rapped the glass tube that showed water properly over the crown sheet, ready to boil and drive the pistons. Hot starting was dangerous: sudden steam could rip the piping apart, seize the pistons; uneven heat could buckle the firebox. But without magic it took an hour or more to raise steam, even in a little engine like *Venture*. And it was midnight.

"Clock," Zelle said, and handed up the timepiece. It was drum-shaped, the span of a hand across and half that thick, a brass case with a glass face and two black hands, showing just a hair past the hour. Copper reached behind Omalfi and hung it on the cabin wall just above the driver's seat.

Omalfi stood straight, closed his eyes, breathed deep, and clenched his fists. The firebox blazed up, and Copper kicked its door shut. Omalfi exhaled, clapped his hands. "All yours, driver," he said. "There's a pillow calling my name." He hopped down from the cabin.

"Thanks, Omalfi," Copper said, and checked the valves and glasses. Steam was building fast, and power with it. One of the tenders struck light to the oil headlamp, and the beam lit up nightmist and bright steel rails for a quarter-mile ahead.

Zelle said "Copper."

He turned.

"How long have *you* been awake?"

Copper made a meaningless gesture and cracked a valve.

"You take a half-day off before you come back, understand?" Zelle said. "Eight hours' sleep before you drive again." She paused. "It's your own rule, Copper."

"I'll bring her back on the nine tomorrow," Copper said, and pulled down the throttle. The wheels ground forward. "Go answer Omalfi's pillow," he shouted back, and watched Zelle's face twist up before she was lost in the steam and the dark and the distance behind him. Copper let out more throttle, cranked the stoker, blew a long low note on the whistle as he left the limits of Saltigos. He looked at the clock: eleven minutes after midnight, eleven minutes late.

And who would care, and who would know, Syvann—or, oh, any number of people—would have said, when no one in the world was holding a clock to him, when damn few were awake at all; but Copper knew. And he knew that the world would change. In time. In railway, click-wheeled, steam-driven, brass-geared time.

Copper shot a glance at the dispatch cases in the corner. For twenty levars, anything you could get into a box would leave Saltigos exactly at midnight, to arrive at Liavek Station near Merchant's Gate within three hours. Copper knew perfectly well that no one used the service for speed, but rather for security; a train moved at three or four times the speed of a coach, and the highway robbers hadn't caught up yet.

Deno had been a coach driver before he joined the Railway, and he'd never stopped thinking like a coach driver. He had no doubt been quite sure he could sober up and get the train into Liavek by dawn, which was when the boxes would be claimed anyway.

Copper knew better. In time, three-hour dispatch would be counted on. And then it would become necessary, just like half-copper newsrags and fresh fish for breakfast and sorcerous weather reports.

And for now—well, for now the Railway needed the twenty levars a case.

Copper listened for the slip of wheels below him, and satisfied that he had traction, gave *Brazen Venture* more steam, making up time that only a handful of people on earth would ever know he had lost.

The clock had just touched the one mark when Copper saw the flicker in his headlamp, something white that cast a long dark shadow on the rails, something on the track. He wound in the throttle, blew a high note on the whistle. The thing stayed there as the engine bore down on it. It was upright and still and looked suddenly terribly human. Copper shoved the throttle all the way in and grabbed the brake wheel, spinning it, clamping the blocks down on the engine's small wheels. Sparks flew, and metal and wood ground against one another with a hideous noise.

The engine slowed to a walk. The person on the tracks didn't move. Copper shouted. No effect. He swung down on the cabin steps, hopped off. The engine crawled on. Copper ran ahead of it, jumped for the white figure standing between the rails. He saw that it was a girl (perhaps fifteen or sixteen years old, in a long white dress) just before he struck her and rolled with her out of the engine's path.

Copper looked up. *Brazen Venture* squeaked to a stop perhaps twenty paces beyond where the girl had been standing. He looked down. Well, there she was, looking up at him, silent, dust on her face and her dress—nightgown, really.

"Would you like to explain what you were doing?" Copper said. There had been a fad for youth suicide in Liavek over the last year, but by all reports it was over, and had leaned more toward quiet poison-swallowing than violent ends—and besides, they were still at least twenty miles away from Liavek, more than thirty from Saltigos.

"I'm on my way to Liavek," she said. Her voice had a strange resonance, as if she were speaking through a hollow pipe.

"The passenger service doesn't start 'til next year," Copper said, and then looked around. There was plenty of moonlight, and the mist was thin, but he didn't see a coach anywhere, or a cart, or even a pony. And the coast road was a long way off—another insistence of the wagoners' association. "How *did* you get out here?"

"I'm on my way to Liavek," the girl said again, then, "Are you the iron-road man? Will you take me to the Liavek Station?"

"I suppose I'm going to, aren't I," Copper said, and helped her stand up. "Rule of stranded travellers—" He stopped, looked around, with a sudden unpleasant thought. Stranded travellers were an old bandit trick. But there was no one out there, just moon-silvered dirt, the Silverspine to the north, and rails to two horizons.

Copper led the girl in white to the engine. As she climbed into the cabin, he noticed that she wasn't wearing shoes—but her feet were pale and soft and quite clean; she couldn't have walked barefoot any distance at all.

She glanced around the cabin once, indifferently, and looked down the tracks. "Are we going to Liavek now?"

"That's right," Copper said. "And then we're going to find a few things out." He released the brakes, poked and stoked the fire, let the throttle out. The rods creaked and they started rolling. "Just to get a head start, do you have a name?"

"Krisia," the girl said.

Copper waited a moment, but the girl just looked up the tracks; Copper sighed and pointed to the dispatch cases. "You might be more comfortable sitting on those," he said, "and you'd definitely be more out of my way."

Krisia nodded slowly and sat. Copper cranked the stoker and worked the throttle out to mainline speed. Then he heard the tick of the clock, reminding him that he'd lost time again, and pulled the lever wide. The wind chirped past the windows. The wheels clicked like a steel heart. Copper said "If you look, there, you can see the lights on the city walls."

There was no reply. Copper said "We have to run all the way around the city—the Station's on the west side, by Merchant's Gate. Look, is someone meeting you? Expecting you?"

Nothing.

Copper turned.

Krisia was gone.

Copper stared, feeling ice in his chest. She had jumped, at speed—but no, she couldn't have jumped, not without his seeing, not without her bumping his *arm,* damn it. He looked back over the rear of the engine, but knew already there was no place she could be hanging on or hiding there. He let go of the throttle lever and bent down by the cases where she'd been sitting: there was a little bit of dust on the topmost box, a faint trace of a damp footprint, evaporating even as he watched.

All right, he thought, it was some kind of magic, an illusion (did illusions leave footprints? He didn't know). But why would anyone cast—

He looked hard at the four locked boxes. They seemed to be the ones Zelle had loaded. He rapped his knuckles on them: solid wood and iron. But then, anyone who could cast an image of a person that was solid enough to be flying-tackled would surely have no problem with a stack of boxes.

Copper turned. He was nearly to the eastern edge of the city, doing full speed and then some. He eased off the throttle, trying at once to make sense of it and not to think about it. He didn't have keys to the boxes. There was nothing at all he could do about them until he got into the Station—and *then* what exactly was he going to say?

Brazen Venture glided around the last curve. Liavek Station stood ahead, its glass roof luminous from within. The artisans worked day and night on it: it was a showplace, a Civic Landmark. The Railway might have to haul valuables at twenty levars the case to get tracks laid and engines maintained, but there was no problem at all with glowing glass pavilions. Copper shoved down the throttle and wound up the brakes, coming to a halt just at the center of the main platform.

No one met him. There was a boy cleaning the windows of the supervisor's office. Copper swung out of the cabin—keeping an eye on the boxes—and asked the boy, "Hey! Where's Tavish?"

"At home, sir, expected a little before dawn."

Copper gritted his teeth. If only all his problems were as easy to dismiss as Deno. "Then you go there and you get him back here now. Tell him Copper sent you."

"What shall I tell him when he fires me, Master Driver?"

"Tell him you're a driver trainee now, and only I can fire you."

The boy bowed and scooted off. Copper sat down in the engine cabin, leaned against the strongboxes, and wondered just what would turn out to be inside them.

The answer, he learned within the hour, was: two sets of legal documents, one dozen uncut gemstones, and a matched pair of flintlock pistols intended as a gift for the Margrave of Someplace-or-Other's wedding. In other words, exactly what was supposed to be in them.

The station supervisor, Tavish ola Shenai, said, "I'm not happy with you, Copper. You know I'm not supposed to open these until the clients take delivery."

Copper said, "You'd have been a lot less happy if the goods had been out of order."

"As would you," ola Shenai said. "Now what about the girl?"

"I've told you about the girl."

"Nothing that makes sense."

"Does magic ever make any sense?"

"Always the rationalist, aren't you, Copper."

"Not always," Copper said under his breath.

"Odd that you should suddenly be blaming magic for things. Next you'll be telling me you've decided to believe in gods after all."

Copper said nothing. His eyes burned, and he rubbed sand out of them.

"Just how long have you been awake, Copper?"

"That's what Zelle asked," Copper muttered, then said aloud, "Not long enough to be seeing things."

"Hm," ola Shenai said. "Well, the room at the Marketplace Inn's empty. You can use that."

"And what are you going to do about the girl?"

"What exactly am I supposed to do about her?"

"I don't know." Copper said, and started for the door, suddenly enormously tired. "Sign her on as a passenger hostess." As he went out of the office, he seemed to feel triumph radiating from ola Shenai like the first rays of sun in the East. The sun hurt his eyes. Ola Shenai hurt his stomach.

He walked through Merchant's Gate. The Market was already hitting its stride, the butchers and bakers calling *Fresh, fresh;* Copper bought a handful of soft new rolls and nibbled them on the way to the Marketplace Inn. He checked into the room the Railway kept for employees on call, which was just comfortable, no more; stripped and crawled between the clean coarse sheets. He was asleep at once, and slept very, very badly.

Copper was awakened from a dream of iron bands and smothering by the boy from the Station. From the angle of the sun, Copper guessed he had been asleep perhaps three hours. "I'm to tell you that Supervisor ola Shenai wants to see you immediately," the boy said, "and that I'm now the First Morning Crew Caller, so you can't dismiss me."

"At this rate, you'll be Managing Director by noon," Copper said. He dressed by touch and headed for the Station, pausing just long enough in the Market to knock back a mug of cider.

Tavish ola Shenai was rather better dressed than at dawn, in a red formal robe with Railway emblems embroidered in gold. He sat behind his desk in the Station office, the sun through the glass trainshed spraying his shoulders with light, his hands folded on the desk in a kind of temple to himself.

There was another man in the office, an old man with hair thin on top and a badly trimmed gray beard. His purplish gray gown was tidy but had seen better days, and his boots urgently needed resoling.

Ola Shenai said, "Copper, this is the Master Wizard Rion Daaveh. Master, this is Copper, one of our engine drivers."

Rion Daaveh made an elaborate seated bow, and said, "The word was spread for information of a young woman. You are the man who saw her?"

Copper said, "I saw something."

Ola Shenai said, "Copper has a reputation as a doubter."

Rion Daaveh nodded. "She was seventeen? Quite slender, with dark gold hair?"

"About that age. And slender, yes, but I didn't really notice the color of her hair. It was late, and dark."

"And you met her on the ironroad from Saltigos to Liavek. Her name was Krisia."

Copper looked at ola Shenai, who said smoothly, "We did not mention a name in the request for information. Nor the location."

Copper said, "That was where I met her. And that was the name she gave me."

Rion Daaveh pressed his palms together in front of his face, let out a long, low sigh. Copper said, "Do you know her?"

"I knew her well, yes," the wizard said. "She was my niece, raised by me from the age of five, when her parents were killed in a coaching accident."

"Don't tell me," Copper said. "Along the road to Saltigos."

"No, oh, no, young man. Their tragedy took place here in Liavek, on the Street of Clay Vessels. It is a matter of public record."

Copper glanced at Tavish, who merely raised an eyebrow.

Rion Daaveh continued. "But Krisia was much given to walking east; she loved the view of the Silverspine."

"She went for walks at high midnight?"

Rion Daaveh smiled gently. "Young man, have you not guessed it? My niece was taken with a disease of the heart—I mean that literally and figuratively as well. She died nearly four months ago." He gestured toward the tracks outside the office window. "I buried her at a spot off the coast road, I can no longer say just where, except that it had a fine view of the Mountains, and the Moon above them."

Copper could feel himself frowning. Tavish ola Shenai looked insufferably smug. Rion Daaveh was just staring at the railway tracks. "Fine," Copper said finally. "Is that all?"

"One thing," the wizard said. "Did she seem . . . happy?"

"I couldn't say." Copper tried to keep his voice level. "We didn't talk much."

"Oh. Then yes," Rion Daaveh said, "that's all."

Copper turned. Ola Shenai said, "We did publicize a reward for information."

"In my name," Copper said.

"It *was* your request. Five levars was the named sum."

"That's the going rate now, to talk to the dead?" Copper found a five-levar coin in his pocket, put it on ola Shenai's desk with rather a crack.

He turned again to go. Rion Daaveh said "Master Driver—I would thank you. I am happy to hear that Krisia's spirit lives."

Copper gave a jerky nod. Rion Daaveh stood up slowly, palmed the coin, and went out of the office.

Ola Shenai said, "Well. Where is the man of ticking clocks and connecting rods now?"

"He's on his way to the inn," Copper said, "to get back to his bed before the sheets get cold."

Copper shut the door on ola Shenai's last comment, something about warm sheets, and too damned intimate.

Copper woke again just before noon, put on his leathers and went downstairs. "I'm done with the room," he told the clerk. "Have it made up for the next driver."

"Sir," the clerk said, and then pushed a sheet of paper at him. It was a half-copper newsrag, the *Mystery Hill Observer*. "Seen this, sir?"

Copper picked it up. The headline read

STRANGE VISITATION ON IRON WAY
Girl's Specter Appears
"I, an Unbeliever, Saw Her," Driver Says

Copper handed the paper back, headed for the door.

"Sir?" the clerk said.

"Yes?"

"Is it true, sir?"

"It's true," Copper said. "I *am* an unbeliever." He went out of the inn, into the market.

A street vendor rolled a sheet of rough waxed paper into a cone, folded up the point to seal it, and ladled pot-boil into it. Copper paid for the soup, bought some soda bread and wine, and wandered down to the Levar's Park to eat. The air was crisp but the sun was warm, and a number of people were out: strollers, dancers, artists. A pair of City Guards trailed their pikes; nothing else attracted their attention. Since the business last year with the wizards murdered by magic, the Park had been remarkably free of violent crime.

Why, no one had been shot dead in the streets of Liavek for *months* now.

Copper sopped the last of his broth with the bread, looked around, set the cup down on the grass a little way from himself and quietly drank his wine. After a moment, a stray cat emerged from a bush and began licking the bits of fish and vegetable from the paper. Copper said, "That's it. We've got to stick together," and the cat's head popped up sharply; then it went back to eating.

Copper spent the afternoon walking at random around the city. He avoided the people he knew; the damned story was in all the newsrags, and he wasn't up to explaining it. He didn't go back to the Station, seriously worried that he might do something violent to Tavish.

But finally he did go back—had to—and found a crowd outside, with what looked like a heaven peddler working them.

It was Rion Daaveh, in a new robe with a gold-colored

sash. Copper moved to the edge of the crowd, just within hearing.

"—yet not soulless," the old man said. "Perhaps this road of fire and metal is only now discovering its familiar spirits. Perhaps the light comes in darkness, in ways we have not suspected. . . ."

Copper looked around. The crowd wasn't exactly spellbound; they were paying no more attention than to any other street novelty. The most interest was shown by two Scarlet Guards, the private troops of the Twin Forces religion. They were supposed to protect the property of the Red Faith, but religions tended to define their property in curious ways.

One of the Scarlets started to turn in Copper's direction. Copper moved on. This wasn't his affair. Nothing to do with faith was.

Copper walked the long way around the Station. Artisans were at work, bending brass for lamps and lead for windowpanes, assembling benches and wall panels inlaid with the Railway monogram. A track gang was laying a second pair of rails under the glass trainshed, to connect with the northbound line to Trader's Town. Iron tieplates were bolted to wooden crossties, then a three-yard length of rail laid and spiked in place. With both rails down, and a cart rolled up to check the gauge between them, the crew wizard shot heat into the rail joints, welding them together.

The tracklaying routine came from Tichen, where there had been railways for nearly thirty years. The Coastal Company had modified it to use mechanical steps for bolting and alignment instead of magical ones, one wizard on the gang instead of five.

Copper had proposed they do without welded rails, have no magicians at all on the track crews. He'd had to withdraw the idea, of course.

Tavish's shift was over; Sandjo, the night supervisor, was in. That was all right with Copper. As he walked into the office, Sandjo was looking out the window, at Rion Daaveh and the crowd. "Kaf's hot in the corner," she said, without turning.

Copper poured a mugful. "Do you know anything about the loud fellow?"

"He and his niece used to work the Park together. Half-levar magics, you know the sort."

"They were both magicians?"

"From what I've heard, she was the talent in the team. The old man mostly argued the deals." Sandjo turned to face Copper. "Could I hear your version of what happened last night? I've got Tavish's and three different rags'."

"Do they agree?"

"No. You should also know that Tavish sent his account with the morning coach to Saltigos. Zelle will know about it by tonight."

"I don't care if Zelle knows." Copper sipped his kaf. "Except that Tavish might have sent it on the ninth-hour express tonight. Made twenty levars for the Railway."

Sandjo laughed. "So what *is* your version?"

Copper told her.

"Could be an illusion," Sandjo said finally.

"It could be a lot of things, Anje." He gestured out the window. Rion Daaveh had finished his speech, and was collecting coins from the crowd. "He strikes me as a natural-born swindler."

"I thought all magicians did. But you're right, he's as trustworthy as a two-copper compass. Still . . . did you see him with that crowd? Whatever he's doing, it's got some kind of energy behind it."

"Speaking of energy, if I'm going to drive the express back tonight, I ought to catch a nap. Is the Inn room open?"

"No, the track foreman from the Trader's Town line is in there . . . and just wait a minute, who said you were going to drive the nine tonight? You *especially?"*

"That's why," Copper said. "Me especially."

Sandjo sighed, pointed at a side door. "There's a cot in the files room. Shall I wake you at eight?"

"Seven."

Copper fired *Brazen Venture* himself, no magic this time. He was half-aware of being watched, Station workers staring at him as he stoked the boiler and oiled the rods. There was supposed to be someone keeping the builders on the job. Copper didn't care. Not his department.

At ten minutes to nine Sandjo came out to the engine, with two dispatch boxes and the cabin clock. She handed them up to Copper, with a grave look.

"Who sent these?" Copper said, tucking the strongboxes into the corner. There was rarely more than one package a week from Liavek to Saltigos.

"One's Admiralty papers," Sandjo said. "The other's from a merchant I never saw before." She tapped her hand on the side of the cabin. "He asked me if you were going to make the run anyway. When I told him yes, he seemed... disappointed."

Copper nodded. "Realized he'd wasted twenty levars."

Sandjo said, "Copper, if you see something tonight—"

"Don't worry about it, Anje. Think of it this way—he just paid your salary for two weeks."

"Yeah. Good trip, Copper."

"Thanks. Good night, Anje."

She waved, and Copper opened the throttle. The engine sighed and began rolling, past the wall of Liavek, leaving the gleaming glass station behind.

Copper was not thinking about the girl Krisia, whoever, whatever she had been. There were other people to think about, real ones. Smiths hammered out boiler plates, forged tight pistons. Cartwrights shrank hot iron tires on wheels, just as they had done for generations, but these tires had flanges to hold rails. Artisans who had made pleasantries for the rich now made gauges and clocks and signal works. Wizards came out of their disappearing houses to work on the line just like spike drivers and engine stokers. When the rails ran, the world changed.

No one else saw the Railway in quite the way Copper did. He had no doubt of that. But it didn't matter. Steam and speed and precision—and the ideas behind them—were in the world now, and it didn't matter what people thought they saw.

There was a white flicker in *Venture*'s headlight, a figure on the tracks ahead.

Copper thought for exactly ten ticks of the clock about maintaining speed, making the thing ahead jump if it was real and sensible, driving clean through if it was something else. But before the fourth tick he knew that he would not. Could not. He calculated distance and speed and braking force, raised the throttle and turned the brake. *Brazen Venture* came to a halt twenty paces in front of the girl, who stood still and calm in the mist and the glaring light, as if she had been perfectly certain that the engine would stop.

Copper swung down, went to her. "Good evening, Mistress Krisia," he said.

"Hello, Master Driver."

"I wasn't sure you'd remember me."

"I don't know how I do," she said. "My memory is very strange, these days . . . May I ride with you?"

"I'm going to Saltigos tonight, not Liavek."

"That's all right. I'm not really certain anymore just where I should be going."

He helped her aboard. "There's a condition of passage tonight," Copper said. "I want you to hold on to my hand. Don't let it go unless I tell you. Do you understand?"

"Yes, Master Driver," Krisia said, and put her hand on his. Her fingers were cold, but no more so than anyone's might be on a night like this. Her grip was quite firm.

"Hold on, now," Copper said, let off the brakes, and opened the throttle. Their speed built quickly. Above the Silverspine to the north, the moon raced like a sloop on white water. Krisia's fingertips pressed hard into the back of Copper's hand, her thumb stroking his palm; he turned for a moment, reminded of what that touch had once felt like, but the girl was not looking at him. She watched the moon. Her hair was, as Rion Daaveh had said, a dark gold, alloyed white by the silver moonlight. Her nails were trimmed very short, like an artisan's or musician's. She had been a novice wizard, Sandjo said. He could see nothing that might be the powervessel a magician needed to work spells; her white shift was hardly appropriate and no jewelry was visible. Unless she wore it beneath . . .

Copper turned back to the tracks, the stoker, the throttle,

and the clock. She still held his hand. That was sufficient.

He did not look back again for half an hour, as the tracks began to curve northward along the coast, some ten miles from Saltigos. Krisia's grip had begun to cramp Copper's hand; he supposed her muscles must be sore, and turned to tell her to be calm, to relax.

She was gone. Copper looked at his hand: there were five small bruises there.

He turned forward again, put a hand on the stoker and another on the throttle, and did not release either until Saltigos terminal was full in his headlights and it was time to brake. *Brazen Venture* came to a stop at the far end of the platform, just short of the switchpoints, and Zelle came running out, lantern in hand.

"Are you all right?" she said, as Copper stepped down, the strongboxes under his arm.

"Yes, I saw her again," Copper said, much too harshly, "and, yes, she vanished again. Here." He handed over the dispatch cases. "Anything going back?"

"Not tonight. Not that you'd be driving it if there were."

Copper didn't answer. He started to walk away, then stopped. "Wait a moment."

Zelle hadn't moved. "What is it, Copper?" she said quietly.

He pointed to the case from the new merchant, the one who had been so concerned that the night run take place. "Open that one."

"What?"

"Ola Shenai told you all about last night, didn't he? Well, I want to be sure this one's in order. If it is, we'll lock it back up and no one but us will ever know."

They went into the station, put the cases on Zelle's cluttered desk. She found the key, opened the strongbox, and said something both obscene and bewildered.

Inside the box was a stack of newsrags, perhaps two hundred copies of tomorrow morning's *Old Town News*. Zelle riffled through them, no doubt looking for something of value interleaved, but there was nothing but the block-printed papers. She said, "Somebody spent twenty times what these are worth to have them hauled out here?"

"It's a new idea," Copper said, "but give it time. Eventually Saltigans won't be able to live without a morning paper fresh from Liavek." And, leaving Zelle standing nonplused over the open box of papers, he went off to find his bed.

Copper dreamt of Syvann. It was bad. It always was. Almost as bad as when Syvann had been alive.

They had met four years ago. Copper had just returned to Liavek; he'd spent two years in Tichen, learning railway engineering, and was trying to help sell the idea of railways to the Liavekans. He supposed later that he must have sounded like a priest with a message, that that was what had drawn Syvann to him. He'd certainly never met anyone who needed a message so badly, who needed a god so much.

Copper wasn't a god, but wet heat makes mirages. In a cooler, drier season, Syvann saw more clearly. Copper was fairly sure she still loved him, but there was the god problem. It was soluble, Copper knew; Liavek was full of gods. But he also knew it was beyond *his* solution.

He knew it was solved when he came home from a line survey to find Syvann in a bizarrely cut robe, the same gold as her hair, practicing a ritual in front of a mirror. She looked very natural in the robe and the pose. Even her smooth bronze skin fit the image, made her seem to be a gold-leafed bronze statue, such as he had seen in eastern Tichen.

She was happy, he knew that. He saw it in her eyes, the distortion of rising heat that let her see something he never would. But he accepted it. And then, in the middle of their second summer together, Syvann was dead. In the street, in the middle of Liavek, in broad daylight.

There had been some sort of a fight, knives and bullets and broken glass. The broken glass was important somehow, Copper had never found out quite why. He had never found out quite anything, beyond the raw facts. The bullets were a fact: there were two great holes smashed in Syvann's body, rather like a pomegranate hit by a spikemaul; the remnant, juice dried to powder, was left on a morgue slab for Copper to identify, and that was all the sense it made, or seemed ever likely to make.

The Guard who pulled the sheet back from the mashed fruit—a Scarlet Guard, not the City patrol—had asked Copper about Syvann's faith.

"She had one."

"Yes. In what?"

"In a god, I suppose."

The Scarlet Guard didn't like that answer at all. He kept on asking until he was convinced Copper was either stupid or mad but definitely ignorant, and there it ended. Copper wondered how this was the Red Faith's property, but he didn't ask.

Copper woke up from the dream of bloody metal, wondering if it had perhaps begun to make some new kind of sense.

It was two hours before noon. He dressed, in a plain cloth jacket, trousers, and cloak, not his driving leathers, and went to Saltigos's Street of Magicians.

The Street was a little oval court with a fountain at its center, and unlike Liavek's more famous Row, one could always find it. The houses were also fairly plain, and generally stayed so. Finding an open house, now, there was the problem. The first two doors Copper tried were securely bolted, and no one answered his very loud knock. The third door had no handle at all.

The fourth was opened by a tall man with a hard body and a harder expression. "I am Lengh Niaru," he said. "What is your business?"

"Magic," Copper said, "but not illusions," and he walked through the open door and the man holding it, down a short hallway to a room hung with velvets and beads. A somewhat fatter version of the man at the door sat at a small brocade-covered table, with a glass of wine and a plate of chops and gravy.

The man chewed and swallowed without hurry, said, "You are Copper, the railway driver, I do believe."

"How long have I had a reputation among wizards? Assuming that you are Lengh Niaru?"

"I am. And you've been known to us longer than you might think, sir."

"Typical pretense of an answer."

Niaru gestured aimlessly. "Typical pretense of worldliness.

But you came here looking for a magical service. I am willing to listen. I don't think we have anything to prove to one another."

"That's fair enough," Copper said. "I want a chain to hold a ghost."

"But you don't believe in ghosts," Lengh Niaru said, not rudely. "It takes a tight box indeed to hold doubt. And a deep grave to bury it."

Copper shrugged. "If you know what I don't believe in, you should know what it is I want." He took a step toward the door.

"I do," Niaru said. "You believe in magic, like an intelligent person, and you want a counterspell. Reasonable enough."

"Does that apply to the cost as well?"

"It depends . . . yes, Master Engineer, it usually does . . . Is your ghost merely invisible? To cancel invisibility is very simple. Or is it impalpable as well? That's a much subtler—"

"She was solid enough to bruise my hand. And then vanished from a moving train at thirty miles an hour."

Niaru stopped quite still, and paled a little. He put down his chop and pushed the plate away. "My dear sir, I knew some of this, but—and I assure you I am not being condescending—has it occurred to you that this might be . . . a real ghost?"

"I don't know what it is," Copper said. "I'm trying to narrow down the possibilities."

"But if it is actually a revenant spirit . . . are you certain you *want* to bind it? Ghosts can be . . . well, vengeful. It's inextricably bound up with their being ghosts."

"Is there a charm or not?"

"Yes. There is."

"How long to make it, and how much?"

"Oh, it could be done by tonight," Niaru said. "It's not a difficult spell at all . . . but there's a limitation I should warn you of."

"That's rare candor," Copper said. "What is it?"

Niaru said levelly, "You must *want* the spirit confined. If your will falters . . ."

"You mean, if I'm afraid."

Niaru shook out a linen napkin and wiped his hands elaborately. "It doesn't matter why. If you cease to want the spirit held, even for a moment, it will go free. I've heard of a man who caught a succubus . . ." He looked at his partly eaten lunch. "You know what's left on your plate, when you finish eating a lobster?"

Copper said, "How much?"

"Ten levars."

Copper got out a cartwheel, tossed it to the wizard. Niaru caught the coin, then bounced it in his palm and dropped it on the table, as if it had burned him. "Are you sure you want to pay me with this one?"

Copper looked at the gold piece, lying on the tabletop with the Levar's face up. "What's wrong with it?"

Niaru picked it up and tossed it. It landed heads-up. He flipped it three more times. Heads all three. "This coin's as full of magic as an egg of chick," he said.

"I thought it was called luck in this country."

"And you think there's no reason for that, don't you."

"So I got some gambler's cheating piece."

"That's twice in a row you've joked about what isn't funny. Strong luck can leave traces of itself on things, gold particularly—"

"Like a bad smell?"

"Third jest, it's your head. I said *strong* luck. Stronger than mortals are allowed. Do you understand me?"

"Well as I care to." Copper reached for the cartwheel. "If you don't want it—"

Niaru snatched up the coin. "You'll have your charm an hour after sunset. If I were you, till then I'd search my heart."

"Now there's a bootless errand," Copper said, and went out.

Copper went back to his room, changed into his black leather jacket and heavy riding trousers. The stable next door hired him a horse, and he headed west, along the trade road until he was out of sight of Saltigos, then to the north, to follow the path of the railway.

It took him more than three hours to reach what seemed to

be the spot. Copper dismounted, hitched the horse to the rails, and began to search. He was not entirely sure what he was searching for—but when he saw the clearing, and the large flat stone deliberately set level upon two smaller boulders, he knew he had found it. The thing would not have been done in a small, furtive basement, he knew.

Copper crouched next to the stone table, found a small brown stain, dripped down from above. He stood, took a step backward, stretched out his arm; then he followed its line until he found the stained knife, half-buried in the dirt where it had been thrown.

There wasn't much blood here. A body contained a lot of blood. But that there was any blood at all must have come as a terrible shock, to a man expecting a miracle.

Copper worked out the rest of it, in backwards order. He went back to the flat stone, took three steps directly away from it, then walked in a circle around it at a three-pace radius. He stopped at a small pile of stones, bent and unstacked them, pulled out a red opal pendant in the shape of a heart, on a fine gold chain.

It would be necessary for a magician, especially a novice, to put her luck vessel out of useful range before the ritual, so that no involuntary magic was done in the hot moment. Removing the thing would call for a little ceremony, a little burial.

Copper wondered what Krisia had been thinking, when the knife came down.

What had Syvann, when the hammer fell?

Copper put the pendant inside his jacket, went back to his horse, and rode for Saltigos.

It was a quarter-hour to midnight. On the Saltigos platform, Copper was oiling the rods of *Black Stallion,* a full-sized road engine, built mostly of iron and steel. It was the largest the Railway possessed, over twice the length of little *Brazen Venture,* its six red-spoked driving wheels as high as Copper's waist. The firebox glowed cherry red, and the stoker auger, driven by the engine's own steam, grumbled as it pulled sea-coal from the bunker behind the cabin.

"I don't like this," Zelle said.

"The parcel came in," Copper said, not as a question.

"Oh, there's a parcel. Brought in by some gibbering fat clown who wanted me to think he was a sea captain—kept pulling his hat down to hide his hair."

"And what's in the box?"

Zelle looked hard at Copper for a moment. "You're damn right I opened it. It's some scrolls. I can't read them, neither can Omalfi."

"Then go get some rest. Omalfi can join you as soon as he lights me up."

"You're supposed to have a live stoker on *Black*."

"That's a Driving Department rule. I just revoked it."

Zelle said, "Copper. What's going on? What's out there?"

"An iron engine on sixty miles of steel track," Copper said. "Fire and metal and that's all."

Omalfi came around the back end of *Black Stallion*. "Could be lonely, then," the wizard said, and then very carefully, "You're sure you don't want company on this trip, Copper?"

"I'm sure. Start the torch, will you?"

Omalfi shrugged and went to the front of the engine. He chanted and gestured, and a brilliant blue-white light appeared in the headlight box. The light was grainy, and made everything it shone on seem curiously flat and decolored, but it threw twice as far as the best spirit lamps, necessary at the speeds *Black* could reach.

Copper climbed into the cabin. "Now hand me up the dispatch."

Zelle did so. Omalfi came around behind her, put his hand on her shoulder. "Copper," he said, quietly, clearly.

Copper turned, his hand on the throttle lever.

Omalfi said, "You know we're your friends, Copper."

"I know that," Copper shouted above the steam and the roar and the rumble of coal, and dropped the throttle. *Black Stallion* moved forward into the night. Copper thought once of looking back, but did not.

It was because Omalfi was his friend that he had gone to someone else for the magic chain. He wanted it to be purchased for cold money; to have no love whatsoever in its making, to be just a thing, a tool.

Once the lights of Saltigos had dwindled, he let the big engine have its head, the stoker thrumming, heat rising from the firebox, moonlight catching the rods like a lightning storm sweeping down the coast. He looked up: Tonight the high moon was made of steel, a white engine racing *Black*. The moon paced well, Copper thought, but she could not win. *Black* was the fastest thing ever made by man, the fastest on earth, and in time they would build engines faster still. Copper looked ahead, along the beam of lucklight, and knew that they would need something better for the eyes of the engines to come; power would exceed the reach of power.

He drove on like that, alone with his dream, the pulse of pistons, the tick of the brass-cased clock, until the distance was covered to the place of sacrifice; he began slowing before he saw her, and had *Black Stallion* bridled to a walk when Krisia appeared in the light.

"Good evening," he said to her, "going to Liavek tonight?" and boosted her into the cabin. She looked around, as if startled by the big machine. Perhaps she was, Copper thought; *Venture* seemed cozy and friendly, in oak and brass, while *Black*'s iron mass could seem forbidding, though *Black* was actually the easier engine to drive. It was all in knowing what the metal truly meant.

"Would you hold on now, mistress Krisia?" Copper said. "I wouldn't want to lose you."

"Of course, Master Copper," Krisia said.

"Thank you," Copper said, and eased out the throttle. They rolled on. Copper turned back to face Krisia, leaned toward her. "And now, if you'll do me a small service—"

He pulled a length of gold chain from his pocket and tossed it around Krisia's wrists; pulled it tight. He wrapped the other end around his own left wrist. "I have to see you home tonight," he said. "I trust you understand."

Krisia gave him an utterly blank look. She did not tug at the chain; she did not even seem to notice it.

Drawing the chain taut between them, Copper turned back to the controls, looked out at the track ahead.

The tracks fell away below the engine. The Silverspine tilted and began to slip by. Wind rushed past the cabin windows as *Black Stallion,* all ten tons of it, rose into the sky. They did not seem to be flying; they did not seem to be moving at all, though Copper's stomach rolled and he felt dizzy. Bracing his feet, he turned.

Krisia was not there.

Someone else was.

A woman in a shimmering blue robe stood across the cabin from Copper, her hands bound with the spell-chain just as Krisia's had been. She was taller than Krisia by at least a span, fully as tall as Copper.

Her face and hands seemed to be made of liquid silver, smooth and agonizingly beautiful. Her hair was a curve of dark-grained metal, her eyes blue star sapphires.

Copper failed at first to speak, and then said, "Was it ever the girl? Or only you?"

"She is still here," the Lady said. "Within me. Or, in another sense, I stand within her. Both at once. Do you understand, o man?"

"Not very well."

The Lady laughed, metal chimes. "Little dark man, who would hold the universe under a glass, yet cannot understand a simple trick of presence." She did not sound mocking; rather like a mother whose child has tried too hard to be clever. She held up her hands, pulled gently at the chain. "But since you cannot be certain who I am, how can you know I am that which you wish to hold?"

If you cease to want the spirit held, it will go free. "You are here," Copper said carefully. "So you are the one."

"Very well. As you see, it hardly limits me." She pointed out the window. The planet was distantly below them now; they were halfway to the moon, stars drifting past, white, red, gold.

Copper kept the chain taut. "If we're to discuss your limits . . . what did you promise Rion Daaveh?"

"That Krisia would become the Goddess of Railways, if given to me freely. And so it shall happen, soon enough."

"When enough people believe in you? That's all you are, isn't it? The sum of people believing in you."

The Lady smiled. "You think that is a small thing, do you."

"You make people kill and die. That's not small. But you . . ." He shook his head.

"You believe in me," the Lady said, "in the evidence of your eyes and your hands? Don't you, Copper?"

Copper could hear the pleading in the Lady's voice, not even disguised. Or perhaps that was the disguise, the appeal, the lie itself.

"How can I?" Copper said. "You've tricked my eyes and hands three nights running. I haven't a stick to measure you against . . . No, Lady, I don't believe in you."

"Others have. Others close to you."

"I thought that might be it. You'd be the one they call the Light. I thought you were a man."

"Another reflection of me is. I am the Light of the night sky, the Moon."

"Reflected sunlight."

"Are you so sure?" She pointed at the Moon, which now filled the view above the engine, shining brilliantly white. "Do I not have my own light?"

"You reflect the sun, or there would be no darkness shading your face." Copper pointed at the huge moon nearby, the shadowed mountains along the terminator.

"O man, o sophist!" the Lady said. "You think this iron beast of yours so mighty, yet against this immensity—" She tried to gesture at the space around them, but Her hands were held, "can you not see how tiny it is? You think you have made a hammer to break the gods, but it will break only your bones and your upstart spirit. When this machine goes crashing into its glass temple outside the city, when you are slivered with glass and scalded with steam, when you lie in your own boiling blood on hot iron, you will know some little of power . . . as will all those who behold your dying. You will fall, o man, and many thousands will kneel."

"I know a little of it now," Copper said, and pulled the spell-chain. "If I fall, you fall with me."

"Little dark man, do you think that your flimsy charm can hold one whose very stuff is magic?"

"I think so," Copper said. "I think even gods are subject to rules. Don't you, blue Lady?"

"Take this chain from me."

"No."

"Take it off or I will shrivel you like a salted slug."

"Do it then."

"Take it off and I will love thee as no woman of dust and blood ever can."

"Nor ever has," Copper said, and pulled the chain tight around their three wrists.

The Lady hissed like a cracked steampipe. Then she stopped, and smiled again, but hesitantly. "Never, Copper? Never?" Copper knew the voice very well. It was Syvann's. The Lady's face had changed too, trying to shift into Syvann's image. But it was not working: the picture was not Syvann but a crooked mask, a sculpture ruined in the firing.

The truth was, Copper knew now, that he had let Syvann go a long time ago; there was no more freedom he could give her.

He pulled the chain from the Lady's wrists, flung it out the cabin window. It exploded into a streak of golden fire against the starry darkness.

"If that frees you," he said, "then you are free."

The Lady struggled, but seemed unable to move at all now. She cried, "I am everything that the moon is, or was, to any mortal who is or ever was. I am the cool blue moon of your dreams, the liquid white moon of your lusts, the bloody moon of your hatreds. All this and many more. What am I to you, o man, that you will not love me?"

"A stone," Copper said. "A worldstone like the one we cling to, barren and not so beautiful, a long distance away across whatever the dark is. You are out of our grasp now, stone . . . but not beyond our reach, I think."

"You will touch me, without loving me?" the Lady said. "Do you know what a touch without love is, o small dark man?"

"Oh yes, bright Lady. I know very well what that is."

"*What do you want?* Power, pleasure, immortality?"

Copper clenched his teeth.

"Deity then? It is possible."

"That least of all."

"Have you no heart at all, little dark man?" The sapphire eyes were wide, though there were no tears in them, and the silver flesh was taut. "*Let me see!*" She looked straight into his eyes: straight into him.

Copper felt his heart swelling up into his throat, banging like the track gangs' mallets, killing him blow by blow. He took a step back, bumped against something: it was the brass cabin clock on its wall hook. He got his hands around it, lifted it to throw at the Lady, feeling its metal pulsing through his fingers, faint tick-tick against the lunatic hammering down his left arm to his heart.

The stars in the Lady's eyes went from white to copper to blood-red, and Her metal lips smiled.

It was what She wanted, of course. For him to smash the clock and acknowledge Her.

Copper put the clock up again. He sagged against the wall. He pressed his fingertips against the clock's glass face, feeling the tick, watching the crawl of the indicator, trying to match his heart to the ticking, his breathing to the sweep.

Human hands made this clock, he thought, his lips forming the words though he lacked the breath to push them out, *and built this engine, and laid the tracks it rides on. All of them were needed, all of them did their part. Lady, Lady, what do we need you for?*

He held still, not quite kneeling. The rush of wind past the cabin had stopped (or perhaps his own blood's hammering had deafened him to it) and the engine revolved, still affecting no sense but the eyes, so that the white face of the Moon was behind the Lady, silhouetting Her against its awful barrenness. The red light in Her eyes went out.

"So now I know," Her voice said, a ringing in a hollow brazen vessel. "Any power would I have given you, any answer, all answers. But you wish not answers, but reasons." She looked down at him. "So die then. With nothing."

The Lady's smooth metal face tore like tissue, crumpled

away. Beneath it was a white face, like chalk, scarred and pitted and blotched. She wept tears of stone that tore rilles down Her cratered cheeks, and dust rose, but there was no fire, no lap of water, no cries of populations driven from broken cities: there was no one there at all.

The face went red, and darkness eclipsed it.

The world was half white, half black, and roaring.

Copper put his hands to his eyes, to be certain they were open. To his right there was darkness and a distant speck of moon. To his left the Liavek city wall flashed past like a stream of liquid. Someone was clutching at Copper's legs. He looked, though he was frightened that it would not be Krisia; but it was. Ahead of the engine was the last, long left-hand curve around the wall, just before the Station.

Where, at this speed, they would crash with enough force to bring the roof down, explode the boiler. Provided they even made it around the bend.

A diagram drew itself in Copper's mind, of curve and momentum. If he opened *Black* up, they would break the rails and go hurtling straight out onto the plains above the Saltmarsh. He and Krisia would die. There might be something left of the engine. The Station would rattle with the noise.

And everyone there would rush out to see the wreck, and marvel at the insoluble mystery of it. No. That would not do.

Copper put his hand on the throttle. He looked down at the girl, who still held on to him.

"Can you smother fire by magic?" he shouted. It was a simple trick, he had heard, one that beginners usually mastered early.

Krisia touched her throat. "If I—if I had—"

The chart was still clear in Copper's mind, the space and time left to them. He knew best of anyone living what it took to stop *Black Stallion* at its ordinary top speed, and they were traveling twice that.

He had done everything he could to stay true to himself, but he had reached the limit of what metal and wood and the craft of hands could do.

Copper reached into his jacket and took hold of the opal

pendant, Krisia's luck piece: he pulled the heart out of his chest and gave it to the girl.

Krisia gave a small cry as she clutched the pendant. She reached out to *Black*'s firebox. She began to chant.

Copper shoved the throttle up and threw his weight on the brakewheel. *Black Stallion* screamed with its whole being. Sparks flew from the wheels. Metal shuddered.

They began to slow.

They took the curve at sixty miles an hour, rocking, bending the rails as far as welds and spikes would take—but not farther. The Station came into view, light through colored glass, waiting for them. Copper held the brake over, looked at the firebox: it had gone dark. They were not rolling now but sliding, the wheels at full stop, grinding against the rails. The brake shoes must surely have burned through by now—would have, Copper realized, except for Krisia's spell. She was a novice. She lacked control. She was terrified, like any sane person would have been. She had made a bottomless pit of cold in the center of *Black Stallion,* and it was sucking heat out of the boiler, the brakes, the wheels. Frost was starting to form on the gauges. They might actually freeze to the rails.

They would have a charm to make sudden heat, he thought, and one for instant cold. The charms would sit in every engine cabin on the Railway, produced as common-trade items by common-trade magicians, and in time no one would even think of them as being magical.

Black slid into Liavek Station wreathed in not steam but cold fog, creaking and squealing to a stop just at the center of the platform. It cracked a siderod, blew a rivet that shot upward, shattering a pane in the roof; Copper threw himself over Krisia as glass showered down. The moon was bright and awful through the open space.

Copper stood up slowly. Standing on the platform, entirely alone, was Rion Daaveh.

Copper helped Krisia to her feet, put her on the platform. "I've brought her home, old man," Copper said, "now see you take care of her." He wanted to make it a threat, but he was much too tired. He supposed that Krisia would leave Rion Daaveh very soon—and even if she did not, she was in no more danger from her uncle. There were things one could only find the courage for once.

And besides, courage or not, the Ghost of the Railway had just been exposed as a fraud. No one would ever believe the old wizard again.

Rion Daaveh looked at Krisia, at Copper, at the engine twinkling with ice and glass fragments, not comprehending the presence of any of them. "Yes," he said finally, "Yes, I must do that. Come here, niece."

Krisia went to him, not even glancing back at Copper. Rion Daaveh knelt to hug the girl, and then said, in a voice thick with what sounded very much like disappointment, "It was only magic, then . . . only a spell after all."

Copper had no idea who the old man was asking, if indeed any of them; and no one at all answered.

Rion Daaveh and Krisia went away. There were some other people by the entrances to the station, but they drifted away into the night. The railway was not finished yet. They would have to find some other way to reach their goal.

Copper sat down on the edge of the platform. He pulled a gold coin from his pocket, tossed it. It landed tails-up. Like iron out of the lodestone's draw, the luck was gone from it. Copper leaned back against the engine, tipped his head way back until it rested on the cabin floor, and looked up through the hole in the glass overhead at the white moon.

He could no longer hear the cabin clock ticking, and the engine's firebox was cold and dead. One could be wound back up, though, and the other scraped and stoked, so it scarcely mattered. Copper continued to look up at the moon, and wondered how many years he would be dead and gone and forgotten when first a human foot trampled her face.

Portrait of Vengeance

by Kara Dalkey

FINGER-BELLS TINKLED AND swaths of black silk rustled to the insistent rhythms of lap drums and the piping of flageolets. Aritoli ola Silba gazed in admiration at the dancer on the stage. No longer did he regret following the advice sent him by Fatar Shimuz, saying that he should see the "Black Swan" dancing at Tam's Palace. Aritoli stroked his black moustache and watched as if entranced.

The dancer's arms undulated like wheat in the wind and her torso beneath the black silk veils rolled like the swells of the sea. The Serpent Dance, Aritoli had heard, had originated among the tribes of the Great Waste as a way to teach young brides-to-be what to do on their wedding nights. When brought to the city, the dance was found to be a profitable entertainment in the less tasteful salons.

But this dancer, thought Aritoli, *strips away the tarnish on the reputation of the Serpent Dance*. Although, by profession, Aritoli was a critic of arts more visual than kinetic, in his estimation the Black Swan was a master of her craft.

The flageolets trilled a flourish and the Black Swan flicked off the veils from her face and head. Cascades of golden hair, so rare and exotic in Liavek, tumbled down and flowed over her shoulders. There was an aloof beauty to her face that brought to Aritoli vague memories of a love long past. As her eyes met his, the Black Swan smiled.

She danced toward him, and Aritoli grinned in wicked delight. *So, I am to be the hapless male in the audience she teases*. It was a common enough antic with such dancers. But as the Black Swan leaned over him, her face became set in an expression of rapt interest, as if she were at last achieving a heart's desire. *It is no game,* Aritoli thought. *Either she is a brilliant actress, or she truly wants me*.

Her bracelets flashed as her arms flowed in swift, graceful movements. Her gaze held his. She whispered, "Look for me when darkness falls." As she stepped back, she playfully cast a black veil over Aritoli's head and shoulders. Then, in a swirl of silk, she turned and danced away. Thunderous applause erupted from the audience, and Aritoli felt the stares of envious men upon him. He settled back smugly in his seat and smiled.

Half an hour later, as the last pink-gold rays of sunset lingered on the rooftops, Aritoli knocked discreetly on the side door to Tam's tavern. The door opened and a small, round man peered out, wiping his hands on an apron. "Excuse me, good sir," said Aritoli, "I would like to speak to the Black Swan on a matter of, er, professional interest." He gestured with his left hand, in which he held her black silk scarf, as proof of her approval.

The little man squinted up at him. "Deremer? She's gone home. Go 'way." The door slammed in Aritoli's face.

Aritoli sighed, then shrugged to himself. *Thank the Forces I am no longer of an age when this would devastate me*. He stepped out onto the Levar's Way to hail a foot-cab.

Presently a stout woman trotted up pulling a fancy number with brightly painted wheels and fringed canopy over the seat. "Cab, Master?"

"Yes. To Number 69, Oyster Street, please." He climbed into the seat, tucking the Black Swan's scarf into his belt, and relaxed on the cushions. The soft pad-pad-pad of the runner's feet melted into memories of the rhythm of the Black Swan's dance, and Aritoli closed his eyes. *So her name is Deremer. Something familiar about that. And her face*. In his mind he watched again the sinuous movements of her body, the swirling of her black silk veils draping her in sweet-scented darkness.

A bump in the road jolted the cab and Aritoli opened his eyes, blinking. He was surprised to see the clear evening had dimmed to a fuzzy greyness. "This fog blew in quickly, did it not?" he called out to the runner.

"Fog, Master? Why this is as clear a night as I've seen this season."

Aritoli peered around but saw only a few blurred orbs of light in the darkening grey. "Where are we?"

"We're hard by the Levar's Palace, Master. And such a grand sight she is, with all her lights, wouldn't you say?"

Aritoli was about to make a snide remark about the runner's poor joke when he realized that he could see nothing at all. His heart jumped in sudden fear. Aritoli drew sorcerous power from the ornate belt buckle that was the vessel of his magic, then tried a simple spell of casting light motes from his fingers. He saw nothing.

"If you please, Master, fireworks are forbidden in the cabs. Company policy."

Aritoli felt his throat tighten with dread. He raised his hands to his face and gently touched his eyelids. His eyes were open and he could not see his hands. *Great Twin Forces. I'm blind.*

The foot-cab made a sharp turn to the right, onto Fountain Circle, Aritoli presumed. He gripped the sides of the cab seat until the woven reeds bit into his hands, and breathed deeply, trying to calm the panicked pounding of his heart. *Is this a trap? The work of thieves?* He did not wish to acknowledge the horror crawling at the back of his mind; that the blindness might be permanent, that his career might be ruined. *An art critic who is blind. There's a pitiful joke. Who would do this? Someone I've offended? Some enemy? I have so many. . .*

The cab lurched left, then came to a halt. "Number 69, sir," the runner announced.

Is it, really? I wonder. Aritoli pretended to have difficulty getting out of the seat, then slumped back on the cushions. He reached into his belt-bag and flicked a large coin in the runner's direction. "Here. Be so kind as to fetch me my manservant from the house. I'm feeling a mite tizzy, er, dipsy . . . well, you know. I fear I may need his assistance."

"Yes, Master!" said the runner and her footsteps padded away.

How large was the coin I threw her? Aritoli thought. *Those blind from birth, I hear, can discern the slightest difference in weight between coins. Those newly blind, I suppose, have a most impecunious time of it.*

Presently two sets of footsteps returned. *Now we shall see.* Aritoli then smiled to himself in bitter irony.

He heard the voice of his elderly manservant, Maljun. "Master Aritoli, are you well?"

Aritoli felt someone lean into the cab. He grasped the intruder's shoulders.

"Master?" said the manservant beside his ear.

With a sigh of relief, Aritoli rested his head against Maljun's neck. "Pretend I am drunk," he whispered, "and help me climb out."

"Easy now, Master," Maljun said gently. "A cup of warm herb tea awaits and sleep will do you good."

Aritoli allowed himself to be pulled out of the cab seat. He stumbled as his feet were unsure where to find the pavement. Maljun's arms wrapped around him and guided him, as Aritoli mumbled a bawdy song.

"G'night, Master!" called the runner. "Sleep well." Her feet and the wheels of the cab rumbled away behind them.

Aritoli straightened up, but continued to let Maljun guide him up the steps and across several thresholds, until he was seated on a soft surface that he presumed to be his sitting-room divan.

"What is it, Master? Are you ill?"

"No, Maljun. I'm blind."

"Master! How—"

"I don't know. It happened only just now, returning home in the cab."

"We should not have let her leave."

"I don't think it was her doing." Aritoli rubbed his face and eyes, but nothing improved. "I don't even know if this is sorcery or some foul trick of Nature."

"Shall I send for a healer, sir?"

"No," Aritoli said hastily, then, "Oh, curse it, yes. But a good one—someone discreet."

"Right away, sir."

Maljun's footsteps rapidly faded and Aritoli felt terribly alone in his private darkness. If he did not fear he would bump into things, he would have stood and paced the room furiously. Instead, he wrapped his arms around himself, as if to keep despair in check, and waited.

After what seemed hours, Aritoli heard Maljun return. "I have brought the healer Marithana Govan, Master."

Aritoli reached out and felt warm, smooth hands grasp his. "Thank you for coming to see me. I have heard your talents praised highly."

"Your name is known to me as well," she replied in a contralto voice, whose tone implied she would brook no nonsense from him.

"Not in a bad way, I hope."

"I don't think you summoned me to discuss your reputation, Master ola Silba. Your manservant tells me you have been blinded, yet I see no obvious damage to your eyes. If you will allow me some tests . . ."

"By all means." Aritoli felt heat near his face.

"Do you perceive any light at all?"

"No."

"Close your eyes, please."

Aritoli felt unsettled, having been unaware that his eyes were open. He had to concentrate to shut his eyelids. *She must have held a candle near me, but I saw nothing.*

Her hands rested lightly across his eyes and cheeks and he felt a tingling across the upper part of his face. He prayed that whatever gods she served could help him. The Church of Twin Forces offered much in the way of stimulating philosophy, but little in the way of miracles.

Presently, she drew back with a sigh. "Well, I can say, at least, that your disability is not natural to the body."

"Which means?"

"It is wizardry. If you wish, I will seek the nature of the spell."

"Yes, of course! Why should I not?"

"Some spells do not wish to be found out," she said cryptically.

He sensed her bending over him again. Soft silk brushed his cheek and he felt her cool, moist breath on his brow. An urge rose within him to reach out and embrace her, more from need for reassurance than desire. Thoughts of the Black Swan returned to haunt him and he imagined black veils swirling in the blackness of his vision. *Sorcery. Could it have been she who cast it?*

Pain lanced behind his eyes and Aritoli screamed. He felt Marithana jump away from him and he clapped his hands to his eyes. The pain remained intense as it ebbed, as though the inside of his face had been burned. He bent over and rested his forehead on his knees, and his lips stretched into a grimace.

"I am so sorry," Marithana said, above him. "I was afraid this might happen. The spell was well planned and well wrought. Whoever did this to you is a very powerful or skillful wizard."

"Oh. Wonderful." The pain had nearly gone and Aritoli rubbed his eyes.

"There is more. It is not a common form of sorcery. I have a suspicion as to its nature, but I would rather not say until I am sure."

"I forgive you," Aritoli groaned, sitting up. "But can you remove the spell?"

"I? No, I haven't the skill. But I can ask one who might."

"Mistress Govan, I will gladly pay you whatever you consider reasonable to bring this person to me."

"I think she'd be rather . . . annoyed to be roused at this hour."

"Mistress, my eyes are my livelihood! If it became known that the art critic ola Silba was blind, my career would be ruined! I will do whatever is necessary to soothe this person's annoyance, if you bring her quickly."

Marithana sighed. "Very well. I'll go now. But I won't guarantee when, or if, I'll return with her."

Aritoli tried to control his own irritation and frustration. "I will bear that in mind, mistress."

"Until later, then."

Aritoli heard the rustle of her garments as she left. Not knowing what else to do, he curled up on the divan, hoping to sleep.

He had no idea what hour it was when he felt someone shaking his shoulder. "Master Aritoli," Maljun said softly, "the wizard is here."

Aritoli sat up, groaning. The boundary between wakefulness and sleep seemed less distinct with no visual clues. *But at least in my dreams I could see. Do those who are born blind see when they dream?* He smelled the aroma of kaf, and a warm mug was placed between his hands. "Thank you, Maljun. Send her in at once, please."

Swift footsteps approached, and Marithana said, "Master ola Silba, I would like to present Granny Karith."

Aritoli had heard the name before, but it meant little to him. "Welcome, mistress."

"This had better be worthwhile, Master ola Silba," she replied in a firm elderly voice. "I've a tapestry to finish this morning."

Well, thank you. "I am most sorry to have disturbed you, mistress," Aritoli said in his best sardonic tones, "But I have this small problem with my eyes—"

"Yes, Marithana told me." Granny Karith interjected. "Now sit still."

With a sigh, Aritoli did so, and felt small, light fingers roam over his face, pressing here and pinching there. He steeled himself for another wave of agony, but the worst he felt was an intense tickling behind the eyeballs.

The fingertips left his face and the old woman said, "Hmmph. As I thought. What were you doing before this happened?"

"I had gone to see a dancer, the Black Swan at Tam's Palace."

The old woman sucked air through her teeth. "She's a bold one. I'll give her that."

"So it *was* she who cast this spell!" *"Look for me when darkness falls," she said. She even told me!* "Yes, she is skilled, I grant her. I wonder who paid her to do it."

There was a silence, during which Aritoli could almost feel the old woman staring at him. "Young man, are you really so wind-brained," she said at last, "that you do not remember Deremer Ledoro?"

Ledoro! The surname instantly brought back memories: A deserted courtyard at dawn; a middle-aged, overweight priest of Irhan waving a flimsy sword and accusing Aritoli of various acts with his wife, some of which were true; a brief, clumsy fight that left the priest confused and bleeding to death on the paving stones; and a little girl watching from a dark corner of the courtyard, screaming and screaming as the priest fell. *That must have been Deremer.* Aritoli fingered the faint scar on his cheek, left from the one blow the priest had managed to deliver.

"I see you remember now," said Granny Karith.

"Yes. And I can understand her wish for vengeance. I might even find it in my heart to forgive her, once I am healed. I assume you can do so?"

"You almost deserve that I try. No."

"No?"

"She planned this well. I hadn't known how much of the book she had memorized."

"What book?"

"Never you mind. All you need to know is that the spell can only be removed safely by Deremer herself. Anyone else who tries will bring back the pain that you've already experienced."

"Oh. Lovely." Aritoli massaged his forehead. "Isn't there anything you can recommend? Anything I can do?"

"Young man, you brought this upon yourself."

"I didn't know the priest was so poorly prepared!"

"You could have declined the duel."

"Declined the—" Aritoli stopped. As a younger man, it would have been unheard-of, cowardly for him to avoid a duel. Now, he wondered.

"Exactly." the old woman said. "Well, mend your ways." Her quick footsteps departed the study.

Aritoli sighed, leaning back on the divan. "What an unpleasant old goose," he muttered.

"I will have you know," said Marithana, "that that 'old goose' is the oldest, wisest wizard of S'Rian magic in Liavek!"

Aritoli was startled, having forgotten that the healer was still in the room. "I am most sorry, mistress. But if that . . . creature is the wisest S'Rian wizard, it is no surprise to me that S'Rian fell so long ago."

"She's right, you should mend your ways. If you cannot be grateful for the help given you, then I will be gone. Enjoy your condition." And another pair of swift footsteps exited the room.

Aritoli buried his face in his hands. "May Karris cut out my tongue and use it for a noisemaker. Has all my tact fled with my sight?"

"Surely it is due to the pain and confusion caused by your loss, sir," offered his manservant.

"You're too kind, Maljun. What do I do now? What hour is it?"

"Near six, I would guess. The sun has only just risen."

"Hmmm. How soon do you think you could make a withdrawal from my funds at the house of iv N'stiven?"

"Usually not until ten, sir. Banker's hours, you know. But if I could convince them there was urgent need . . ."

"Yes, good, but do not be specific about the reason. Let them think I have gambling debts or some such. And have the cab runner wait when you return. We will leave again immediately."

"May I ask to what destination, sir?"

"To the one place where I can expect an optimistic answer, if I pay enough—Number Seventeen, Wizard's Row."

"Number Seventeen, gentlemen!" the runner called out in a lusty voice.

"Thank you, good fellow," said Maljun and Aritoli heard the clink of coins. He pulled the hood of his cloak lower over his face, hoping there was no one nearby to recognise him.

"Thank *you,* sir!"

"You understand, we have not been here."

"Who? Where?"

"Very good."

Aritoli felt Maljun grasp his arms and he was guided out of the cab. The strongbox Aritoli carried felt very heavy. With careful steps, Aritoli's feet felt the way over the curbstones.

"Here is his gate, sir."

There came a faint squealing of metal on metal, and Aritoli stepped forward at Maljun's urging. As he did so, he blinked in surprise as patterns of white light flickered before his eyes.

"Maljun! I can see again . . . sort of." As he spoke, the light resolved into the outlines of a house with a garden fore-court, filled with statues. But the scene was like a surreal drawing rendered in white chalk upon black slate. The statues were of nude couples posed in various erotic positions, and they seemed to writhe as he passed. "Do you notice anything . . . odd about this place, Maljun?"

"As I understand it, sir, this house always appears odd to visitors. Perhaps you are referring to the flowers that line the walk, which are bowing graciously to us as we proceed?"

Aritoli saw no such flowers in the moving chalk drawings that served him for sight. "Um, I meant the statues, Maljun."

"Begging your pardon, Master, but I see no statues."

"Oh. Never mind."

Aritoli felt pressure on his arm causing him to halt, and suddenly a door was sketched in front of him by an invisible hand. In the middle of the door appeared the head of a gargoyle with a long, lolling tongue.

"That is an unusual door ornament," said Maljun, hesitantly.

Assuming that they might be seeing the same thing, Aritoli said, "I believe you are supposed to pull the tongue, Maljun."

"Are you certain, sir?" There was a faint pleading in Maljun's voice.

"I am afraid so." Aritoli heard his manservant sigh heavily beside him and saw a sketch of Maljun's hand reach out and gently tug on the gargoyle's tongue. In the distance, he heard a resounding "BLAAAAT!"

"Ah, such lovely bells," Maljun said.

"Uh, yes," Aritoli agreed, resigned to the bizarre.

"Well, well, what have we here?" said the gargoyle, becoming an animated sketch in Aritoli's eyes. "The bland leading the blind?"

Aritoli had heard stories of how to deal with this creature. "Enough, Gogo, we have come to see The Magician."

"You can't very well *see* him, given your current condition, can you?"

"That is what I hope he can correct, Gogo."

"What? Don't you like my helpful drawings? Tell me, great art expert, what do you think of my skill?"

Aritoli fought hard to keep his temper in check. "It is . . . unique, Gogo. Now kindly—"

"Is that all? Unique? Well, if you don't like it, I can always change it." The sketch of the gargoyle head swirled and flickered until it resolved into the downwards view from a very high cliff.

Battling vertigo, Aritoli covered his eyes, only to find it did no good at all—the scene was still there. He said slowly between clenched teeth, "I have brought a lot of money, Gogo, now let us in!"

Abruptly the scene shifted again, to an opening door. "Well, why didn't you say so in the first place?" Gogo said cheerily. "Enter and be welcome." Beyond the open door lay a chalk rendition of a winding path paved with silver coins, lined with trees that dripped diamonds.

"What understated elegance, wouldn't you say, sir?"

"Forward, Maljun," Aritoli growled.

"You should have listened to her," said Trav The Magician, who was sketched much younger than the reputation of his age and skill warranted. Aritoli wondered if that was simply the way Gogo wanted him to see Trav. He had thought of confirming his impression with Maljun, except that he wouldn't trust that version either. Trav went on, "When Granny Karith says something is so, you can believe it." In a bantering but dangerous tone, he added, "And I'll thank you to refer to her more politely in future."

"Of course. My apologies," Aritoli said, wondering at the respect the old woman seemed to command from others. "But are you telling me that you also cannot remove this spell?"

"Oh, I suppose there are several things I could do. They would result in your being sighted, but quite mad from the pain. I presume you would find insanity as much a detriment to your career as blindness. Or would you?"

Aritoli stretched his lips in a thin smile. "Some would say no. I prefer to keep both my wits and my sight. I am willing to pay a great deal, you know. This is extremely important to me."

The white outline of Trav shrugged and smiled and threw up his hands. One of them came back down a little slower than the other.

Stop playing games, Gogo, Aritoli thought with annoyance. "So you cannot help me?"

Trav toyed idly with something on his desk. "One idea seems not to have occurred to you. Most spells dissipate when their maker dies."

Aritoli paused, surprise then revulsion coursing through him. "Are you actually suggesting that I have Deremer killed?"

Trav blinked back. "You have said this is extremely important to you. And that you have considerable funds to invest in the matter. Sorcery isn't the only skill for hire."

Aritoli stood. "If that . . . *obscenity* is all you have to offer in the way of advice—"

The sketch of Trav caught Aritoli's arm. "No. I do not advise it. But you have killed one Ledoro already. I had to know."

"Yes, I have killed one Ledoro. When I was young and foolish. Now I am middle-aged and foolish, and the thought of killing Deremer had indeed never crossed my mind. I have never wished harm to Ledoro's family, not even to the priest himself. And Deremer," he added softly, "had reason for this. She is skilled, and graceful and determined. She is much like her mother."

The sketch of Trav nodded, and he released Aritoli's arm.

"You ease my mind. But, I fear, there's nothing more I can tell you. Only Deremer can remove that spell."

"Your pardon," said Maljun, mildly. "I am no wizard, but is it not true that spells also dissipate at the wizard's luck time on their birthday, when they must reinvest their magic?"

"Normal spells, yes," said Trav. "But this is a S'Rian spell involving deities, and gods have . . . other ways of doing things. Deremer quite clearly wanted the spell to be permanent."

So how could I ever convince her to remove it? "In that case, I have no hope left." Aritoli let his spirits sink. *I wonder if the Green Priests would want another convert. I have few responsibilities. But I hear the House of Responsible Life tends to add complications, not remove them. Where might I buy a swift poison? Would I have the courage to drink it?*

Someone grasped his shoulder, and Aritoli looked up to see the white lines that formed Trav's face collide into a frown of concern. "One genuine bit of advice," said The Magician, "Make no irreversible plans. She has dealt you a blow, but you will be defeated only by yourself. Your blindness is only part of her vengeance. Your despair is the rest. You needn't allow her that part. She has already made one mistake. Perhaps she will make two."

"What mistake is that?"

Trav's image grinned. "She let you live. You can make her regret it."

The Magician's grim humor was infectious and Aritoli managed a weak smile in return. "I will consider your advice, then, good Magician. Maljun, we have taken much of his valuable time. Open the box." Aritoli reached his hand into the strongbox and counted out seventeen gold levars. "For your pains."

Trav hefted the coins in his hand as if weighing them. His chalk-sketched eyebrows rose. "For *my* pains?" He sighed and looked at Aritoli. "If pain commands a price these days, this is more yours than mine. And I think you are going to have need of your gold." He handed all but one coin back to Maljun.

Aritoli could not think of how to respond, so he gratefully bowed and left with Maljun at his arm.

The courtyard path was sketched with only plain cobblestones, lined with large, irregular rocks, very similar to one that lay in Aritoli's own garden, brought there by a child he had once befriended. The child had taught him how to see a world of things in a simple stone.

Aritoli felt his eyes grow hot and something wet ran down his cheek. "You are cruel, Gogo."

"There is more to seeing than what the eyes perceive," was her gentle reply before the white lines faded, leaving Aritoli once more in darkness.

"You have a two o'clock appointment with the Copper Street Studio . . ."

"Cancel it," Aritoli said, finding it hard to keep the bitterness from his voice. He had spent the night mulling over the words of The Magician, but finding little solace in them. Deremer would never willingly remove the spell, nor could Aritoli think of a way to trick or force her to. *And I used to be such a clever fellow. Where are my wits now? Did they fade with my sight?*

"You have a dinner engagement with the Countess Tchai."

"Extend my sincerest regrets, saying that . . . an opportunity has arisen that I could not let pass."

He could almost hear Maljun frown. "Is that not—"

"A trifle crass? Yes. Better she believe that I am being my usual fickle self, than to come around with questions and sympathy if I plead illness."

"As you wish, Master. Now on tomorrow's schedule—"

"Let that wait until tomorrow." *Assuming I will have one.* He felt his hand on the desk curl into a fist. "You know, Maljun," he said softly, "I find myself wishing I could see anything again. Even paintings by the Shatter-eye School. Even that awful play at the Desert Mouse theater. What was it called, Maljun?"

"*The White Dog,* sir."

"Yes. Even that."

"Please do not dwell on your condition, sir. The Magician was right, where there is life there is hope. What will you do today, sir?"

"I feel the need for more of what you have just given me—inspiration and guidance. I will go to the Temple of the Twin Forces and spend the day in contemplation."

There was a moment's pause. "Very good, sir. When shall we leave?"

"I would leave at once, Maljun. But I will go alone." As his manservant was about to protest, Aritoli went on, "Do not fear. I will go in disguise and have the priests assist me when I arrive. I need you to take care of business for me—to spread word of my being alive and well and in many places at once, and to retrieve another box from the iv N'stiven's."

After much cajoling, Maljun finally agreed.

But the box, as Aritoli carefully did not mention, contained his will. And the temple to which he went, disguised and alone, was not the Temple of the Twin Forces. Instead, he went to the very place served long ago by the man he killed—The Shrine of Irhan, the God of Beauty.

As Aritoli was led by the cabbie into the Shrine, the first thing he noticed was the scent of flowers, spiced with cinnamon and ginger. In the distance, he heard the cheerful burbling of a fountain, and a flute played sweet and high. A cool breeze caressed his face, relieving the heat of the day. *Can I truly wish to die, when I can still experience this?* Aritoli wondered.

"Nice place," said the cabbie beside him. "Too bad it's all cluttered up with those gewgaws all over."

Aritoli chuckled and for once felt grateful for his blindness. Though the Shrine had been designed with the most elegant structure, he'd heard that devotees had loaded the place with every sort of "beautiful" offering imaginable; ornate silver-framed mirrors, statues covered with gold filigree, woven wall-hangings dripping with glass beads, and so on. These surely would have offended Aritoli's eyes more than the dark.

"And who are we," said a young, male voice, approaching, "to tell our worshippers what gift is and is not worthy of Irhan? A thing's beauty lies in the heart of the one who gives it, not in its mere appearance."

"Well," the cabbie began.

But Aritoli pressed a coin into the cabbie's palm and said, "That will be all."

"Yes, Master." The cabbie's footsteps rapidly retreated.

Aritoli was left alone with . . . what? He tried to imagine the face and form of the young man who had spoken. Did he have lovely dark eyes like that actor at the Desert Mouse? Was his hair the gold of Deremer's or the glossy black of the Countess ola Klera? Aritoli ached with not knowing. *Yes, death is the only answer. I cannot live like this.*

"You are too early for visitor's hours," said the young man, a question in his voice.

"I come to give an offering to Irhan."

"You may leave it with a priest at the side entrance, or return in two hours if you wish to present it yourself."

"I do wish to present it personally, but not publicly. And it is not a tangible object that can be given to a priest."

There was a pause. "What . . . sort of offering did you have in mind?"

"The opportunity to decide my fate."

"What interest would Irhan have in such a thing?"

"I have owed it to him for a long time. I killed his high priest, Emarati Ledoro." Aritoli had thought about this the whole previous night; what to do if the blindness were deemed permanent. This was the act that would no doubt have pleased the Green Priests, had he joined them. At this moment, Aritoli felt the sublime release from worldly care, so often mentioned by other faiths. He relished the idea of going to a mighty stroke of iridescent lightning. What an artful end to an adventurous life!

But instead of shouts of anger, there came only an awkward cough. "I see," the priest finally ventured. "You are . . . Aritoli ola Silba?"

"I am." Aritoli removed as much of his disguise as he thought decent. As a sign of "good faith" or perhaps the finality of things, Aritoli had not worn the belt that contained his invested magic.

"It was before my time," said the priest, "but I have heard of the incident. Wait here and I will tell the others you have come."

Aritoli waited, his thoughts drifting between quiet enjoyment of the cool, perfumed room and vague worries about Maljun. He felt little fear. *Whatever happens, it is preferable to a life in darkness.*

He heard the rustle of silky robes, and Aritoli stood a little straighter.

"Come forward," said a rich, deep voice. "We will summon Irhan for you."

"Thank you. But I require assistance. I have . . . temporarily lost my sight." Aritoli was surprised at his own lie. *Even though death or worse awaits, I still protect my image. If Irhan is a god of Vanity as well as Beauty, as some claim, this is certainly where I belong.*

Gentle and respectful hands grasped his arms and guided him surrounded by whispering cloth and subtle perfumes. Wind bells chimed merrily nearby. *May whatever waits beyond life be this lovely,* thought Aritoli, *though undoubtedly I do not deserve such.*

He was brought to a halt, and he stood very still. Aritoli heard the priests begin to move all around him. From the swish of their robes and the rhythmic cadence of their feet, he knew they were dancing. *How I wish I could see them!*

Aritoli could not tell how long he stood, surrounded by the music of the dance. But suddenly a part of him he could not name felt a Presence nearby.

"You are early." The voice that spoke had an exquisite resonance and timbre that made Aritoli shiver. He had no doubts as to who was speaking.

"An urgent matter, Holy One, has disrupted our schedule. Master Aritoli ola Silba, the one who slew the High Priest Ledoro, has presented himself for your judgement."

"Ah, Aritoli." The beautiful male voice sighed, sounding annoyed, amused, and fond all at once. "I wondered when you would come to me."

"I regret," Aritoli's voice cracked and he had to swallow before continuing, "Most Beautiful One, that my visit is not entirely my own choice. The daughter of High Priest Ledoro, Deremer, has exacted revenge upon me for her father's death. She has taken from me my most precious possession—my sight. Without it, my life is useless. Therefore I have come to you, thinking you are most fit to be my final judge. It is you I have ultimately offended and—"

"One moment!" Irhan sharply commanded. "It offends me that one here cannot appreciate the beauty of my temple. Although healing and spellbreaking are not among my Holy Gifts, I must do something to rectify this. Stand still."

Aritoli felt a slight pressure on his brow and cheekbones. A bright, golden light burst shimmering before his eyes. Hands on his shoulder turned him around, and Irhan said, "Behold."

Aritoli blinked, and his eyes teared. He could see! The interior of the Shrine of Irhan shone radiantly before him, and to his profound shock everything in it was *beautiful*. The gilded, overstuffed pews that only days ago Aritoli would have found repulsive were now breathtaking to behold. The tapestries and statuary and gilt-framed mirrors, that he once would have thought gaudy, were awe-inspiring. Aritoli looked at the priests standing around him, their faces, young and old, shining with the poignant beauty of each individual soul, and he fell in love with every one of them at once.

To live like this . . . always surrounded by beauty . . . what heaven it would be. I could take whatever punishment Irhan may give if he lets me live with this—Aritoli's thoughts paused as his gaze passed over a gallery of paintings. There were simple studies of flowers, uninspired renderings of landscapes, horses, and big-eyed children. Each blazed with its own glory, independent of the spirit that created it, or the subject it depicted. Aritoli felt his heart sink. *The most worthless painting in Liavek would appear as beautiful as the greatest masterpiece*. He buried his face in his hands.

"No?" said Irhan.

"No," Aritoli moaned. Then he caught himself, knowing it was unwise to reject a divine gift. "Great Irhan, if I see all things as having equal beauty, then though I have gained sight, I have lost judgement. I have so long lived by my judgement that this, to me, would be like losing my sanity. I have no wish to live blind or insane. If your judgement is to take my life in retribution for the loss of Emarati Ledoro, then do so." Aritoli bowed his head in resignation.

There was a brief silence. Then Irhan said, "Who am I, Aritoli? Am I Roashushe, to sweep away whatever offends me beneath wind and wave? Am I Narkaan, to freeze you in ghastly fear? Am I Brongoi, to destroy you with thunder and fire? Who am I?"

Aritoli swallowed and replied softly, "You are Irhan, Lord of Beauty."

"Indeed. And it is not my way to destroy in a flagrant display of might. You might say I act more in the fashion of the House of Responsible Life, whose works I rather approve of when I'm feeling morbid. This incident that concerns us has upset a balance that must be restored."

"Yes, Holy One." Aritoli felt a curious mixture of relief and disappointment.

"This matter must be resolved in a harmonious fashion. Consider the situation, Aritoli, as if it were a painting—a portrait if you will, whose theme is vengeance. The subjects of this painting are you, Emarati, Deremer, and Me. As you well know, for a portrait to be pleasing, all elements must be present in a harmonious balance."

Aritoli frowned, unable to grasp what Irhan was saying. He had been prepared to lose his mind into the Void Beyond, which made it difficult to bring it back down to earth for the effort of thinking. "But this particular tableau, Holy One, cannot be assembled, if for no other reason than that Emarati is dead."

"There are no impossibilities where divine honor is concerned, Ari. If you wish this matter to come to closure, then you will see that it is done. When this tableau is assembled, then shall you hear my judgement."

"But—"

"One bit of advice I will give you; the setting of this work will be upon the sand of Ka Zhir."

Aritoli shifted uncomfortably on the hard bench, pulling the smelly, worn cloak tighter around him. His false beard itched dreadfully, but he dared not scratch at it too much. Instead, he tried to calm himself and listen to the guttural but musical language of the Zhir sailors who clinked their mugs and glasses at a table nearby.

The darkness of his blindness was almost reassuring after the intensity of Irhan's beauty-sight. Still, Aritoli longed for either normal sight or death, which was why he was willing to sit in this tavern, the Golden Masthead, and listen to the Zhir sailors it served, in order to gain a clue to Irhan's riddle.

Maljun coughed nervously beside him. Someone off to Aritoli's left said, with a heavy Zhir accent, "Why do you stare at us, old man? Have you not seen Zhir before?"

"Perhaps," said another voice, "he wishes to be reminded what a real man looks like. He is so old, he has forgotten."

Aritoli spoke up, "We are held in rapt attention by your wonderful stories of the sea and faraway places, gentlemen." Aritoli hoped his command of the Zhir language was good enough. "But there is one story in particular we are listening for."

"Storytellers are usually paid for their services."

Aritoli pulled a five-levar coin from his pocket and held it out. "This is all I have," he lied. He felt the coin quickly snatched from his hand and imagined the sailors examining it closely.

"This tale is important to you then, eh?" said a sailor.

"It means my life to me." *And that is no lie*.

"Ask what tale you wish," said the sailor heartily. "If we don't know it, we'll make up one even better."

"Ah, but the tale I want must be true," said Aritoli.

"All tales contain some truth."

"Indeed, but this one must have more than wisdom as its truth. I need to know where, upon the sand of Ka Zhir, is a place where the dead may stand among the living."

There was silence for a moment. Then came a harsh babbling as the sailors conferred among themselves. "This is a tale we do not know, blind one. We can tell you of ghost ships that appear on Midnight Bay, or the spirits of drowned sailors who haunt the Kil Strand waiting to drag unwary swimmers under. But—"

"The only thing close to what you ask," said another, "is this; there is a tent on the beach by the harbor in which an old woman sits day after day. She is called The Gatekeeper. People come to see her and leave her tent ashen-faced. They say she has the power to summon the voices of the dead."

"Do you believe she can do this?" asked Aritoli.

"I do not know, blind one. But I, myself, will never enter her tent to find out. Too many dead enemies have I."

This brought laughter around the sailors' table and Aritoli knew they would not return to the subject again. "Let's go, Maljun," he whispered to his manservant. "We will learn no more here."

To Aritoli, the darkness of his study should be no different from the darkness he experienced elsewhere, yet there was a comfort in the feel of the room that he could not name. He regretted that he would have to leave it, even if only for a tenday or two.

"Your valise is packed," said Maljun, entering. Aritoli knew his manservant had doubts about the entire venture, but he was well trained enough to carry through with it.

"Thank you. The difficulty now is seeing that Deremer follows us. You did spread the rumors?"

"Yes, Master. Certain parties have been informed that you have found a wizard in Ka Zhir who can easily cure a slight ailment of yours."

"Good, but that will not be enough to bring her. She could wait until I return to see if the rumor was true. Damn, I wish there was something more I could do."

Hesitantly, Maljun offered, "You *are* still a wizard, Master."

Aritoli snorted. "Yes, a wizard of light and illusion. What good is that when I can see no light? Can I be a wizard of darkness instead?" And then he stopped. *Yes . . . perhaps I can. There are relations, connections I might use . . .*

"Master?"

"Maljun, bring to me the black silk scarf I brought home the night I was blinded."

"It is right here, Master."

The soft veil of silk, still fragrant with Deremer's perfume, was draped across Aritoli's open hands. "Yes," he whispered, stroking the cloth, "This might do very well. Bring me my belt."

"At once, Master." There was no need for Maljun to ask

which belt, and shortly the belt whose ornate buckle contained Aritoli's luck was placed in his lap.

Aritoli nodded his thanks and wrapped one end of the scarf in his left fist, the other in his right. Drawing upon the luck in his belt, he concentrated upon Deremer, and easily he could imagine her smiling face as she danced.

We are bound, you and I, Aritoli thought, with will poured through his magical power. *Bound by an act of bloodshed. Bound by darkness. The darkness that is in your heart is matched by the eternal night before my eyes. By your spell upon me, you have bound yourself to me, and where I go you will follow until the spell is broken.*

He felt something flow out from him—an invisible magical thread. It was small, subtle, yet Aritoli knew when it had reached its destination. And it did not break. *She did not expect or sense it.* "Yes, Maljun. She will follow."

"Is she there, Maljun?"

"A woman in a brown abjahin has been trailing us, Master."

"Good." Aritoli waved his raven's head cane ahead of him, tap-tapping the cobblestones of the Zhir street. Surrounding him were the smells of ginger and garlic, and the heavy perfumes of exotic flowers. "We are at Noyang Market, aren't we, Maljun?"

"Passing the southern end of it, Master. We will come to the beachfront shortly."

Aritoli felt perversely pleased with his newfound ability to use his other senses. *Would smell or sound seem this rich to me if my sight were returned?* "The day is bright and sunny, isn't it, Maljun?"

"No, Master. It is overcast."

"Oh." *Soon,* he reminded himself, *soon this matter will be finished, one way or another.*

"Careful of your step here, Master. This is where the sand begins."

Aritoli felt himself guided to the right a little and he stepped onto a soft, yielding surface. Overhead there were the cries of seabirds, wheeling in an endless search for fish. In the distance, Zhir dockworkers moaned out their worksongs. And beyond that, the soft whoosh of ocean waves upon the shore. The air was full of the tang of salt and sea. *What might this have looked like, had I kept Irhan's beauty-sight? Would the sand seem strewn with diamonds and gold? Would the sea be emerald and silver? Would even the grey clouds above seem like doe-skin velvet?* For a moment, Aritoli regretted his pride in denying that Holy Gift. Then his step faltered in the sand and Maljun caught his arm. With a sigh, Aritoli turned his concentration back to walking.

After what seemed like an hour, Aritoli heard the thunder of heavy cloth flapping in the wind.

"Here is her tent, Master. Shall we go in?"

"Does Deremer still see us?"

"Yes, she watches from down the beach."

"Let's go in, then. The cat always prefers to chase the mouse behind the curtain."

Aritoli let Maljun guide him in, and he heard the tent door cloth clap shut behind them.

"There is a chair here, Master. Sit."

Aritoli cautiously did so, as an old woman said, "Welcome, sirs, to the tent of the Gatekeeper." There was something out of place in the voice. *If this is an old woman, she yet has some youthful fire in her.*

"It is said you have the power to summon the dead," Aritoli ventured. "Is this true?"

"Through me, their voices may be summoned, yes. Do you seek a loved one who has passed on? Merely say the name and the soul will come."

"The one I seek is not, I fear, a beloved relative. And for the moment we must wait for another to arrive before we begin."

"Very well."

By the Twin Forces, may she not be a fraud! Too much depends on this. I hope her skill is enough to satisfy Irhan's riddle. Aritoli fingered a gemstone in his pocket—the parting gift from Irhan. At the appropriate time, Aritoli was to summon the Lord of Beauty with it. *If I am wrong . . .*

"Where is Deremer?" Aritoli growled.

"Shall I look outside, Master?"

"No. Then she'll know she's expected." Aritoli pulled the black silk veil out of his shirt and concentrated. *Follow! Come and finish what you have begun!*

Suddenly the doorflap cracked open and a perfume wafted through the tent that brought back memories of swirling black veils and pounding drums. Before anyone else spoke, Aritoli said, "Deremer Ledoro. What a pleasure to see you again."

There was a moment's pause. "I know you cannot see me, ola Silba," Deremer's low voice purred. "I cast the spell that darkened your eyes."

"Yes, I know."

"And by now you should know there is no wizard in the world who can remove it but me. Your trip here is futile."

"Is it? I think not, Deremer. Actually I came here not to be healed, but to consult with your departed father. I wondered if he'd approve of what you've done."

"If that is a jest, ola Silba, I do not find it in the least amusing. I can do far worse than I have, you know. I have exacted justice where even the mighty Irhan would not. My father would be proud to see this, ola Silba. I dearly wish he could be here. It would bring his unjustly treated soul peace."

"It is not wise to gloat, my dear, and I assure you this is no jest. By all means, let us bring your father's soul peace. Mistress Gatekeeper, what must we do?"

"Merely call the name of the person you would summon," said the old woman.

"This is nonsense," said Deremer in a tone less sure than she doubtless would have liked.

"Emarati Ledoro!" Aritoli called out. "Your daughter and your murderer would speak with you."

"Who . . . who . . . Deremer?" a tenor voice, tentative and uncertain, wavered in the air.

Perfect, thought Aritoli, *That is much as I remember him.*

"What trick is this?" Deremer hissed.

"No trick," said Aritoli. "Yes, Emarati, I called you and Deremer is here. It is time a certain matter was settled."

"How amazing," said Emarati's voice. "I never . . . Deremer, my child, how are you?"

Tightly she replied, "I will not speak to a ventriloquist's casting."

"She is quite well, Emarati," said Aritoli, "though a trifle upset at the moment. She needs proof that you are truly Emarati."

"Ah, Deremer, my little Derchi . . . how I missed you. Remember when you dressed up in my face cream and robes, and called yourself a priestess of Irhan? You were five, I think. Do you remember? Have you devoted your life to Irhan?"

There was a pause, during which Aritoli wished fervently that he could see Deremer's face.

"Irhan!" she cried, "Father, he betrayed you! I would never serve him. Never!"

"Yes . . . yes, he did," Emarati sighed. "But he had reason."

"Reason? There is no good reason that he let you die. I will punish him for you, Papa. Just as I have punished your murderer, ola Silba."

"Punish? Oh, no, little Derchi, don't—"

"Before this goes further," Aritoli said, "there is one more player missing from this drama." He turned a portion of the gem in his hands. Golden light streamed down from above. *Oh, no. Am I to have the benefit of his glamor-sight again?*

But it was not quite the same. In the middle of the tent stood an exquisitely handsome young man. All else around him was dark and drab by comparison. The sparse furnishings of the tent were dingy and grey, and even Deremer's golden hair seemed mousy and dull.

"Ah, Ari," said the radiant god, "I knew you were resourceful enough to bring us together."

"You!" cried Deremer. This was followed by a string of epithets worse than anything Aritoli had ever heard in sailors' taverns.

"What a pity," said Irhan, placidly, "That camel dung should come spewing out of such a lovely throat and mouth."

Deremer choked on whatever words she was about to say.

"Derchi, stop," said Emarati. "Irhan did not protect me in the duel, because I overstepped myself in asking him to."

"Ah!" said Deremer, "Irhan is a god who thinks it too much to protect his priests!"

"I thought *I* was the one on trial here," said Aritoli, half-amused.

"And so you are," said Irhan. "The subjects of our tableau are assembled."

"And who is to be my judge?"

"I am your judge!" Deremer said, rounding on Aritoli. "And I have already passed sentence."

"I think not," said Irhan. "You may be witness for the prosecution, perhaps, but the right to be judge falls to another. Emarati, will you pass judgement on us, whom your daughter claims wronged you?"

"Yes, Papa, tell me what to do."

"There has been no wrong done to me," said Emarati, "that I did not deserve."

"What!" exclaimed Deremer.

"Irhan failed me because I had failed him as a priest."

"That cannot be true," Deremer whispered. "You were a great priest, Papa."

"I'm afraid not, Deremer," Emarati began. "You see, I misunderstood the meaning of the worship of Irhan. I felt a High Priest in the Shrine of Beauty must be beautiful. But my concept of beauty changed into vanity as I aged. I combed my hair over my baldness. I bought corsets to hold in my girth. I put clay ointments on my face to smooth the deepening wrinkles, and spent hours at the tailor's, fitting clothes that hid every defect. Soon I forgot my priestly duties, in the pursuit of a beauty I could never attain." With weariness, as if speaking was an effort, he finished, "I should have stepped down from the priesthood long before, but my pride would not let me."

Yes, thought Aritoli, remembering, *this rings true with what I recall of Emarati. His obsession with his appearance, to the exclusion of all else, was why his wife Mehari was so receptive to my attentions.*

"And so," said Irhan, "Aritoli stepped in to do the removal instead."

"How *dare* you!" cried Deremer.

"Dare? I?" said Irhan. "Was it not you who dared to attempt to subject me to Rikiki's curse?"

Aritoli marveled at the arrogance, or courage, of Deremer that she would extend her vengeance to a god.

"Ah, Derchi, do not do such things. I deserved my fate. It was my foolish pride that led me to challenge ola Silba. Foolish to ask my god to protect me when I had no skills in swordsmanship and faced a younger man. On this side of life I have learned one thing . . . to forgive. I forgive Master ola Silba. You should forgive him too, Derchi."

"No!" shrieked Deremer. "Papa, I did this for you! I blinded him to avenge you! Aren't you proud of me, Papa? Aren't you?"

"Oh, Derchi," Emarati sighed sadly, "I should not have neglected you and your mother so."

"Papa, I hated them for you. I'd destroy them for you." Tears began to run down her face and her shoulders shook with sobs.

"Oh, no, Derchi. No, no." Emarati spoke soothingly.

He might have made a good father, thought Aritoli, *had he not been a priest of Irhan.* He looked at Deremer's strong, tear-stained face. *How she must have loved him, to have driven herself so.*

"Well," said Irhan, "our judge has given his verdict. He has forgiven Master ola Silba of the deed. Therefore, Deremer, you must restore Aritoli's sight."

"No!" Deremer wailed, and she sat abruptly on the tent's sandy floor, burying her face in her hands.

"This leaves our portrait of vengeance unbalanced," said Irhan. "Therefore, Deremer, prepare to receive *my* vengeance."

Aritoli did not know how much of his current borrowed vision reflected reality, but he watched in horror as Deremer became wrinkled and shriveled and bent. Her rheumy eyes grew wide as she looked down at herself and she moaned.

"No!" Aritoli shouted. "Irhan, I beg you, cease!"

"What?" said the Lord of Beauty, frowning.

"Don't you see? She did this out of love for her father. She wanted to do something he would have found praiseworthy, that would have earned his love. She couldn't know it was not what he wanted. She saw me as her father's murderer. She couldn't know that her father asked for death as surely as a man in a dory who throws his oars away at sea. Restore her, Irhan. I forgive her."

A smile crept across the god's lips. "Well, it would seem forgiveness is an underlying theme of our gathering. I will restore her, if she restores your sight."

"No, Irhan, do not blackmail her—" but as he spoke, Aritoli felt his eyes twitch and prickle, and he shut them, putting his hands to his face. He blinked out tears and slowly opened his eyes as the sensations faded. He saw sunbeams slanting through the crack of the tent door, dappling the sandy floor with pools of pale light. He looked up and saw the Gatekeeper's ancient, craggy face, a man-shaped cloud of golden dustmotes, and Deremer's young, intent face as her hands completed a sorcerous pattern. And Maljun—his worn visage a study in loyalty and patience. It was the most beautiful scene he'd ever beheld, because it was his true sight restored. "Thank you," he whispered.

"And so our scene is complete," said the golden cloud that Aritoli realized was Irhan. "I could not let you remain blind. I need you as an arbiter of beauty in the world. You have served me in more ways than you know." In a glimmer of golden lightning, Irhan was gone.

Aritoli looked at Deremer and tried to smile at her.

She scowled in return. "I still hate you," she said.

"So long as you do not feel indifferent to me, I am pleased. You impress me, Deremer."

"You make me sick."

"From what other artists and their patrons tell me, you are in good company."

"I'll listen to you no more." She slowly stood and reached for the tent flap.

"I've been thinking of reviewing your dance for the Crier," said Aritoli. "Favorably, of course. You are an excellent dancer, you know."

Deremer stared back at him, her expression showing more

confusion than hate. Then she flung the tent flap aside and strode out onto the beach.

Aritoli sighed and leaned back in the chair.

"That was well done," said Emarati's voice above him.

Aritoli started. "Excuse me, Emarati. I'd forgotten you were here, more or less."

"Yes. I must go. This speaking is . . . difficult. Ah, Mehari sends her regards."

"She is there? With you?"

"It was she who taught me forgiveness, for she forgave me."

"I am pleased for you, Emarati. May you both have joy, wherever you are."

"I do not know what lies ahead for us, but I thank you. Be well, ola Silba."

"The crystal has gone dark," croaked the old Gatekeeper. "He will say nothing more."

Aritoli bade Maljun to pay the old woman handsomely, and he strolled out of the tent. He blinked, his eyes unaccustomed to the light. Yet he delighted in all he could see; dark-eyed children playing on the sand, colorful birds wheeling in the sky, sunlight sparkling on the sea. Maljun stepped up beside him and they walked together back towards the city of Ka Zhir.

"Will we be staying here awhile, Master?"

"Eh? No, Maljun, I want to return to Liavek as soon as possible. I want to quash whatever rumors may be starting in my absence. Also, I think I may commission a painting. A group portrait. What do you think, Maljun?"

The old manservant wore a slight smile. "An interesting idea, Master. You know. . ."

"Yes?"

"I was wondering about one rumor in particular that is said about you—"

"Which rumor is that?"

"The one which says that whatever deity presided over your birth figuratively placed your heart in your eyes. I was wondering if that deity might have been—"

"Irhan? Tut, Maljun, he hardly seems old enough to have presided at my birth."

"Appearances can deceive, Master."

"Ah, but seeing is believing."

The laughter of the two men was soon lost in the cries of the birds and the quiet roar of the waves.

The Skin and Knife Game

by Lee Barwood and Charles de Lint

THUNDER DRUMMED IN Saffer's room, as if a madman had been let loose at a set of kettle drums. Saffer groaned and burrowed her head deeper into the twist of blankets on her bed. She wished desperately for the storm to move on. As though in answer to her prayer, for one brief moment there was a lull. Then the thunder started up again.

Poking her head up from out of her nest of bedclothes, she squinted at the bright light coming in through the window. How could she be hearing thunder when the sky was so blue it hurt to look at it? Her squint tightened, then focused on the door to her room which was vibrating with the thunder.

"Open for the Guard!" a deep voice cried in the next lull.

Saffer continued to stare stupidly at the door. The Guard? Sink them. What did they want with her at this hour of the—

The thunder started up again.

"All right!" Saffer shrieked, then immediately clutched her temples to keep her head all in one piece. In a much softer voice she added, "I'm coming." Sitting up very carefully, she stretched a hesitant foot towards the floor.

Stumbling to the door, she swung it wide to blink at the pair of large, gray-clad Guards.

"Demar wants to see you," one of them said.

Saffer winced. Demar. That figured. Trust her brother to have her roused at—

"What time is it?" she asked.

"Almost noon."

"Already?"

"I wouldn't keep him waiting," the guard told her. "He's in a mood."

Lovely. Her head was ready to split and Demar was in a mood. "What am I supposed to have done this time?"

The guard shrugged. Saffer sighed and stumbled back into her room. Fumbling about in the small remedies bag that hung from the end of her bed, she finally closed her fingers about a little pouch that contained one of Marithana's hangover cures.

"Can I get dressed, or is it a come-as-you-are sort of party?" she asked as she sprinkled some of the mixture on her palm. Pulling a face, she swallowed it dry.

"Five minutes," the guard said, then closed the door.

Saffer replaced the little pouch in her remedies bag. She rubbed her hands over her face, then ran her fingers through the short hair on the top of her head. The seven braids hanging behind her felt heavier than the Levar's purse this morning and she draped them carefully over her shoulders to take their weight off her aching head.

Going over to the window, she stared out for a few moments, trying to remember what she could possibly have done that would entail her brother sending a couple of his men round to pick her up. Odd's end. She hadn't been in a decent scrape since Dumps had left the city to work the railroaders' camps with his card tricks.

A sound at the door—still loud, but identifiable as a knock now—roused her enough to get dressed, hurriedly splash some water on her face, and join her unwanted travelling companions. About the only good thing for this morning, she thought as she trailed along between them, was that Marithana's hangover cure was beginning to take effect.

Demar took one look at Saffer and frowned. She was decked out in the current fashion—baggy Zhir-styled trousers and a tight shirt, topped with a loose jacket, all in pastel shades of mauve and pink. Her face was puffy from the previous night's drinking and her hair was a snake's nest of braids spilling to her shoulders.

"You look like a clown," he said.

"Oh, don't be such a dried old toad. This is all the rage."

Demar sighed. When she tried her best winning smile, he didn't allow himself to react.

Demar had Saffer's chestnut brown hair, but he was taller than her by a head. He was lean and rangy, thick-wristed, with a lightness to his step that came from years with the Guard. Looking at his sister with her lopsided smile made him think that half those years had been filled with pulling her out of one scrape or another.

"What is it you think I've done this time?" Saffer asked finally.

"You'd better come with me," Demar said.

Saffer gave him an odd look. "Oh, don't go all sinking officious on me," she began.

Demar cut her off with a wave of his hand and led her down the hall. He wouldn't speak until they entered another room in the guardhouse. Lying on a cot in the center of the room was the bruised and battered body of a young man. The guard who had been tending him left the room when Demar gave her a nod. On another cot by the wall lay a girl a few years younger, one leg twisted and thin.

Saffer blanched, but she stepped forward to take a closer look all the same.

"Are . . . are they dead?" she asked.

"The girl is. The man's taken a bad beating, but he'll live." Demar studied his sister, watching her reactions. "Do you know them?" he asked.

"No. Should I . . ." Her voice trailed off as she got a closer look at the man's face. "Kerlaf," she murmured. She turned to look at her brother. "I met them last night. I had a commission at The Luck's Shadow and he was there with—" she glanced at the body of the girl"—with his sister, Ayla. Demar, how did you know I knew them? Odd's end, I only met them last night."

"The man had your name on his lips when he was brought in."

"Truly, Demar. I went straight home after the party and collapsed on my bed until your thugs dragged me out of it." Her gaze drifted back to the pair on the cots. "Poor Kerlaf. He really cared about Ayla. You could just tell by the way he took care of her."

"So the last you saw of them was at The Luck's Shadow?" Demar asked.

Saffer nodded.

"That's a wizard's inn, isn't it? Is he a wizard?"

"Ayla was—sort of. I never really got to talk with them about it. But they were there with me. I met them on my way to the party and they looked so bedraggled that I brought them along and snuck them in. They looked like they could use a bit of fun."

That was Saffer, Demar thought. Always willing to pick up any stray dog.

"What happened to them, Demar?"

"Nobody knows. A couple of guards found them in Fortune Way and brought them in just an hour ago. When the man—you said his name was Kerlaf?"

Saffer nodded.

"When he mentioned you by name, I had you brought around straight away. They're not from the city, are they?"

"They used to live here a long time ago. I got the impression that they'd been away and only just returned, but I didn't get much of a chance to talk to them. I was working, you know." Her gaze drifted back to Ayla.

"And you're sure there's not more to this than you're telling me?"

Saffer looked away from the dead girl's face. Swallowing hard, she shook her head.

Demar sighed. "Will you take responsibility for them, Saff? They hadn't even a copper to their names."

"I can put Kerlaf up at my place, I suppose, but Ayla . . ."

"If she stays here, she goes into a pauper's grave."

"Send her to an undertaker in my name," Saffer said. "I'' go by later to make the arrangements." Though who k where she'd get the money.

"I'll see to it," Demar said. "You'll want some help getting him back to your place?"

Saffer nodded.

"I'll get those two 'thugs' to help you."

He could tell that she wasn't in the mood to smile, but she touched his arm to let him know that she wasn't just being sulky.

"But if you hear anything . . .?"

"I'll tell you right away."

"That's all I wanted to hear." Taking her by the arm, he led her back to his office.

After seeing that Kerlaf was comfortable in her room, Saffer spent the rest of the afternoon making the funeral arrangements for Ayla. It took the last of her money, plus some that she had to borrow from Meggy Thistle whom she ran into in the Levar's Park. She'd also been at the party at The Luck's Shadow the previous night and was an old friend of Saffer's.

"Mind you," she said as she handed Saffer the coins, "I'll need this back before the end of the week. I thought I'd wander up toward Trader's Town for a week or so and see how well the railway men are paying these days. I was going to ask you if you wanted to come. We could've had a bit of fun *and* collected a copper or two while we were at it. I've heard they're starving for good entertainment."

"Don't I know it," Saffer replied. "Dumps is up there right now, cardsharping his way through their wages. Say hello to him for me if you see him."

Meggy shook her head. "Not likely, Saffer. I want to stay on the *good* side of the railway men."

"I'll get this back as quick as I can," Saffer said, holding up the money Meggy had lent her. "Thanks again."

Meggy nodded, but just as Saffer turned to go, she caught her arm. "Now I remember," she said.

"Remember what?"

"I had something to tell you and it just drained out of my mind the moment I saw you. Remember the big woman at the party last night, the one that looked more like a baker than a wizard? She had the little yapping dog that thought it knew every tune better than we did."

"I remember her. Her name was Teshi, wasn't it?"

Meggy nodded. "She was by looking for you."

"For *me*? What for?"

"She didn't say. Maybe she has another commission for us."

"Then why didn't she talk to you about it?"

Meggy shrugged. "I don't know. Anyway, I sent her round by your place."

Wonderful, Saffer thought. Her brother thought she was up to no good, she had a patient in her bed, she'd just spent all her money on a funeral for someone she hardly knew at all, and now a wizard was looking for her. She just hoped that she hadn't done something stupid at the party last night while in a beer-silly mood.

"She's probably been and gone by now," Meggy said.

Saffer nodded glumly, not believing it for a moment. After thanking Meggy again for the loan and promising to pay it back as soon as she could, she hurried off for home.

According to her landlord, the wizard had been and gone by the time Saffer returned to her room. Upstairs, Kerlaf was still imitating a man-sized lump on her bed. After fussing about with his pillows and blankets, she went and sat in her windowseat. There she indulged in a soliloquy while plucking the odd note from her cittern and staring off through what little view there was from her window.

"It's not so much that Demar doesn't trust me," she said, "as that sometimes I wonder if he isn't right. Maybe I *do* just bring trouble on myself." She plucked a few notes from the cittern's double strings, then a chord. *Ting, ting, kring.* "I didn't have to bring them along to the party, but they did look so forlorn, and I just knew there'd be all that food there that was only going to get thrown out in the morning." *Kring.* "And no one really seemed to mind, what with Ayla being a . . . was it an herbalist or an astrologer?"

"She was an astronomer, actually."

Saffer blinked with surprise at the reply to her question.

She looked at the bed, but Kerlaf hadn't moved, little say spoken. Then her gaze went to the door.

The wizard Teshi stood there. She was a short, friendly-looking woman, plump with short curly grey hair, dressed in voluminous robes that glimmered with a rainbow effect. Huge gaudy rings, all gold and silver and with far too many large gems, glittered on her hands. Her eyes twinkled, but there was something in their blue depths that made Saffer feel a little intimidated. She found it hard to look away. It wasn't until Teshi broke eye contact to look at Kerlaf that Saffer blinked and set aside her cittern. Then she spotted the little mop of grey fur with the big dark eyes that had accompanied the wizard.

"I don't want to seem rude," Saffer began, "but—"

"What am I doing here?" Teshi replied.

"Something like that."

"It's because of Kerlaf's sister," Teshi said. She turned from the bed and sat down on its edge so that she was facing Saffer. The little dog began to explore the room. "She does star charts," Teshi explained. "Did star charts. I was planning to commission some from her, but then I heard the horrible news. This sort of a thing . . . You'd think we were in Ka Zhir or something."

She gave Saffer's clothes a sharp look, but Saffer managed to ignore it. Saffer thought about her patient and his sister. News certainly travelled fast. Half of Liavek had probably known about it before she had.

"I took rather a liking to them," Teshi finished, "and thought I would see if I could do anything to help. Whoever did this shouldn't be allowed to get away with it."

"Well, the Guard's looking into it," Saffer said.

"Yes, but they have so many things to look into. If we can lend them a hand, I doubt they'd mind."

"You don't know my brother."

"I'm sure I don't."

Saffer shook her head. "That's not what I meant. Demar's in the Guard and he told me I was absolutely *not* to meddle in this. Odd's end, he'd kill me if—"

"We caught the attackers and delivered them without his having to lift a finger?"

"He wouldn't be happy."

"Nonsense."

Before Saffer could argue any more, Teshi had turned back to Kerlaf. She laid her palms on either side of his head. The air seemed to glimmer around her for a moment, then Kerlaf's eyelids flickered and his eyes opened. Saffer left the window-seat and stepped close. He had, she decided, the nicest pair of clear blue eyes that she'd ever seen.

"A-ayla . . .?" he murmured.

"Ah . . . she's not . . . ah . . ."

"She's dead," Teshi said softly.

Kerlaf's gaze went back and forth between them, then his eyes clouded with pain. "I . . . I remember," he said and he began to weep.

Saffer had never had a grown man cry on her before. She gave Teshi a beseeching look. The wizard nodded and gathered Kerlaf up in her arms.

"Maybe you should get him something—tea, or soup," she told Saffer.

Saffer backed away to the door. "I'll see what the landlord's got on," she said.

But they weren't listening to her. Kerlaf's body shook with great shuddering sobs. Teshi held him against her, murmuring comforting noises. Biting at her lower lip, Saffer hurried downstairs to the kitchen, grateful for something to do. The wizard's little dog followed at her heels.

By the time Saffer returned with a steaming bowl of beef broth, Teshi and Kerlaf were sitting on either end of the bed. Kerlaf's eyes were bleak with his loss, but he was no longer weeping. Saffer remembered her first look into them last night and then again a few moments ago, when Teshi had brought him around. The guileless clarity that had attracted her was gone, replaced with a sorrow that went beyond despair.

"Can you remember what they looked like?" Teshi was asking him. "The people who attacked you."

Kerlaf blinked. It took a moment for him to find his voice.

"It wasn't people," he said finally. "It was a woman—the one who ran the boarding house."

"What woman?" Saffer asked.

"Her name was Bica. We rented the room when we arrived yesterday afternoon—it was cheap and clean, and when you don't have much, that's enough."

"I don't know her," Teshi said. "But this isn't my part of town. Saffer?"

"I know *of* her," Saffer replied. "Everyone in the Alley does. She's this crazy old woman who runs a rooming house a few blocks down from here. I don't know anybody who's stayed there."

Teshi's eyes narrowed.

"No," Saffer said. "It's not because she's dangerous or anything. She's just—too weird. My friend Meggy was going to rent a room from her, but she got the creeps and never moved in. The thing is . . ." Saffer hesitated, looking at Kerlaf. Odd's end, you'd think he could take care of himself against some old spinster. "She's not tough or anything, you know? Just a crazy old woman."

"What did she do?" Teshi asked Kerlaf. "Did she have others with her?"

"No one else," Kerlaf said. "She . . . she gave us hot spiced milk when we returned to our room last night—a welcome cup, she called it, and then . . . the next thing I remember was her standing over me. I was on the floor and Ayla was beside me, so still. She must have drugged us only I didn't finish all of my drink. I tried to rise, but she hit me with something. I started to pass out, but she just kept hitting me, and Ayla . . . I knew Ayla was already . . . I knew she was . . ."

He didn't weep again, he just closed up. His eyes went bleak and he slumped against the headboard.

"If I wasn't so . . . so sinking weak . . ."

Teshi and Saffer exchanged glances.

"We'd better tell my brother," Saffer said. "Demar can—"

Teshi shook her head, her eyes cold and hard as diamonds. "Let me deal with this Bica," she said.

"I don't think that's such a good—"

Something flickered like fire in Teshi's cold eyes and

Saffer suddenly remembered that this was a wizard she was arguing with, not one of her friends.

"All right," she said. "Sink the Guard. Let Demar dump me on Crab Isle when he finds out. What do I care."

Teshi's dog jumped onto the wizard's lap and she patted it absently. "Twig and I, we look after our friends," she said. "Even when we've only just met them."

"Fine," Saffer said. "Perfect." And do you know any spells to get one off of Crab Isle? she wondered.

Teshi rose. Twig leapt to the floor and danced eagerly by the door, while the wizard laid a comforting hand on Kerlaf's shoulder.

"I'll be back," she told Saffer, and then she and the little dog were gone and Saffer was alone with Kerlaf.

"Ah . . . you really should try some of this broth," she told Kerlaf.

Her patient made no reply. Lovely, Saffer thought. Not that she blamed him. But looming larger in her mind than Kerlaf's grief were her own worries about Demar. He was going to kill her.

The dead woman sat upright in the chair. The day was wearing to its end outside, but it was always dark in the cellar where the corpse sat. In the flicker of the lantern light, its features almost seemed alive. But the corpse was mummified and tied to its chair. Its withered cheeks were gaunt. Its skin clung like dry leather to its limbs. Dark hollows lay where its eyes had been.

Across from the corpse sat a living woman. She too had a wrinkled face, but her eyes glittered darkly like a crow's as she stared at her dead companion. Her hair was a faded salty yellow and hung limply past her sloped shoulders.

"He went and stayed alive," she told the corpse, "and Bica doesn't like that. He'll bring Guards, he will, and maybe wizards. You'd like that, wouldn't you? Maybe the wizards will put your soul back in your body, or set it free—I'm sure you don't care, just so long as you can get away from Bica. But Bica has a plan, you know. Bica will just find him and cut his throat and then no one will know that Bica had anything to do with it."

She grinned at the corpse, exposing long yellow teeth in poor condition.

"Maybe Bica should bring him back here to be with you and then you wouldn't be so lonely. Would you like that?" She cocked her ear. "Oh, you'll have to speak up, or Bica will keep him for herself." She listened a second time, then rose to her feet. "Well, Bica gave you a chance to speak, but it's too late now. Bica's made up her mind. It's the knife for him and the dark cellar for you."

Catching up the lantern, she held it up to the dead woman's withered features. "It's almost night now," Bica told the corpse. "Soon Bica will go out and find him and play a game of skin and knife with him. Do you remember that game? It's the one Sadabel played on Bica before Bica tore out his heart. See this? See it now?"

She lifted her blouse to show the dead woman the scar tissue on her abdomen.

"You peel the skin back, bit by bit. And then you cut a muscle here, and another there. And then you twist the blade, just a touch, until the blood's running freely. And then you peel some more skin back. It's a fine game, isn't it?

"Remember when Bica played it with you? You didn't like it. You kept crying for Bica to stop, but Bica remembered that you had a little power. Bica knew that you'd helped Sadabel hurt her, so Bica had to cut away, cut, cut, cut, until there was just the skin left to cure and the bone left to wire, and then the puzzle to put all back together again.

"But you're still here, aren't you, and don't you look fine? Oh, yes. Bica didn't want to send you away. Bica wanted to keep her eye on you. Like Bica should have done with Sadabel so that she didn't have to keep killing him, over and over and over again . . ."

Teshi stopped by her rooms in The Luck's Shadow after leaving Saffer and Kerlaf. She stayed only long enough to change, then left by the rear, transformed into a shabbily-dressed woman by the simple magic of a disguise. Her beautiful robes and jewelry were replaced with well-worn clothing that was too large for her, while her fingers glittered with rings of polished tin and brass set with great chunks of brightly coloured glass. She carried a bag over one shoulder, and a small disheveled bundle of fur dogged her footsteps as she headed towards Rat's Alley.

She paused across the street and eyed the battered three-story dwelling. Twilight lay thick on the streets, but the building was dark, giving it a gloomy look. The door was an odd-coloured green—the paint chipped and flaking, she discovered as she crossed the street to approach it. She was about to knock when the door opened.

Teshi took a step back and Twig growled while hiding behind her ankles. The woman who opened the door leaned on a knobby stick of a cane and glared at them until she spied the bag on Teshi shoulders.

"Looking for lodgings, are you?" she asked.

Teshi took another step back. An unpleasant odour hung about the woman that grew more pronounced when she opened her mouth.

"Don't be shy, don't be shy. Bica's got room enough for everyone, isn't that the truth?"

"I haven't much money," Teshi began, but Bica waved that notion off.

"Paugh! Bica likes to help people and, in turn, people like to help her. Bica always has room for those that need it, don't you know. You can pay a little and help out a little . . ." Her eyes narrowed slightly. "Do you know any magics?"

Teshi shook her head.

"Too bad, too bad. Bica likes to trade lodgings for magics, especially guardspells." She leaned close and Teshi held her breath. "There's some that don't like old Bica, you know. They live up there." She pointed straight above them.

"What—on the upper floors?" Teshi asked.

"No, no. In the sky. In the moon. Bica's far too clever for them, though."

When Saffer had described Bica as a crazy old woman, Teshi realized, the young cittern player hadn't been exaggerating. She felt Twig still rubbing nervously against her ankles so she hoisted him up into the crook of her arm.

Bica eyed the dog with sudden suspicion. "Where are you from?" she demanded.

"Not from the moon," Teshi said.

"So," Bica said after a long moment of silence. "You want a room?"

Teshi blinked, then nodded. "Yes, but—"

"Oh, don't you worry about your little dog. Bica loves animals, doesn't she just."

She put out a hand to Twig—who suffered a rough pat with only a little trembling—then turned and led the way inside. The room she offered Teshi was the first on the right from the front door. Leaving the wizard to inspect it, Bica bustled off, "To get you a little welcoming gift, and wouldn't that be nice?"

Teshi studied the rented room. In different circumstances, it would have been amusing. The room *was* clean, but it was such a crazy quilt of colours that it made her head spin. Bica must have furnished her house from the pickings of Fortune Way—but only after a more thorough cleaning than anyone else would want to get close enough to give the various articles. She sighed and turned to Twig. The little dog sat in the middle of the room, fastidiously wrinkling his nose.

"Yes," Teshi said. "There certainly is an air of—" Bica chose that moment to return with a tray and two steaming mugs of spicy milk. "—A charm about the building," Teshi finished.

Bica nodded. She smiled, but the revelation of her yellowed teeth only made her look worse. "There is something about these old buildings, isn't that the truth?"

She put the tray down on a table by the door and handed Teshi a mug. Then before she picked up her own, she muttered something about that shade not hanging quite right. As soon as Bica crossed the room, Teshi surreptitiously exchanged the mug she'd been given for the one still on the tray. Twig barked a warning.

Teshi caught a glimpse of Bica with her knobby cane in her hand. Then the cane hit her head as though powered by the force of one of the new railway engines, and she collapsed to the floor, her milk mug spilling from her hand. Twig growled as Bica approached his fallen mistress, but the old woman swung the cane at him and he had to back off. She chased him all the way to the front door, coming closer and closer to hitting him with each blow, until he finally turned and fled out onto the street.

"Bica likes to eat dogs!" the old woman screamed after Twig before slamming the door. Her momentary ill-humour at the dog dissolved as she stood over her newest victim.

"Thought Bica wouldn't know you had a new body, did you now? Thought you could fool her, but Bica's too smart. Always was, always will be. And this time Bica knows what to do with you. It's the skin and knife game for you, and won't that be fun?" She paused long enough for Teshi to answer, but the wizard lay limp on the rug. "Oh, yes," Bica nodded. "It'll be such fun, wait and see."

Saffer was sitting in her windowseat, working on the particularly intricate bit in the middle of a reel called "Wrap Up and Roll." Winny Lind, the bones player, had showed it to her on Meggy's whistle once and, while it wasn't quite a cittern sort of a tune, Saffer had always wanted to learn it. With Kerlaf asleep once more, and Teshi still gone, it seemed the perfect thing to keep her mind off her troubles.

She had just about got the three rolls of triplets that were giving her the most trouble when she happened to glance out the window. Surprised, she started to lean over the ledge, then quickly ducked her head back in. Demar was out on the street, heading for her lodgings.

Perfect, she thought as she laid down her cittern. She gave the bed a glance, but Kerlaf was still asleep. Maybe she should curl up on a pillow and pretend to be asleep as well. Demar would peek in, see them sleeping, and then—

Demar's characteristically loud knocking interrupted any further planning. Was that the first thing they learned when they joined the Guard? How to knock down doors with their knuckles?

"I know you're in there!" Demar called through the wood.

Saffer swung the door open and lifted a finger to her lips. "Will you keep it down? I've got a sick man sleeping in here."

Demar gave the bed a quick glance. "Sorry." He caught the door before Saffer could close it on him. Taking her by the arm, he pulled her out into the hall where he was standing and then shut the door. "We have to talk."

"About what?"

"Let's start with the wizard you had in your room this afternoon."

"Demar, have you been spying on me?"

"Only as much as you've been holding back."

Saffer tried a fierce frown on him, but it did no good. "It wasn't my idea," she began, then told what had happened since Teshi had arrived. As Demar listened, a storm gathered in his face.

"Saffer," he said grimly. "I warned you what would happen if you held back on—"

"Odd's end, Demar! She's a wizard. What was I supposed to do? Stand in the way and get turned into a frog or a newt?"

"Wizards don't do that kind of a thing."

"It happened to Dumps—he told me so himself."

"Do you believe everything he tells you?"

"Saffer shook her head. "No, but—"

Demar held up a hand to cut her off. "Please, Saffer. No more."

"What are you going to do?" she asked as Demar turned to go.

"Talk to this Bica *and* your wizard. We have laws in this city, Saffer, and a Guard to see that they're obeyed. Both you and Teshi are in a lot of trouble."

"But—"

"I want you to stay in your room and don't budge until I send someone around to collect you."

"But—"

Demar took a step towards her. Saffer skittered back into her room and closed the door on him. But when she heard him going down the stairs, she crept out into the hallway again. As Demar went out the front door, she bolted out the back, meaning to make her own way to Bica's rooming house. But in the alley that the back door opened onto, she almost stepped on a little bundle of fur.

"Twig!" she cried when she recognized it. Then her heart lurched inside her. If the little dog was here, alone, *what* had happened to his mistress?

Twig gave a bark.

"Aren't you a clever little thing," Saffer murmured. She scooped him up and, holding him against her chest, took off at a run for Bica's once more.

The dead woman in Bica's cellar had company now. Teshi was tied to a chair, just as the corpse was. All her clothes had been stripped from her, every belonging from the small bandage on one ankle where her sandal had been chafing to the tiniest of her rings. It all lay in a pile at the far end of the cellar, well beyond Teshi's reach.

Humming to herself, Bica sat in a third chair. Lamplight spilled from the copper-based lamp on the table beside her, lighting both the corpse, which stared straight into eternity with its sightless gaze, and Teshi, whose head was limp against her chest. The melody that Bica hummed was one that Saffer might have recognized. It was a Zhir knife-sharpening song and Bica honed away at her knife with a whetting stone as she hummed.

From time to time, Bica tested the blade against her thumb. Then she went back to her sharpening, her own eyes glittering like a carrion bird's as it dropped from the sky to feed.

When Teshi finally regained consciousness, the first thing she saw was the dry weathered skin of the corpse's face. Its dark eyeless sockets gazed emptily back at her. That, combined with her nakedness, the coolness of the cellar, and Bica's humming, sent a shudder through her body like a wave.

"Awake now, are you?" Bica murmured.

Teshi lifted her head and turned it slightly so that she could see her captor.

"Didn't think Bica would recognize you in that body, did you? But Bica's no fool. Bica always sees right through the skin—don't you know that by now?"

Teshi's gaze went from the woman's mad eyes down to the long wicked blade that she was sharpening.

"We're going to play a game," Bica said. "The skin and knife game. Bica's let you go free too many times, so this time you'll stay with Bica forever, just like your lover has. Bica's going to wrap your soul around your bones, then sew it all up in your skin and then won't you look fine?"

Teshi remembered Saffer's argument about leaving this to the Guard and wondered why she hadn't done just that. She strained against her bonds, but the ropes were tied too tightly. Her gaze lit on the pile of her belongings. Her luck was invested in a small gold band that she normally wore under her larger gaudier rings. She could sense it lying there, just across the cellar. But it might as well have been on the moon for all the use it was to her now.

"Looking for your power, are you?" Bica asked with a grin. "Bica's got the power now, wizard. You should have plunged your knife straight through Bica's heart instead of teaching her the skin and knife game, isn't that the truth?"

Teshi saw something change in the madwoman's eyes—just for a moment. There was a flash of anguish, a weight of pain for which there could be no measurement, but it was quickly suppressed. The fire returned to Bica's eyes, glittering and mad.

"I've never met you before," Teshi said quietly, but firmly.

"Isn't that a laugh?" Bica said to the corpse. "Our good friend Sadabel doesn't remember us." She looked back at Teshi and held up the knife. "Bica thinks you'll remember quick enough, and won't it be fun, won't it just?"

She returned to working on her knife's edge and began to hum once again. Teshi stared at her, then at the corpse. Bica had called her Sadabel. Teshi tasted the name, trying to recall why it sounded so familiar. When the memory finally came to her, she shuddered again.

Bica looked up with a grin. Testing the knife against her thumb, she set the whetstone aside and stood up.

"Bica thinks Master Knife is ready to play," she said.

• • •

Though Twig protested, Saffer refused to go round by the front of the rooming house. She made her way by the back alleys, holding the little dog so that it couldn't run away. By the time she reached Bica's back door, she was out of breath and had to lean against the dirty wall.

Some rescuer she was going to be. She'd come in looking like a guttersnipe and—oh, what was she even doing here? If Teshi—who was a wizard—was in trouble, what could she possibly do?

She realized that Demar must have already arrived. That was why she was here, she told herself. If Bica could deal so easily with Teshi and Kerlaf, what mightn't the old witch do to her brother?

Steeling her nerve, she pulled a length of wire from where it was hidden in the sole of her left shoe and began to work the lock on the door as Dumps had taught her. It was hard to keep a grip on Twig, who was squirming to be let down, and work the lock at the same time, but finally she was rewarded with a satisfying click. Replacing the wire it its hiding place, she cracked the door open and peered inside.

Demar arrived at the green door of Bica's house and brought his fist down against its wooden panels. Once, twice, again. He waited a moment, then repeated the hammering. When no one came after a quick count to twenty, he reached for the doorknob. But before he could touch it, the door swung open and a shabby old woman who could only be Bica stood there leaning on a cane and studying him with small glittering black eyes.

"Oh," Bica said. "What's this? A guard looking for lodging with old Bica? Isn't that fine."

Demar rubbed a finger lengthwise against his lips. "Er, not exactly," he said. While the old woman was probably a few bricks short of a load, she didn't exactly appear to be the villainous madwoman that Saffer had painted her.

Bica fluttered her eyelashes grotesquely. "What? Have you come courting old Bica then?"

Demar took a half-step back. "I'm looking for the wizard Teshi," he said in his most formal tones.

"Ah, the wizard." Bica revealed her yellowed teeth in a grin. "Of course. The important wizard." She stepped aside. "Come in, come in. Don't be shy. Bica doesn't bite."

Demar nodded uncomfortably and moved past her. "I just have to ask her a few—"

Before he could finish, Bica hit him from behind with her cane and he went stumbling to his knees. He stopped his fall with his hands, but she hit him again, across the shoulders, then once more on the back of his head. The floor turned black and swallowed him.

Bica pushed at him with her cane. When he didn't move, she cackled to herself. "Bica's blows are worse than her bite," she told him. Laying aside the cane, she grabbed his shoulders with surprising strength and began to haul him down to the cellar.

There was no one in the kitchen when Saffer crept inside. She closed the door behind her, then scurried across the room, one hand around Twig's muzzle to stop him from making an outcry. When she poked her head around the doorjamb, she was just in time to see Bica dragging her brother down the hall. Twig squirmed in her arms, but she clamped him to her chest with panicked strength and ducked out of the old woman's sight. Not until she heard Demar's boots hitting each stair that led down to the cellar, did she dare peek around the corner again.

The hall was empty. The door leading to the cellar stood ajar. Swallowing drily, Saffer crept to the landing and peered down. Oh, Demar, she thought. If she's hurt you, I'll . . . I'll . . .

She didn't know what she'd do. She didn't know *what* to do. Run to the Guard and call them in? What if they arrived too late? What if they thought it was just some joke and didn't come at all?

Oh, why did this sort of thing always have to happen to her?

Bica's laughter came drifting up the stairs and Saffer knew she couldn't wait any longer. Gathering the tattered bits of her courage, she eased her way down the stairs, stepping close to where they joined the wall and praying they wouldn't creak. By the time she reached the bottom, she was a walking tangle of nerves, tautly wired and ready to flee at the slightest provocation. But then she looked into the room from which Bica's laughter came.

She saw Teshi first. The wizard was tied naked to a chair. Her position might have seemed humorous if it hadn't been for the withered corpse tied to another chair and Bica standing over her brother, tugging off his trousers with one hand, a big gleaming knife in the other.

Saffer froze. She wanted to rush to her brother's rescue, but every muscle in her body knotted and she couldn't move. Then Bica turned and saw her. With a shriek she dropped Demar's trouser leg and brandished the knife at Saffer. But while Saffer still couldn't move, Twig surged out of her arms and attacked the mad woman, yapping madly.

Bica swung the knife at the little dog, missed, tried to kick it. Twig dodged each of her blows, ducked in and took a nip out of her pale leg, then dodged away from the next slash of the knife. The flurry of action was enough to unlock Saffer's paralysis. With a shriek as piercing as Bica's, she picked up the first thing that came to hand—a chipped statuette of Andrazzi the Lucky that was standing amid a pile of junk on a table by the door—and charged the madwoman.

Bica lifted the knife to meet Saffer's attack. Twig launched himself at her calves and bit through to the bone. Bica wailed. The statuette in Saffer's hand came down with enough force to shatter against the madwoman's head. Bica stumbled, her weight on her unhurt leg, her arms flailing to keep her balance. She tripped over Twig who was attacking her good leg and then fell over Demar's body. The knife twisted under her and she fell onto it, then rolled over.

Her cries were pitiful as the blood pumped from the hole in her stomach. Saffer took one look at the wound, then turned to retch in a corner. She continued to retch, dry-heaving long after Bica had finally expired. It was Teshi's voice that finally brought her around to free the wizard from her bonds.

Teshi held Saffer tightly, then steered her towards the stairs. "Go on up," she said. "I'll see to your brother."

Saffer stared at her, wide-eyed with shock. "I never meant . . . I didn't . . . She just . . ."

"Go," Teshi ordered softly.

She waited until Saffer had reached the top of the stairs, then slowly turned back to the room.

Two days later, Demar was still off-duty. He sat in the common room of The Luck's Shadow, nursing an ale, his head wrapped in a swath of bandage. Saffer sat beside him, much subdued. Teshi was across the table from them, Twig on her lap, daintily eating the little fishsticks that the wizard fed to him, one by one. Kerlaf, his bruises a hundred glorious shades of purple, yellow, and blue, sat beside her.

"Sadabel and Kitani—it was a great mystery when they vanished," Teshi said.

"But where did Bica fit in?" Kerlaf asked.

"We can't be sure," Teshi said, "but my guess is that she was Sadabel's apprentice. From the old scars on her torso and what little of her rantings I had the chance to hear, it seems Sadabel and Kitani had been torturing Bica. Somehow she managed to kill them both. Kitani you saw in the cellar—Bica cured her skin, then sewed it back up again with the dead woman's bones inside. As for Sadabel . . . I doubt we'll ever know exactly what happened to him."

"But . . . but why was she killing people?" Saffer asked.

"She thought they were Sadabel, come back to have his revenge upon her," Teshi explained.

"No doubt she killed him in a place where the body was easily disposed of," Demar said, "then came back to deal with Kitani."

Teshi nodded. "Only to live in fear of Sadabel's return."

"That poor woman," Saffer said softly.

Kerlaf shook his head. "I've no pity to spare for her."

Saffer looked at him, at the bleakness that still lay in his eyes, and didn't bother to argue with him. All she knew was that Bica had been a poor mad creature and the weight of her death lay on Saffer's soul.

Demar put his arm around Saffer's shoulders. He said nothing when she turned to look at him, just gave her a squeeze, but it was enough. He hadn't said a word about her following him, nor anything to anyone about how she and Teshi had interfered with Guard business.

"Did you know," she said, "that you look like a camel-driver with those bandages on?"

"Watch it, camel," he told her sternly. "You could still end up in the Guardhouse for a day or two."

Saffer smiled for the first time since the events in Bica's cellar and laid her head against his shoulder.

"That's better," she said. "You were being so nice to me that for awhile there I thought you didn't like me anymore."

Demar looked at Teshi, but the wizard only rolled her eyes and went on feeding Twig his fishsticks.

Strings Attached

by Nathan A. Bucklin

"I'd like some strings for my cittern," I told the old fellow.

He was tall and grey-haired and hard to impress. "Try these, young master," he said, a little too smoothly. "Magically guaranteed to stay perfectly clear and bright in tone for fifty days. Wound by the finest string-maker in Liavek."

I considered. "And what happens after the fifty days?"

"They disappear," he said without a trace of guilt. "So it's a good idea to replace them after forty-five days or so, just in case."

All I asked was that they last me through tonight. "What do these strings cost?"

He didn't blink. "A levar and a half."

I didn't have that amount on me, but I wasn't going to come right out and say it. "Could you show me some other ones? I don't like the idea of strings that are going to disappear."

"I have just what you need." He turned around. I busied myself staring around the room at citterns, baghorns, Zhir hammered-harps. When he turned back with a superficially similar set, I was resting my hands on the rippled glass countertop and humming to myself.

"Only one levar," he continued. "Guaranteed to hold a tune for six months. Just tune them once, play the opening verse of 'The Kil Island Fisheries,' and you'll never have to touch your tuning pegs until the next time you change them."

One levar. Only. "And what if they slip out of tune while I'm playing the verse you named?"

"In the forty years this store has been open," he said slowly, "we've only had one complaint."

"That's one complaint too many. And what about the songs that I play in unusual tunings?"

"Most citternists don't use unusual tunings." He was imperturbable. I was hoping he'd figure out how tight my finances were, so I didn't have to humiliate myself by admitting to it. "But I can sell you the Instant Retuning Spell of—"

"Strings!" That's all I want. Do you want me to take my trade somewhere else?"

"Your pardon." He turned again, traded the strings for an old and dusty packet. "The cheapest strings in the store and possibly the finest. They are good for—"

"I know what strings are good for!" It wasn't the old man's fault. I was anxious about this evening's concert, and taking it out on whoever was close. And I did have cause to be angry at the printer, who had delayed printing most of the posters until yesterday, but I'd somehow held my tongue when picking up my order. "Tell me the price," I finished, struggling to get a grip on myself.

"Ten coppers." He smiled suddenly, but I didn't believe it. "If you promise never to come in here again, I might make it nine."

Not trusting myself to speak for fear of making things worse, I counted out coppers from my belt-pouch. I'd paid the printer; I'd paid Thrae for rental of The Desert Mouse for the evening, almost every copper I could afford between us. Ten coppers for the strings just about cleaned me out. Very well, I told myself, tonight I skip dinner. After the concert, though, Iranda and I will celebrate.

The storekeeper simply handed me the strings, no wrapping or receipt. I took them without thanks and went back outside. This was no way to start the day. I really wished the old son-of-a-camel no harm, and most days I didn't let my frustrations get the better of me. If I felt any calmer in the next hour or two, I would go back and try to apologize.

My friend Iranda was putting up the posters, big ones with my name on them in fancy script writing. Tonight's concert was to be my first. I had reason to be proud; I had never known a street musician to reach the concert stage without serving at least a five-year apprenticeship in the public houses. As for me, I hadn't felt like wasting the five years; my youth had suddenly become a selling point.

"Well, did you get your strings?"

"Yes." I showed her the packet. "I hate to leave you alone, but I should really break them in a little. Are you sure you won't come back to my room with me?"

"I don't know what bothers me more, Liramal," she said reflectively. "When you pretend you don't care about me, or when you pretend you do."

"You're my friend." The sun broke through the clouds for an instant, catching Iranda's fair hair at just the right angle to bring out its unreal beauty. "And the way the day's going, I've got a feeling I might need you to keep me out of trouble."

"I'd like to keep you company," she said, "but there are at least fifty more posters to put up."

"And plenty of tacks?"

"Plenty. Look. How about if you go back to your room and do whatever boring things you have to do, and I meet you in front of the Tiger's Eye in an hour? That should give you time."

"Barely," I grumbled. But it wasn't as if I wasn't going to be seeing her again today; and—probably deliberately—Iranda had sidestepped the tense situation that always seemed to develop when we were alone in my room or hers. Iranda could be remarkably sensitive.

I wandered through the Canal District with more purpose than most passersby probably would have suspected. I allowed myself so few days off from playing in the Levar's Park that the long walks I loved seemed like unimaginable luxury. A basket shop, a silversmith's shop, a gambling parlor caught my eye as I wandered the Street of Thieves (actually a respectable commercial street, due in part to its name). Here and there on the palm and cypress trees there were posters, put up haphazardly by Iranda as we'd walked this way earlier in the day. "Liramal, Balladeer to His Scarlet Eminence the Regent, Appearing at The Desert Mouse." I could wish for a better theater, or at least a theater with a better name; but the Desert Mouse was at least known, and those who saw my posters would know where to find me.

Home was an upstairs room at Mama Neldasa's. I had my closet under the eaves; Mama had my music on Luckday nights. And Luckday nights had always been busy, ever since I'd become well known; I more than earned my keep. I opened my door, sat down on the three-legged stool, kicked off my sandals, rested my feet on my pallet, put my cittern face up in my lap and began to change the strings.

String-changing is a bore and a chore; I'd learned to put up with it by making it so systematic I could think of other things while I did it. I tuned the lowest pair of strings down to a tension so low they both barely rattled, and did the same with the next pair up. Then the highest two strings, for variety; then the two pair in the middle.

At some point in untuning the cittern, I stretched out my right foot, just enough, and touched the set of strings where they lay on the pallet. And I felt something.

I have no magic of my own, and most of the time I can only tell when magic's being used by how things look. If you're walking down the Levar's Highway and you see a cypress tree turn into a palm and back, and someone in front of it is making frantic gestures with one hand while the other hand fondles some useless bauble, anyone can tell there's magic being worked. But sometimes—

Sometimes it's not the way the spell looks that's the giveaway. I had been walking down the street when Pilavi the wizard stumbled on the broken step outside the herbalist's shop. I saw him limp back into the shop, cursing and demanding that the stonemason be summoned. And I saw him sit down on the walk, casting a simple spell to make the step be solid until it could be repaired.

I had lost interest and was walking away when something happened. Maybe it was my luck time, but I'll swear by the Twin Forces that I felt it when the step changed. And similarly, I could feel that my newly bought strings were radiating magic.

I didn't have time to go back to the store and argue, and my own strings needed changing desperately. I'd planned on changing them the previous night to let them settle. Except the *Praluna* had shown up in port, I'd gone down to say hello and received a hero's welcome, and we'd wound up singing old Zhir folk songs until almost dawn. (I am probably the only minstrel in Liavek who has ever helped raise a swamped Zhir ship. Trust me, the story's too long to retell here.) Besides, whatever I'd told the storekeeper, I didn't really believe that all magicked strings were worse than all regular strings. The magicked ones just had surprises built in.

I was used to surprises. After all, I'd lived a third of my life on the street. I polished the cittern with my usual care and put on the new strings; first, tenth, second, ninth, and so on. About the time I had eight of them on, I tried a barred 7th formation. It was missing a couple of notes, and the tuning wasn't quite there yet, but it sounded clear and crisp—or was it, perhaps, a little too soft?

Down below in the dining room I heard laughter and applause. Then one voice came through, radiating above the others, talking about archery. Today the Archers of the White Rose were meeting in that dining room, talking about their exploits, their equipment, their kills in the hunt. Mama would earn a hefty wage for her cooking for this afternoon's banquet. And that wasn't even mentioning the ones who'd come in from Hrothvek or Saltigos and would be staying the night. But for me, the speaker was only a distraction.

Determinedly, I began to strum as hard as I could, singing "Pell and Onzedi" at the top of my lungs. Clearly, there was nothing wrong with either my voice or my ears. But the strings were producing nearly no volume at all.

There was a timid knock at my door. It was Zawan, Mama's main serving boy. "Could you keep your voice down?" he said hesitantly. "We got a complaint from one of the archers."

Life was mad today. My strings were too soft, and my voice was too loud. I thanked Zawan for the message—he was a nice enough kid; I'd known him for over a year—and went downstairs the back way, not even detouring through the kitchen to say hello to Mama Neldasa.

A block shy of the Tiger's Eye, my day became even worse.

I'd started to play and sing as I walked. After all, the cittern hung as naturally from my shoulders as a leaf from a tree, and I had a sneaking suspicion that playing for strangers throughout the streets of Liavek ultimately made more people come to the Levar's Park in search of me. Somehow, the strings were quite loud enough outdoors; it was as though the room I'd tried them out in walled off the sound. So I was singing, improvising both words and music as I could do when exceptionally chipper, and almost ran into a stranger.

He was a big man, old, with a full head of long grey hair and a full beard of the same shade. "Madmen!" he muttered, looking right through me as I tried to step around him. "They charge you half a levar for a basket of fruit my family can eat in a day! Tell me, minstrel, have you heard of the like?"

I admitted that I had not, and tried again to go around him.

He reached out one gnarled hand and grasped me by the wrist. "Not so fast, boy," he said. "Play me a song. Something about fruit-sellers."

I couldn't think of a song about fruit-sellers, and could hardly play with his hand around my wrist. I told him so.

He released me. "Two coppers I will give you," he said, removing my main reason for resisting. "Two coppers, and no more! Do you understand?"

I looked ahead toward the Tiger's Eye, and didn't see Iranda. That made the difference for me. I didn't think I was late for our meeting; maybe two coppers for one song was worth it, right now. "Picking Time in the Orchard," by the Saltigan minstrel Arulen, had one of the prettiest melodies I knew. Besides, if you turned the words around, they might be interpreted as a song about how the pickers worked all day to make the fruit-sellers rich. I played him the opening few bars:

"The fruit trees are laden, the ladders in place,
My work is as plain as the frown on my face—"

But the strings were terribly, impossibly, out of tune. I tried to reach out and tune a peg, still singing, but it only made matters worse.

"Who cares if you're fevered, who cares if you're sick;
A copper a bushel for all you can pick—"

The old man interrupted me furiously. "And you call yourself a minstrel?" he screamed, causing several passersby to stop and look at him curiously. "Take that instrument of yours and junk it! And be off with you!"

Under the circumstances, I didn't feel justified in asking for my two coppers. I detoured around him without a word and went to wait for Iranda.

The solemn and efficient woman who ran the Tiger's Eye had told me once that she'd rather I didn't play outside her door. I imagined that money tossed into my hat might otherwise be spent on her premises; she certainly hadn't said I was a bad musician, or that she didn't like me. Still, as I waited for Iranda, I tried a tentative chord or two. Oddly, it now sounded perfectly in tune, except for the one string I'd altered in a panic while playing.

Iranda showed up out of breath and empty-handed. "They've all been put up," she reported. "Some of the posters we put up last week around the Desert Mouse have been ripped down, so I put up some new ones."

"Sounds reasonable. But what shall I do about these strings?"

"Your new strings?" Iranda asked blankly. "What's wrong with them?"

She listened patiently while I explained the day's events. When I finished, she heaved a deep sigh. "Liramal, I wonder how you ever managed to survive on the street as long as you did. Common sense says all you have to do is go back to the store where you bought them, say they aren't good enough, and get another set."

"Common sense tells me that if I can make them do, they're good enough. Besides, I'm not sure that weasel at the music store won't cheat me again."

"So go to another store and buy another set. Forget about these."

"Whistler's Corner is closed due to illness in the owner's family. Maridonci and Daughter is too far to walk in the time we've got left. Krum's baghorn shop sometimes has cittern strings, but more often doesn't. And besides—" I patted my belt-pouch. The two coppers left in it clinked rather than jingling. Iranda got the idea.

"Can you at least go back to the store and find out the nature of the spell?" she finally said.

"That might be a good idea," I said uncertainly. It felt strange to trust the explanations of a man whose wares were so unreliable. "And I do owe him an apology for getting mad. Except, considering the way these strings have been acting, I'm still mad."

"You might have cause to be," said Iranda.

There was one street, the Street of Shadows, that led more directly to the store than did the Street of Thieves. Most Liavekans didn't use it for a thoroughfare because it went up and over a small, steep hill. I avoided it because I'd grown up on it and my mother still lived there. I didn't know what she'd have to say to the son she'd kicked out of the house five years earlier, and I didn't care to run into her by accident and find out. It was lined with tightly packed old houses, mostly owned by young working families who couldn't afford to live anywhere else. Iranda and I took it almost at a run; time was getting shorter.

At the bottom of the hill we found the little boy.

I think Iranda noticed him first. She would; I knew her to be fond of children. The boy was sitting in the middle of the street, not crying, just looking very, very forlorn.

"What's your name?" Iranda asked him. I was carrying the cittern and panting too hard to talk; the interruption provided a welcome breather.

The boy looked up at her with eyes that seemed an impossible blue. He was three or four years old. "Sandiros," he said. Belatedly, I noticed that his face and arms were all bruised, and I remembered the way I'd been treated as a child.

But his tunic and trousers were torn and covered with dirt, and I realized that a beating wouldn't account for everything that was wrong with this child.

I couldn't make out more than two words in three of Sandiros's childish tones, but it was becoming plain what had happened: he had started somewhere up the hill, had decided to roll down, had completely lost control of himself and fallen all the way down, and now he wasn't sure where home was but it was too far to walk.

May the Twin Forces bless me for what I must do, I recited. Someone should take care of Sandiros until his parents could be found. The Twin Forces must surely know how I tried to keep them balanced: good and evil, red and green. Over the years, though, I felt I had earned more green than I wanted. Now I had a chance to make it up.

"I think I know what we'll do," I said. "I'll just walk up the hill, playing and singing as I go. People will stick their heads out windows and maybe run outside, and before you know it, you'll find somebody who knows where Sandiros lives, and we'll be done."

"Leaving me stuck with carrying the kid," said Iranda glumly, but she picked up the boy and slung him across her shoulder. I took time out to see if he wore either a necklace or a bracelet of any sort—my mother had given me a bracelet with a homing-spell on it, once, so I could play outside and she wouldn't have to watch me so closely—but apparently not. So I began to play and sing.

> "One day young Sandiros was playing outside,
> No sign of a camel to give him a ride,
> His mother had left him to do as he would,
> She patted his shoulder and told him, 'Be good.'"

The lyrics were neither better nor worse than what I ordinarily improvised. The tune was an old Zhir folk song, "On Shimar Street," that I'd been unable to remember when a crewman of the *Praluna* had asked me for it last night. Still, the chords came easily to my fingers. Heads were indeed popping out windows as I climbed the hill. One young man hanging laundry on a line stopped and watched me closely. A girl of about ten playing dice in the small yard of her house dropped her dice and followed me for a few paces. I think Iranda said a few friendly words to her, but I can't be sure. Young Sandiros was whimpering faintly. Poor kid, he must be sore all over.

A door flung open and a thin, sallow-faced woman with a paintbrush in her hand came running outside. "You!" she said to Sandiros. "Get down and come into the house this instant!" I stopped singing, though my hands continued with the chords to "On Shimar Street." "And you," the woman continued in a milder tone. "Where did you learn that song? My husband is Zhir, and we courted to that song!"

"I—" I stopped playing, confused. Come to think of it, I didn't remember where I'd learned that song. It seemed as though I'd always known it. "I don't know. But you'd better see to your little boy. He tried rolling down the hill in the street, and I think he's bruised all over."

Iranda deposited Sandiros on his feet. The boy ran to the woman who must be his mother and hugged her around the knees. She picked him up and held him to her, patting his back. Yes, it was possible to be a mother on the Street of Shadows and still love your son. The scene was making me acutely uncomfortable, and I looked away.

"Perhaps we should be going," said Iranda.

At that the woman seemed to come to life. "Not without telling me who you are! You've saved me countless troubles. Let me at least know your names. Oh, how can I repay you?"

"Just come to my concert tonight," I said. Sometimes it paid to be mercenary. Besides, if this evening didn't at least pay for itself, I would really be in trouble. "I'm playing at the Desert Mouse, the hour after sunset, near the Levar's Park. Bring some friends." I waved jauntily and started walking. Iranda followed me and soon caught up.

The house I'd lived in until I was about twelve was halfway down the other side of the hill. I felt an incredible inward tug of feelings as we approached it: a longing to stop and look in the familiar windows, a desire to start running and not stop until I was several blocks past it. I had shown the house to Iranda in the dead of night once the previous year. Remembering, she put a reassuring arm around my back. It didn't help.

In front of the house I slowed and stopped. I was thinking of the one cittern piece my father had learned, back when he was still alive and I hadn't claimed his fine cittern for my own. The piece was called simply "Serenade," and my mother had always listened enraptured when he played it. Almost without thought, I played the first chord formation, then the second. Within four bars I had it up to concert speed and was putting my whole heart into it. Was that my mother I saw at the window? I couldn't tell—yes, it was. But I couldn't tell if she was listening. To my left, Iranda was watching me closely, and—no doubt—wondering.

All too soon, the piece was finished. I was blinking and trying to keep my hands from shaking. They had just played through a song they didn't know, flawlessly.

Iranda walked with me down the rest of the hill, perplexed more than anything else. "And what," she demanded, "was that all about?"

"I don't know," I said honestly. The impulse to try to communicate with my mother had vanished as quickly as it had come, but I still had plenty to think about. The strings. Talking to the old shopkeeper. And if this concert didn't come off, I thought, I would really be in trouble.

"So what's on your mind right now?"

Everything. "I was wondering whether that old man at the music store will give me a new set of strings."

"What if he won't? Will you put your old strings back on?"

"Not a chance. They can't hold a tune, and three or four will break when reapplied."

"Borrow a cittern from somebody else," she said thoughtfully.

"From whom? Most of the people playing on the street use the cheapest citterns available."

"Liramal, I'm sure if you think about it, you'll realize you have other friends." Iranda had made this mistake before: she assumed that because she cared about me, other people also must. In fact, the best that could be said about me was that I had surprisingly few enemies.

"I'll think about it," I said.

At the foot of the hill, we turned right. It was a two-block walk to the music store, Harps and Strings; an immense Zhir hammered-harp hung overhead outside the door. Iranda and I entered together.

"Well, young master," said the old man behind the counter, "Is there more I can sell you? Picks? Polish?"

"Actually," I said with some difficulty, "I came for a couple of reasons. I came to apologize for being rude earlier in the day." The old man didn't twitch an eyebrow. "And I came to discuss the strings you sold me. I would like to trade them for another set."

"An apology given only under pressure," said the old man, "is no apology at all." I tried to return his steady gaze, but couldn't; he was right. "And I should have known you would have trouble with the strings of Libonas. You play only from impure motives."

"Impure motives?" I started to take a step forward, feeling the tension of anger in my face. Iranda tugged at my left tunic sleeve. The old man, looking a bit frightened, ducked back a step.

"I play to stay alive," I said quietly. "To make up for a childhood of being alternately beaten and ignored. To keep from feeling worthless."

"To earn the attentions of the young women of Liavek," said the old man. "To make yourself famous while others your age are still serving their apprenticeships. To show that you're better than other people."

"I—" I clenched and unclenched my right hand, several times. He was wrong about the young women of Liavek. And he had no business saying the other two, even if he was right. Iranda tugged even harder at my sleeve.

"I don't need your business," the old man said at last, "and I think you'd better go."

Still pulling at my sleeve, Iranda did what I could not trust myself to do: she asked him a question. "Can you tell us in what respect the strings of Libonas differ from other strings?"

Suddenly, he smiled. It was a hard smile, all teeth and jagged edges. "Libonas himself would not have told you," he said. "Therefore, I will not. Young lady, I bid you a good day."

I expected the fabric of my tunic to tear, the way Iranda was tugging at it. But I let her drag me outside; the old man wouldn't have told me anything anyway. After a few breaths standing outside in the late afternoon sunshine, I thought of something.

"Iranda? You've met Brethin iv Secawin. I can't use his cittern because it's left-handed and specially built, but he has students. Maybe one of them will let me use his cittern in return for a free admission."

"I'm relieved," Iranda said. She let go of my sleeve, patted my arm once, and smiled. "I was afraid you were just going to stand there all day and fume." Then she had a second thought. "Brethin—how easy is he to find, when he's not actually on stage?"

"That's a tough one." When Brethin was in with a student, he might not answer a knock; when he wasn't with a student, he was probably playing three nights out of five at the only public house on Kil Beach. "I know where his studio is, but it's halfway across town."

"We'd better take a footcab," Iranda said. "The way you've been wearing yourself out, you won't have anything left by concert time."

We hailed a footcab only minutes later. The man between the shafts was dark of skin and hair, maybe a bit better muscled than the average. "Ah, a musician," he said as he stopped for us. "Mind if I sing while I trot? It makes the miles go faster."

By that time I was past caring. "All right," I said. "Maybe you'll sing something I know."

So the cabby sang, and Iranda sang harmony as usual, and I played and tried to find a third part. The new strings carried loudly through the streets of Liavek. We played rowing songs, and marching songs sped up a trifle, and one song I'd heard only from the Tichenese railroad workers. The cabby was right: singing did make the miles go faster. As we pulled up in front of Brethin's, we were finishing a rousing chorus of "Pot-Boil Blues."

The cabby accepted five coppers, two from me and three from Iranda, but graciously resisted her attempts to tip him. "My pleasure," he said with a boyish grin. "I'm going to be a singer someday." He held up his right arm, and I realized with a shock that it ended just shy of the wrist. "There's little enough other work I can do."

The waiting room for Brethin's studio was large and well furnished. A nervous boy about two years younger than I sat on a finely varnished walnut bench across the room. Every so often he sneaked a look at his cittern in its leather carrying bag, as if to make sure it wasn't going to walk off and leave him. The room smelled of incense. Sunlight shone on a tapestry hanging by the door. Yes, Brethin's success made him enviable. No, I couldn't hate him for it. Iranda sat next to me in a chair just like mine, save that hers was upholstered in sunbeam yellow and mine in black. She was being patient. I was glad someone could be.

Finally the door popped open and Brethin stuck his head out. "There you are, Medosh," he said to the student. "I just wanted to let you know that we're running behind schedule, and—Liramal! What are you doing here?"

It wasn't much of a welcome, but I'd learned to take what I was given. "I need your help," I said. "The sooner, the better."

"I'll do what I can." He nodded a quick greeting to Iranda, who nodded back. His eyes met mine at last, and his eyebrows raised in a silent question.

"About Libonas," I managed to say. "And his strings. What do you know of them?"

"In a few minutes." A smile crossed his face. "Medosh, meet Liramal and his lady friend. Liramal, keep my student out of trouble for a little. I'll be out soon." He closed the door and was gone.

Medosh was squirming on the bench. Plainly, he was even more afraid of dealing with me than with Brethin. People who never have to live on the street don't toughen up properly; some ways, I'd been lucky.

"May I see your cittern?" I asked politely at last. It was a handy conversation-starter between two musicians. And Medosh could always say no.

Without saying a word, he lifted his cittern out of its bag, which collapsed into a mound of leather on the floor. I handed him mine in a fair exchange. Maybe I'd learn something from hearing someone else play it.

Medosh's cittern was old, with many cracks on both face and back. The strings were wrapped negligently around old and rusty tuning-posts. I played a chord, carefully striking each string individually. It was hideously out of tune, about the way mine had been during the argument with the old man. I readjusted the strings for what seemed like ten minutes but was probably more like two. It was useless. The strings were so old and inconsistent that when I got a chord in tune on the second fret, the same chord played on the fifth fret would be hideously off. Clearly, if I was to try and rent a cittern from one of Brethin's students, I would not ask Medosh.

Meanwhile, Medosh was experimenting with mine. His face lit up when he strummed an A chord and got a clear, tuned, harmonious sound. Then he tried D, E7, and then A again. To me, it sounded perfect. I stopped playing Medosh's cittern, then, as Medosh began to sing.

> "The lady came from far Tichen
> All dressed in silken finery,
> She'd come from there, I know not when,
> To tour a local winery—"

I listened abstractedly as Medosh finished the song. He wasn't good yet, but he wasn't bad. He was the sort of student someone like Brethin wants, to make him famous as a teacher as well as a performer. Iranda and I applauded softly. Medosh's face was all smiles and excitement.

"It's wonderful, Liramal," he said as he handed the cittern back. "I don't sound anywhere near that good on my own."

"Get a new one," I said. "This one doesn't begin to do you

justice. Go to Whistler's Corner; they're always willing to bargain."

"Someday," Medosh said dreamily as he accepted his own cittern back. "When I'm good enough."

Brethin interrupted our conversation by opening the door. He was scowling, and I didn't know whether to take him seriously or not. "Medosh, why don't you ever play that well on your own cittern?"

The young woman who stood behind him eased her way past. Her cittern was three-quarter-sized; appropriate for a small-built beginner, perhaps, but scarcely for a concert performer. She was out the other door without a word to me. Let her be, then; I had other ideas besides talking to Brethin about getting a cittern from one of his students. Medosh was sitting there, eyes downcast. Iranda was looking at me expectantly.

I spoke. "Brethin, what can you tell me of Libonas strings?"

Brethin answered quickly. "First of all, Libonas isn't the name of a string-maker. Libonas was a balladeer who played on Kil Beach until two months ago. He was called Libonas the Fainthearted, because he seemed to fear his audiences. One day he approached me and asked what magic I knew to make him less afraid."

"You know magic, then?"

"I have not invested my luck," Brethin answered. "Nor will I. Sometimes I go to a wizard on Wizard's Row and tell him what I need, and then he and I together devise a spell that will meet my needs. But it is the wizard who works the spell, not I."

Medosh was looking at Brethin with awe in his face. Iranda was trying to smile reassurance at the boy, but didn't seem able to catch his eye. Me, I had my one question. "Yes, but what of Libonas and his strings?"

"I sent Libonas to Wizard's Row," Brethin explained patiently, "to get a spell that would help his fear. It seemed to work, for a few months. Then one day before an evening's entertainment, someone heard a gunshot, rushed into a backstage room, and found Libonas lying there dead with a pistol in his hand. I delivered his cittern and twenty sets of strings to

Harps and Strings, and began to play at the Golden Cove in Libonas's place. I know little else."

"And what wizard did you send Libonas to see?" I asked.

"Esculon," Brethin said shortly. "Number 12. Medosh—I think it's time for your lesson."

In ten seconds Iranda and I were sitting alone in the waiting room. The sun was getting lower in the sky every minute.

"Libonas died," Iranda said. Her face was pale; her hand stole into mine. "What if it's a spell that absorbed the anxieties of all those who face performing? But then when the spell wears off, all the accumulated anxieties hit you all at once and you—you kill yourself."

"I wouldn't build up that much anxiety in ten years," I said, trying to be reassuring. Still, I was uneasy. I wanted to live to be older than Brethin, and twice as famous. "And what does the spell have to do with strings?"

"It could have been worked on the cittern, or on Libonas himself," Iranda said, as though she were trying to convince herself. "But the strings were easier because they were smaller and handier to carry."

I had faced death before, or thought I had. No sunbeams, no incense, no tapestries, no soft hand in mine—I didn't want to think about it. "All right. But what are we going to do about the spell?"

"I can go down to Wizard's Row," Iranda said with sudden decisiveness. "I can find Esculon, and ask him to give me the counter-spell, while you're testing the sound of the room at the Desert Mouse. But I'll have to hurry!"

"While I'm testing the sound—then you can't take the strings with you."

"But I can find out the nature of the spell that's on the strings," Iranda said excitedly. "And see whether you're in any danger using it tonight at the Desert Mouse."

I fumbled briefly in my belt-pouch, but my last two coppers had gone to the one-handed cabby. "We can't do it," I said miserably. "Wizards always expect to be paid."

Iranda reached into the pouch at her own belt, pulled out five coppers. "And this is all I've got left," she said. "I'll give it to him and tell him to expect the rest of his payment tomorrow."

I stared at her blankly. "Iranda," I managed, "why are you doing all this for me?"

Iranda looked me straight in the eye. "Liramal, do you know that I love you?"

"Yes," I said. I felt about as uneasy saying it as I did playing for important audiences. "And do you know whether or not I love you?"

"Yes," she said steadily. "But don't worry; I won't tell anybody. Not even you. Now we'd better get out and tend to our business."

I reached the corner of Lane of Olives and Sandy Way. Hesitating just a bit, I went into the side door. The players' waiting room was right off the door. It had a red-tiled floor, seemed to be half-filled with fake weapons and costumes and props from old plays, and somehow made me feel right at home. I entered with a swagger, wishing Iranda were with me.

Thrae was in the waiting room, doing some last-minute straightening. She was tall, slender, dark-featured, grey-haired, and made me wish I'd known either of my grandmothers. "Liramal!" she said, a bit too poised to be called surprised. "I was expecting you. You said you'd be here quite early."

"I'm early enough," I said. "I want to see how well the sound from these strings carries. They're new." The room smelled of fresh flowers. In fact, there they were, a well-arranged basket against the far wall.

"Ah, yes. You have to do your share of preparations, too." Thrae nodded toward a chair at the back of the room, on which I'd draped my stage uniform for that evening. "Is your friend who sings harmonies going to come by later?"

"Yes." There didn't seem to be any point to explaining the whole story. "Thrae—could you stand out in the gallery and tell me how my sound is carrying?"

"Why, certainly." We left the room and went our separate ways. When I reached the center of the platform, Thrae was sitting on a bench about halfway across the room.

I played the first verse of "The Ballad of the Quick Levars" and stopped. "Is that okay?" I called out.

Thrae pondered for a few breaths. "It sounds fine," she said.

"Sounds fine from up here, too," called down a man with a scrub brush in his hand. He was in one of two balcony boxes, up against the far corner of the building, high over my head. "At least the cittern is okay. The singing could be a little louder."

"That's enough out of you, Lynno!" Thrae sounded amused more than anything else, though. "Although it's funny—down here it was the other way around."

"You mean the cittern could be a little louder?" I interpreted.

Thrae considered. Then, having decided it was not worth her while to shout, she walked up to the edge of the platform. "The cittern was fine. The singing might have been a little too loud. You have an amazing set of lungs, Liramal; I don't think anyone in my company has better."

"So I should sing softer for Thrae, and louder for—what's his name—Lynno," I mused, as Thrae wandered back into the gallery and sat down again. Yet I had obviously played the cittern louder for Lynno, and softer for Thrae. In fact, volume—

It hit me at that instant.

The cittern had sounded softer at Mama Neldasa's because of the archer's convention downstairs. I hadn't chosen to play softer; it had simply happened. Yet riding around town with the one-handed cabby, I'd had all the volume I needed, so the cabby could sing over the sound of his own footsteps.

And young Medosh—Medosh hadn't played well because he wanted to play well, I was willing to bet. He'd played well because I would have had no patience with amateurish garbage. I'd wanted good music. I'd gotten it.

And the lost little boy—Without knowing how I knew it, how I remembered it, I'd played a song his mother had courted to. Would she have stuck her head out of the house if I'd been playing anything else?

But a few minutes later in front of my mother's house, I had stopped of my own volition. In fact, it had been I, not Iranda, who had first started walking down the Street of Shadows. The strings had helped find the little boy's mother, and had known exactly what to do when I was trying to catch the attention of my own. The strings aided me. They did not control me.

That left the old man who'd just gotten into an argument with the fruit vendors. Plainly, he was still mad. So I played, and it was hideously out of tune. What more could strings do, to provoke the fight the old man most desired?

I had the perfect legacy from Libonas the Fainthearted—strings that would always give the listeners exactly what they wanted.

It was too late to catch up with Iranda. She was en route to Wizard's Row, where she would pay what Esculon demanded, find out what I already knew, and return here thinking she had news of utmost importance to tell me. So I went back to the room by the side door to wait.

Dressed and warmed up, I sat calmly in a chair in the waiting room. My cittern rested comfortably in my lap like a much-loved pet. I was playing snatches of old ballads, fragments of songs I'd written myself, an occasional warmup exercise, and sometimes just running my fingers over the strings.

My blessed, cursed, wonderful strings.

Someone knocked twice, then burst in without waiting for my reply. It was Iranda, looking out of breath but happy. "You're safe," she exclaimed. "The only spell Esculon sold Libonas was one to make the strings please the listener. And you'll be doing that anyway, I expect!"

"I know," I said, watching the expression on her face change. "I worked it out just after you left. Iranda, did you think to ask Esculon why Libonas was dead?"

"You figured it out yourself," she said, dazed. "I'm pleased. About Libonas—remember that Esculon is a wizard, not a mind-healer. But he said that when he met Libonas, the minstrel was set to die of unhappiness because of his inability to please his audiences. Esculon did everything a wizard could do to make things better, but it didn't work. Apparently Libonas had other problems."

"Had Esculon heard of Libonas's death?" I asked.

"No, he hadn't," Iranda said. "I broke the news to him. When he heard it, he refused any payment for our discussion. He said he wouldn't profit from evil deeds as long as he had a choice. But he also said not to worry about the strings. If even half the audience is friendly, you'll be fine. Or you can always pick one friend in the audience and play to her. Like me."

"And if you join me on stage for two or three songs," I said, thinking out loud, "I can play to Thrae. Or Lynno."

"I've stood by you through years of good and bad times, Liramal," Iranda said intently. It was the tone of voice she used when she was trying to tell me something important. "Today's been different, though. Do you know why?"

I considered. "Maybe you'd better tell me."

"Usually," Iranda said, still serious, "you muddle through life as best you can while someone else figures out what's happening. Today, you figured it all out yourself. You really didn't even need me to go see Esculon."

I considered. "I guess you're right. But does it matter?"

"Stand up," Iranda said. "And get your cittern out of the way."

I stood up, not knowing what to expect—

Iranda kissed me.

It was a shock; like accidentally grabbing the wrong end of a fireplace poker; like touching one of the stinging eels the fish markets sometimes sell. Yet at the same time, I knew I had been waiting for this moment for years. I had been waiting for the right woman, and she had been waiting for the right time.

We let go, both gasping for breath. Then there was another knock on the door. Iranda opened it. It was Thrae.

"Sorry to bother you," Thrae said. "But there's a woman at the front door to see you, Liramal. Says she's your mother."

"I'd love to see her," I said. "After the concert." So the

strings could claim one more small victory. And so could I. What would Mother think of Iranda?

It was time. Giving Iranda's hand one last squeeze—not for luck; for confidence—I walked briskly out onto the platform stage. And the audience greeted me with applause.

The Last Part of the Tragical History of Acrilat

by Pamela Dean

THAT YEAR IN Acrivain, the spring thaw arrived in the middle of the month of Heat. Farmers wondered glumly if they could get in a fall crop of beans before winter, returning, fell over its own heels; the priests of Acrilat breathed easier and dared to make an inventory of the granaries. Heat was the element of Acrilat's indifference, as cold as that of Its interest, and they needed this respite.

Three thousand miles away in Liavek, the weather arranged itself as it always did in Heat. The brazen sunlight fell out of a vicious blue sky and stung the skin like molten metal; the dust lay in heaps like the autumn leaves or spring snows of more reasonable climates; every growing thing looked as bright and brittle as if it were made of painted paper; and visitors from more reasonable climates got sunburned.

And yet it was not quite the same. The strong dry heat of Liavek had usually a preservative effect on all smells, good or bad; but this year neither the orange tree nor the orange peel, not the blooming nor the cut and festering jasmine, neither the clean tang of freshly-drawn beer nor the sour lingering taint of it spilled later were evident in the still air. There was only the smell of dust. While not regretting the beer in the least, as she paced her aimless way among the hot, bright streets of Liavek, Jehane Benedicti was nevertheless perturbed. She turned into her own back garden and sniffed vigorously at the drooping tomatoes. Yes, that sharp cat-related smell was there; so was the dim presentiment of the ripening fruit and the drowned-purple redolence of nearby poppies. Everything smelled as it ought, if you attended to it. But the general air was as sterile as winter, and the whole garden looked like a basket of dried flowers.

A sunburn still felt precisely like a sunburn, even when you tried not to attend to it. The Benedictis had lived in Liavek for twenty years and knew how to behave in the summer. Jehane and Livia had gotten sunburned just the same, Livia because she was deliriously happy and Jehane because she was pleasantly melancholy. Livia dealt with the matter by developing a high fever and retiring to bed in a shower of complaints, where she required the services of every sister that she had. Jehane, having sniffed the tomatoes and derived from the results only puzzlement, dealt with puzzlement and sunburn alike by retiring to the cellar with six cushions, twelve books, and a jug of orange juice.

In Acrivain, thought Jehane, they say that love and a cold cannot be hid. In the topsy-turvy land of Liavek one would inevitably receive a sunburn as the reward of love. Livia had gotten hers sitting on the beach with the unsuitable young man she had finally been allowed to become engaged to. Jehane had gotten hers in the far less satisfying pursuit of loitering in the Street of the Dreamers, moping enjoyably at the Tiger's Eye, which the object of her affections visited like a stray cat on its rounds.

Things had gone too far when somebody with skin the color of a fish belly and a mind like a good clock could stand gaping in the afternoon sun of Liavek for two hours. Livia was only twenty-two; in Acrivain, they would be beginning to treat her as Liavek treated its fourteen-year-olds. And she had, moreover, actually been courted by the young man in question; she could afford a sunburn. Jehane was four years older and much cleverer. It was time she found something to do with herself. She thought, upending the jug and finding it empty, that she might begin by trying the ale in the keg. Her mother brewed it every year, because that was how one did things in Acrivain. She then drank one mug, declared that the taste reminded her of home so powerfully that she could not abide having it in the house, and made one of Jehane's brothers sell it. The latter part of this yearly ritual had been overlooked in the excitement attending Livia's betrothal.

Jehane filled the mug to the brim and took a healthy swallow. It tasted like aloes and cats' piss and sourdough. "That's Acrivain for you," said Jehane, and took another mouthful.

Her youngest sister, Nerissa, found her there some hours later. Nerissa was looking for her cat, who had chosen to mount an attack on the dried fish stored in the cellar. Jehane, sitting happily in a welter of cushions with her third jug of ale half-empty between her knees, startled Nerissa half out of her wits.

"Nissy," she said hospitably. "Just the girl I want to see."

"Hana? I thought you were sick. What an awful smell of beer. Has the keg leaked? *Hana,* you're drunk. Whatever is the matter? Has Livia taken all the willow bark? I'll kill her, the hoarding monster. Come upstairs before you catch your death, and I'll bring you something better than ale."

"I lack advancement," announced Jehane.

"What?" said Nerissa, fluently.

"I need employment," explained Jehane. "Like yours. I want to work in the House of Responsible Life."

"No, you don't," said Nerissa. "And they wouldn't have you; you're too cheerful by half. Come on, Jehane, do get up. Can't you go work at the Tiger's Eye?"

"No," said Jehane. "I'm too besotted by half. And I won't get up until you've had some ale. It's the drink of our homeland, Nissy, and you've never even tasted it."

"I'll get Mama."

Jehane laughed.

"Well, you're not quite out of your senses, are you?"

"Drink some ale, Nissy."

"If Mama finds out we'll have no peace for a month. Mercy, Hana, it tastes dreadful, like abandoned bread dough."

"It gets worse," said Jehane, "but after a time, you don't mind."

"You've been mooning over Silvertop again, haven't you? When are he and Thyan getting married?"

"Not soon enough," said Jehane. "That's why I want to work for the House of Responsible Life. I'm not cheerful at all, Nissy, I feel like one of Floradazul's exercises in mayhem."

"Jehane, you are more cheerful on your worst days than I am on my best. They won't have you. There's nothing they could teach you."

"If I don't find something to do, Nissy, I shall go mad."

"Acrilat will preserve—" said Nerissa, and stopped.

"Exactly," said Jehane. "Have some ale."

The Desert Mouse was preparing for an Acrivannish play. So far as Deleon knew, it would be the first Acrivannish play ever performed in Liavek. This was not the triumph it appeared. Thrae, who owned the theater and exercised over each of its operations an erratic but iron control, had insisted that, instead of reconstructing from memory any of the classic Acrivannish plays, Deleon should write his own. He was Acrivannish, so it would be Acrivannish.

Deleon would have protested more vigorously had he not been persuaded that this odd stricture was his fault. He had suggested that he sneak into his parents' house, where he had not set foot for nine years, and abstract one of his father's books of plays. He and Aelim had thought the suggestion funny, and had elaborated on it happily during rehearsals for the annual production of *The Castle of Pipers*, which any of them could have performed as a one-player show while asleep. Thrae's insistence on an original, modern Acrivannish play probably stemmed from the fear that Deleon and Aelim would indeed break into the Benedicti household and, if not actually be arrested as thieves, at least suffer some unpleasant scene with Deleon's family that would put them off their work for a month.

She had had the playbills printed already, which Deleon considered the height of foolishness. He had renamed the play three times since its inception. Half the parts were not yet firmly cast. He was struggling, in the middle of the third act, to fuse into some coherent whole his original grand tale of spying, murder, and serpentine intrigue with an unwanted family drama that had reared its multifarious head suddenly in the second act and seemed likely to drag his entire plot off course and wreck it on the rocks of what Aelim said was a comedy of manners and Deleon privately thought of as lower-class melodrama.

He had been sitting here with the pen resting on the paper long enough for all the ink to leak out and make a monstrous blot. Deleon snatched the paper off the table; yes, the ink had gone right through and made an elongated black stain on the red cloth covering the table. The red cloth was a cloak belonging to Calla, and she was supposed to wear it in *The Violent History of the House of Dicemal*. No, in *The Catastrophic Tale of the Prince of Moons*. No, Thrae had rejected that title, too. In Deleon's bloody play. Would Thrae let that one by? *The Bloody Play.* She might laugh, bu she wouldn't let him do it; they would have to reprint all the playbills. What was the blasted thing called? *The Revenge of Acrilat?* No, that was a real play by Petrane. And the ink was still on Calla's cloak.

"Damn," said Deleon, belatedly. His sister Jehane would have known how to get the ink out—yes, of course. "Aelim? Where's that rice powder?"

Aelim was lying on Deleon's bed, because there were books piled all over his own. He wore a pair of red silk trousers that also belonged to Calla, which he had mended for her and then put on absently when the stationer's girl brought another stack of paper for Deleon. (They couldn't afford such services; but Deleon had promised to put her in the play.) Aelim's skin was the color of strong black tea, his hair was blue-black like the seaweed you saw at low tide, and his eyes, Calla had once said, were breathtaking brown, which sounded silly until you looked at him. Deleon, doing so, thought that he was really far more beautiful than Calla, who was too thin and too fidgety. But Calla made his throat hurt like the early flowers of Rain that would be gone in a week. Aelim he regarded more as he would some very beautiful book or sculpture that he intended to keep for a long time. This attitude vexed him. He didn't think it would vex Aelim in the slightest, but it was better not to find out.

"I took it back to the theater," said Aelim, after returning Deleon's scrutiny with one of his long, opaque looks. "Malion was asking for it."

"He can't need it; we're not rehearsing yet."

Aelim sat up into a thin beam of sunlight, and the profound darkness of his hair took on hints of blue. Deleon smiled at him. Aelim didn't smile back. But he said, in the dry voice that meant the same thing, "Perhaps he spilled black ink on a cloak of Thrae's."

"Cold water, then, do you think?"

"The dye will run," said Aelim. "That's only clutch-shell red. You'll do better to think of a reason that Mellicrit goes about with a black spot on his cloak."

Deleon snorted, and then said slowly, "Well, Rikiki's right ear!" If Mellicrit's sister had thrown a bottle of ink at him in their youth, which she very well might, the vixen, then he would wear that cloak ten years later so that she could— "Aelim," said Deleon, picking up his pen, "we'll make Thrae print up a new run of posters with your name on them also. Ahead of mine," he added, and began scribbling.

Four pages later he flung the pen down and said, "Thrae's mad."

"Not she," said Aelim, who had lain down again with his arms behind his head. He had been doing a lot of this lately, and explained when challenged that he was learning his part, which was neither settled nor mostly written. "She may drive us all mad one day, but she'll stay cool as sherbet, and find a play where every character's a lunatic."

"Five Who Found Acrilat," said Deleon. "My father's got it."

"I daresay," said Aelim, sharply for him.

"It's a very fine play."

"I daresay," said Aelim, in an easier voice. "Why is Thrae mad?"

Deleon pushed his chair back and went to sit on the edge of the bed. "Acrilat may be a very poor sort of god," he said, "but he makes a splendid play."

"Why is Thrae mad?" said Aelim.

It was too hot to argue. "Because she trusts me to finish

this play in time, and to make of it something of which she won't be ashamed. She doesn't trust any of us to do anything else. She reminds us when it's rent day, she keeps a jar of Worrynot in her study for us, she lectures us night and day on the art of playing, she won't let us go barefoot in the theatre. But she thinks we—and especially I—can pull off this play as if it were just another *Mistress Oleander.*"

"It's her revenge for *Two Houses in Saltigos,"* said Aelim. He reached up a long brown arm and slid his cool hand under the hair that stuck to Deleon's neck. "Better for you to enact your own tragedy, she thinks, than to be perpetually inserting tragical interpretations into her comedies."

"We're creasing Calla's trousers," said Deleon.

"They'll have to be washed and pressed anyway," said Aelim. "They're all over sweat and dog hair. I wasn't thinking when I heard the bell; I had them in my hand, so I put them on."

"What were you thinking of?"

"How long ago it was that the Acrivannish alphabet diverged from the Zhir. I think the inscrutable men who speak like beasts, in *Thy Servants and Thine Enemies*, were Zhir. You said that was written about three hundred years ago?"

"Yes. That's when my play happens, too."

"Does it happen in Acrivain?"

"The first act does. The second happens I know not where on the sweet brown earth."

"And the third?"

"Oh, Aelim, I don't know. I don't know how this is going to end. I don't think I can kill all these people."

"You'll disappoint Sinati," said Aelim, dryly. "She has never died on platform in her life and she's like a mouse in a bakery about it."

"Oh, I'll kill Sinati with pleasure," said Deleon. "But if I do, then the rest of them go too."

"Why?"

"She's Second Queen. You don't kill queens and get away with it. At that, it might be amusing to write about people who did."

"Well, it wouldn't be wise. You don't want to write about the virtues of killing heads of state."

"Why not?"

"Leyo? Whom is the theater for, in Acrivain?"

"Acrilat," said Deleon, surprised.

"And would you write about the virtues of killing Its priests?"

"Why not? It kills them all the time."

"Rikiki give me strength," said Aelim. "I forgot that all the Acrivannish are mad. Deleon. In Liavek, plays are for the Levar. Don't write a play in which a queen is killed and her dispatchers prosper. It's unkind and dangerous."

"The character's not a ruling queen," said Deleon. "She's just the wife of the ruler. She's forty-six years old and she has eight children. The Levar is a child, Liavek is ruled by His Scarlet Eminence, and neither of them is coming to the play."

"Thrae says Andri Terriot is coming."

"Aelim, what is the matter with you?"

"Trust me. Don't make Sinati a queen. Make her a priest."

"In Acrivain, the dispatchers of priests don't prosper."

"Don't set it in Acrivain. Set it in Ka Zhir; set it in Liavek; set it in the Airy Elsewhere if you like. You're not writing a history."

"If Sinati were a priest," said Deleon slowly, "Acrilat might send somebody to kill her, if he couldn't send her mad."

"Sinati hasn't the imagination to be sent mad," said Aelim.

"Well, the character isn't truly like Sinati. But she has the will of a camel. So. If they had proof that Acrilat had told them to do this thing, they would be safe."

"But not admirable," said Aelim, in an odd voice.

"What?"

"Killing someone on the word of a mad god?"

"Some of them aren't admirable," said Deleon. "But I want you and Calla to be admirable. Aelim! Acrilat needn't come into it. If you and Calla were to construct the proof—"

"Leyo, will you do me the favor of settling on names for your characters? Calla and I are not going to conspire against anybody's god, however mad."

"Mellicrit and Chernian, then."

"Chernian means 'I might have been yellow' in S'Rian," said Aelim.

Deleon dropped his face into Aelim's fragrant bare shoulder and began to laugh. "Tell me a word that means, 'I delight in the irrelevant,'" he said, "and I'll name your character that."

"If Thrae agrees with your casting."

"I can't tell you, Aelim, what a joy it is to me, to be always reminded of everything I want to forget."

Aelim slid his fingers further into Deleon's hair. "It is the price I exact," he said, "for being made to forget all I want to remember."

"Why don't you put Calla's trousers in a safer place?" said Deleon.

Outside the sun beat the smell of dust up from the narrow street.

Nerissa Benedicti was annoyed. It took her some time to figure this out. She was accustomed to feeling frightened, oppressed, hopeless, smug, neglected, disliked, protective, affectionate, and furious. Lately she had from time to time surprised herself feeling happy. But a negative emotion with the approximate weight and staying quality of a hungry mosquito was new to her.

The nature of her problem came to her on an oppressive afternoon, three days after she and Jehane had drunk Acrivannish ale in the cellar and she had been forced to explain to her sister just exactly why she could never work for the Green priests. Jehane was the only person Nerissa had ever seen told of the nature of the House of Responsible Life who had not laughed at its fundamental concept. Jehane had hated it, and Nerissa had found it advisable to work longer hours.

She sat now in the room assigned to Verdialos in the House of Responsible Life, copying crumbling scrolls scribbled hundreds of years ago by people whose minds were not on their handwriting. She was supposed to keep her mind on hers, so that the copied accounts of all these ingenious demises could be sent to the printer. Everybody else was tremendously excited at the notion of having more than three copies of the Green Book, and copies that you could read as casually as the *Cat Street Crier.* Nerissa, having been engaged in copying the originals for almost two years, was largely unmoved. She knew how many gaps and guesses there were in her accounts; how many times she had asked someone to help her and how many times she had gritted her teeth and invented something plausible. She also knew just how disturbing the accounts were. She was beginning to wonder if some of the early Green priests had not perhaps been a little crazy. Was that why they had made the rule against magical suicides, to keep out the crazy people?

Not that it seemed to have helped. Gorodain, Serenity of the whole Green Order—its head insofar as it could be said to have one—had obviously been as addled as Acrilat, running about murdering wizards and adhering to the principles of the original order, which had been not a decent, philosophical church of suicides but rather a school of assassins. Verdialos had been first haunted and then preoccupied, and on occasion actually sharp, ever since they caught Gorodain. Nerissa supposed it was a shock to him. Gorodain was his superior and his advisor; had even been, perhaps, to Verdialos's muddled and tortured youth what Verdialos was to Nerissa's.

It was at this point that Nerissa realized that she was annoyed, and only annoyed. Verdialos had been neglecting her, but it wasn't his fault, or hers either.

She had sat here idling and made a monstrous blot on her page. "Nnnng!" said Nerissa, who no longer swore by Acrilat, found the Tichenese curses Jehane knew to be unsatisfactory, and was unacquainted with any others. She fumbled in the drawer of her table for the rice powder.

With his usual gift of timing, Verdialos walked into the room, preceded by a huge tangle of green linen. Nerissa couldn't decide whether to smile or throw the ink at him. Then, as he put the cloth down on his desk, from which its top four layers promptly fell onto the floor, she just stared. He had cut his hair. He would never be prepossessing, but even the silly bowl-cut he had gotten, the kind you gave the children who wouldn't sit still for anything more, made the perpetually hopeful expression of his face justifiable; he no longer looked like a man smiling while his house burned.

Nerissa was unnerved. She knew that Verdialos had a mind like a shiribi puzzle and the persistence of a cat that knows where the leftover chicken is; but it was more comfortable not to be reminded of these things every time you looked at him.

"Did Etriae do that?" she said.

Verdialos smiled, which was even more unnerving. "Over my protests, she did," he said. "She considered that the Serenity of the Order ought not to look as if his mother neglected him."

How did he so often come so close to what she was thinking? That talent ought to make him a splendid Serenity of the Order, if it didn't drive everybody to distraction. There was no point in offering felicitations; he didn't want to be Serenity, it was just another responsibility he would have to see safely fulfilled or bestowed before he and Etriae could die happily by whatever bizarre means they had agreed on when they were married. "So that's where you've been!" said Nerissa.

Verdialos stopped smiling. "Have you been fretting?" he said. "Surely you've enough to do?"

"I missed you," said Nerissa, who had not intended either to miss him or to say so. It's the relief, she thought, that he isn't going to go off and kill himself now that I'm all provided for.

"I thought you might," said Verdialos. He poked about in the pile of green linen and came up with a little book bound in poisonous purple velvet, locked with a minute brass lock. "When you've read this, you'll need to come to see me again. But you won't like it."

Except for the color and the lock, the book was just like all the blank books Nerissa used for her journal and her stories. Her parents kept a vast quantity of them in the attic; she and Deleon had pilfered them for five years, and Nerissa had been taking them for ten more, and you could hardly tell that any were gone. Nerissa thought that she might try asking her mother about them, even asking permission to use them. She could, after all, buy her own with her salary from the Green priests, if her mother said No. It had never occurred to either

her or Deleon to ask permission. That it occurred to her now was almost solely, she thought, to Verdialos's credit.

"Where did you get that, Verdialos?"

"Your brother gave it to me."

Nerissa put her hands in her lap, very carefully. Some of the most unpleasant moments of her recent life had also been to Verdialos's credit. After a respite to put her off her guard, he appeared to be starting another offensive.

"When?" she said.

"In Wine, the year before last."

"Did he give it to you for me?"

"He didn't write what is in it," said Verdialos, divining as usual what worried her. "He took it on his twelfth birthday, and kept it for you. Then he asked me to keep it for you."

"It's why he ran away," said Nerissa. She was extremely cold. "Give it to me."

"You won't—"

"Of course I won't like it. It's why he left me. Now *give*—"

"No," said Verdialos. "His own book is why he left you."

Nerissa merely looked at him. Until he had said what he intended to say, he would not give her the book.

"Do you remember your twelfth birthday?" said Verdialos.

Nerissa thought about it. "I remember my fifteenth," she said.

"So you ought," said Verdialos, unsmiling.

"On the fourteenth," said Nerissa, considering, "Jehane gave me a pen, and Cook made creamed turnips and Livia rushed from the table and was sick all over the new tile floor in the hallway." It had been a long time since she thought about that. Now, suddenly, she giggled. "Somebody ought to put us in a play," she said.

"Bear it in mind," said Verdialos. "Now, the thirteenth birthday?"

"Jehane made a rhubarb pie and forgot to put in the sugar," said Nerissa, and giggled again.

"What did Jehane give you?"

"Embroidery silks," said Nerissa, gloomily.

"And the year before?"

"I can't remember."

"What about your eleventh, then?"

"That was a bad one," said Nerissa. "We were still looking for Deleon. It seemed wrong to celebrate. I think—yes. Jehane made me a cake that was supposed to look like Floradazul, but it looked a great deal more like a rock with green eyes. She used marbles for the eyes, and Isobel broke her tooth on one. Cook was furious. I don't remember that anybody else noticed."

"Have any of your sisters mastered the domestic arts?"

"Oh, all of them, except Jehane and me. Jehane wouldn't be bothered. And I expect," said Nerissa, with a touch of the old bitterness, "that Mama was tired by the time she got to me."

"And your twelfth birthday?"

"I don't think I can have had one. I don't remember. Buds of 3313—oh. That was the month Marigand got married. They probably didn't have time."

"You're frowning," said Verdialos.

"It was odd," said Nerissa slowly. "I thought Livia and Jehane were planning something. Livia liked me that year, I don't know why. But whatever they were planning, they must have given it up."

"Your parents were supposed to give you this book on your twelfth birthday."

"But they couldn't because Deleon had stolen it."

"Do you know what it is? Did Jehane ever say anything to you about it?"

Nerissa no longer felt inclined to giggle, but the sting of all these reminiscences had still, somehow, been drawn. She felt as she did when she was rummaging among the scraps of old scrolls, finding the top of this page from one, the middle from another, the bottom from another that was not the standard size, and triumphantly piecing them together into a coherent account. "No," she said. "Not Jehane. Isobel. She said that when one became a woman one received such a book, but I was backwards and would have to wait. I wonder what she knew."

"Possibly nothing," said Verdialos; and held out the book.

"I really don't think I need it," said Nerissa.

"It is not a manual for schoolgirls," said Verdialos. "It's the story of your conception."

"Comfort for Acrilat," said Nerissa, but she took it.

"Come and see me tomorrow morning," said Verdialos.

"In Gorodain's room?"

"No," said Verdialos. "This room will do very well."

"I'm sorry," said Nerissa. "Was he a friend of yours?"

"I don't know," said Verdialos. "Am I friend of yours?"

"I don't think so. I think you're waiting. I might manage it one day."

"Gorodain," said Verdialos, "had ceased to wait, for he knew I would never manage it, being only a weak fool." He smiled again. "But you know all about that," he said.

He went away, leaving the heap of linen lying half on the table and half on the floor. Nerissa turned the ugly little book over once, and then stuffed it ruthlessly into the pocket of her skirt. She would read it at home. She knew what was in it, or all that was in it that mattered. She knew they hated her; perhaps this would tell her why. Or, worse, would it tell her that they had not, to begin with, hated her at all, that she had done something to make them?

She was copying her page for the third time when Calla put her head around the frame of the door. "Nerissa? A moment?"

Calla had been about the place for a year or so; she was the only newcomer Verdialos had brought in since he encountered Nerissa on the banks of the Cat River on the morning of her fifteenth birthday. Nerissa envied her helplessly. She was small, slender, dark, and striking, with eyes like amber and an incredible fall of black hair from which any light struck gleams of red. She had a voice like silk, a piercing wit, and an absolute fearlessness that Nerissa envied above all. Nerissa did not know what she was doing in the House of Responsible Life.

"Come in," said Nerissa. "I'm only making a botch here."

"Verdialos asked me to tell you," said Calla, rather breathlessly. "The Desert Mouse is performing an Acrivannish play. He thought you and perhaps one of your sisters would like to go with him. We'll open the first of Fruit, if nothing catastrophic happens."

"Oh, splendid! Which one?" Nerissa had never been to the theater in her life; but she and Deleon had read the old plays until the edges of the pages crumbled and their father threatened to burn the books if Nerissa and Deleon couldn't show them some respect.

"*When Lilacs Strew the Air,*" said Calla, her voice threaded with laughter.

"I haven't even read that one. Who wrote it?"

Cella gave her a long, opaque look. "Somebody obscure," she said.

"I should love to go. I'll ask Jehane. Thank you, Calla."

"How's your cat?" said Calla, rather abruptly.

"She's graduated to rats," said Nerissa.

Nerissa had to break the lock on the book. It did not give her very much trouble. She did wonder who had been negligent, Verdialos or Deleon. Or was this another of Verdialos's little plans? Was there some benefit to her pursuit of a beautiful death in breaking that lock? Nerissa laid aside the ripped velvet and dangling threads of the book's cover, and began to read.

The account was not long. Her mother had written three pages, her father three lines. Their feelings she knew already; the reasons for them caused her to make a number of violent resolutions. It was all very well to blame Acrilat for such things; but Acrilat needed a chink to get in by; and the chinks in the minds of every member of this family must be the size of barn doors. How could people who had known each other for more than twenty years and had once, presumably, been fond, behave so to one another? How could they make their bed a battlefield and all the small facts of their history only arrows to shoot at one another's eyes? She would never marry. Never. She would have nine cats and a good library, and raise kittens. Granny Carry, who had given her Floradazul, could advise her on the fine points, if there were any. Perhaps Jehane would like to come live with her also. It would be employment, certainly, though it might not offer advancement.

Floradazul jumped onto the bed and sniffed at the broken book.

"Hello, O vessel of death," said Nerissa.

The calmness of her voice pleased her very much. Her cat laid her ears back, climbed onto Nerissa's knee, and began washing Nerissa's thumb.

"I wouldn't do that if I were you," said Nerissa, rubbing her between the ears. "It's very likely poisonous."

"Did you read it?" said Verdialos. They sat in his small green room, drinking tea. The room smelled of lemon oil, which meant Etriae had been here; of old leather, from all the books; and of the tea, Prince Fyun's Folly, which Verdialos had given Nerissa ever since he discovered that the name made her grin. The tea itself had a dim and peculiar taste, and was the color of Calla's eyes, but it smelled pleasant. Overpowering this familiar blend was the strong, prickly odor of dust. Etriae must have been in a hurry.

Verdialos was looking at her, rather as if she had turned out to be, not the leftover chicken, but only the sauce from it, too full of sea-grass flavor to please his taste. "It's comforting, isn't it," said Nerissa, "to have been right all your life?"

Verdialos opened his eyes very wide; he had not expected her to say this. He considered her unnervingly for several seconds. Then he said, "I wouldn't know." She had not in all their acquaintance heard such a tone in his voice. He usually talked as if he were thinking about something else, or as if he had just run a mile, or as if he were getting a cold. He spoke with very little breath, very little emphasis, and very little warmth. She had heard him speak loudly and sharply, but she had never heard him speak as if he were paying no attention to anything else on the entirety of the sweet brown earth, except herself.

She was going to cry. She had not cried when Deleon ran away; she had not cried when her nephew died; she had not cried when her cat died; she had never cried when her parents put aside her dearest wishes as irrelevant importunities, or any of the times Isobel pinched and Livia carped and Gillo and Givanni laughed at her.

"Oh, Verdialos," said Nerissa, her voice loitering on the threshold between laughter and tears, "I wouldn't know either."

"What a mercy for you," said Verdialos. "We shall make you happy yet." He reached across the desk in a gesture very unlike him, and laid his hand palm up on top of the newest list of runaways. Nerissa leaned her forehead on his wrist and cried all over it.

She was just beginning to run dry when Verdialos said, *"Floradazul!"*

Nerissa lifted her head and looked into the bright yellow eyes of the black cat. Floradazul had brought her an extremely large mouse; oh, heavens, no, it was a half-grown rabbit.

"You drop that," said Nerissa wetly.

Floradazul obeyed her. Nerissa scooped the cat up, and Verdialos examined the rabbit. "It's not hurt," he said.

"Jehane hates it when she kills rabbits," said Nerissa.

She rubbed her cheek against Floradazul's flat, dusty head, and into her thoughts there stole the odd sideways perceptions, dimly seen, sharply scented, clearly heard, attuned to small, swift, sudden things, of the feline mind. Before she caught the rabbit, Floradazul had been ranging all over Liavek, and had sat for some time watching a linnet that, maddeningly, perched on a signpost and would neither alight on the ground nor fly away. Nerissa was still very unskilled at interpreting what she saw through the cat's eyes. The Magician had told her that she might never see much that was meaningful. That was what you got for creating a magical artifact that was a means and not an end.

She tried to read the sign. All the information was there, but it had meant nothing to Floradazul. The Desert Mouse. That was Calla's theater. If she could read the sign, she could check its correctness with Calla. An Acrivannish play by Deleon Benedicti. Nerissa has never heard of him. And then, of course, she knew that she had. Her missing brother was writing plays for Calla's theater. Did Verdialos know, or was this some charming scheme of Calla's? Calla was clever; but Verdialos was a match for her. Whosever idea this had been to start with, Verdialos must know; he was far too careful not to find out exactly what play Calla wanted him to take Nerissa to. He had decided that it was time for her to meet Deleon again.

I'll meet him, I will, thought Nerissa. And I'll bring my sister, oh, yes, Verdialos, I'll bring every sister I have, and every brother, and Mama and Papa too, if I have to lie away my hope of holiness. Let him hide for nine years, to this favor he must come. See if you laugh at that.

Verdialos was looking at her. They still needed to talk about the little purple book. "I'll wash my face," said Nerissa, "and you wash your arm. And Calla is going to have to copy that list again. She'll be furious."

"Calla will laugh," said Verdialos.

His voice was a little odd. Nerissa looked at him steadily over the head of Floradazul, who was purring like the incoming tide. If he knew what she was thinking, he was still not bold enough to say so; or his plan did not require it. "I hope she will," said Nerissa.

In Thrae's cluttered study, the company of the Desert Mouse was arguing with itself. They had seventeen days until the play opened. Thrae refused to cast any of the characters until Deleon finished the play; they could not, of course, rehearse until the characters were cast, and they were used to thirty days of rehearsal before even the most mediocre and familiar of comedies. They had all, over Deleon's protests, read what he had written, and they all agreed that this play, however rewarding, was going to be difficult. Naril, their magician, was worried because most of the special effects came at the end and thus had not yet been determined. Malion, who was even older than Thrae and normally kind and circumspect to a fault, thought that they should cobble together a quick production of *How They Came to Eel Island,* something they did every two years, and save Deleon's play for the month of Wine or even, perhaps, Fog. Sinati, who cherished hopes of the lead in Deleon's play, had raised a howl of protest, which instantly ensured that, whatever they thought, both Naril, who was presently her lover, and Lynno, whom Naril had displaced, would agree with her. Calla, reasonable as always, thought Thrae should cast the characters so that they could begin rehearsals. Aelim said blandly that he couldn't see what the fuss was about; if they couldn't conquer a three-act tragedy in a tenday, perhaps they should all go make paper for a living. Naril, whose mother did just that and who had never fathomed Aelim's sense of humor, became rather heated at this, and Deleon deemed it time to intervene.

"I'll have the play finished by tomorrow," he said.

He felt Aelim looking at him, but kept his own eyes steadfastly on the lined, elegant face of Thrae.

She raised both eyebrows at him and said, "You must take what time you need, Deleon; we'll contrive."

"That's all the time I need," said Deleon.

"How many extra players do you think you'll want?" said Calla, and surprised Deleon into looking at her. She was slouched in the chair they sat in when they came to be scolded, wearing the mended red trousers and a green tunic embroidered with red snakes. Her expression conveyed a clear warning, but her question was not calculated to help him back out of the wrong street he had just taken.

"How many can we afford?" he said to Thrae.

"That's not the question," said Thrae, briskly.

That was precisely the question. It was infuriating of them to be so kind and tolerant in just the wrong way and at exactly the wrong time. "Three," said Deleon, knowing he was doomed.

The crease cleared from between Calla's eyebrows, and the worried twist went out of Thrae's mouth. Lovely, thought Deleon, now they can sleep tonight.

"Del?" said Naril. "Do you know about the effects yet?"

"I want a blizzard," said Deleon, completely at random, "that is also a thunderstorm. The grandmother of all thunderstorms. And I want a burning castle and falling trees. But all the fire is to be blue and white, except that around Sina—around Brinte. And at the very end, I want all the effects to vanish; not just the fire and snow, but the sets we've talked about. I want people standing on the bare platform wearing just the clothes they walked on in."

Naril looked taken aback and then extremely pleased. Deleon, who could feel Aelim's concentrated gaze like the heat of a candle on the side of his face, considered the rest of them one by one. Yes, he had been successful. They all thought, hearing him state so definitely what he wanted, that the play must indeed be near completion. All except Aelim.

"I'll arrange to have it copied, then, Deleon," said Thrae, "and call the extras for Sunday." She spoke with her usual serenity, but there was a very faint warning in her eyes. She wanted to believe him, but she knew him too well.

Today was Rainday. Thrae was going to have to pay more than she ought, to get that play copied by day after tomorrow. He would have to give it to her early tomorrow. He was a fool, and Aelim was going to call him one the first chance he got.

"I'll bring it in the morning," said Deleon, and grinned charmingly at her. Thrae was accustomed to the blandishments of players, and merely said, "Good, then," but Deleon caught Calla scowling. She disapproved of using their art at such moments. She would disapprove a great deal more if she knew that Act Three was unborn and unconceived.

Thrae and Malion went off together to argue about which extras they would approach, and Sinati came up to Deleon, with Naril tagging possessively behind her. She smelled of jasmine; Naril smelled much more reassuringly of white soap and cinnamon.

"Del," said Sinati, "if you want me to get Brinte, make her odd to look at; tall, or yellow-haired."

"Perhaps she could have a squint?" said Calla. She wore, as always, the scent of Ombayan tiger-flowers; but she also smelled of dust. She had probably been climbing about in the attic after Thrae's cat again. "Or a hunched back?"

Sinati, who was the only player in the entire company who could use magic to change her appearance, and was possessed of a melting dark beauty and a vanity to match it, gave Calla the best reproachful glance in her repertoire, the one the traitor Ruzi's betrayed lover had given him. Calla burst out laughing.

Aelim said, "Leyo. If she had a dragging limp—"

"Anybody can perform a dragging limp," said Sinati.

"I know," said Deleon. "You shall limp as much as you

like, Sinati; that will do very well. But for Thrae's instruction, we'll make Brinte bright blue."

They all gaped at him; Calla stopped laughing. "Deleon, if it isn't *intrinsic to the plot,*" she said, in an excellent imitation of Thrae, "she'll just throw it out and cast whom she pleases."

"It's intrinsic," said Deleon.

"It must be a very odd play," said Sinati, clearly trying to sound bright and looking very dubious.

Aelim sat down suddenly on Thrae's Tichenese carpet, dropped his face into his hands, and began to laugh.

It was possible, thought Deleon, that he was the only person present who had seen Aelim laugh before. "He's read it already," he said to Calla.

Calla gave him a level and opaque look.

"But I thought it was a tragedy," said Sinati, in her dangerous voice.

Calla snorted, reached down, and pulled Aelim's hair. "Of course it is," she said. "That is why he is laughing. Get up, you wretch, and take Deleon home so he can turn Brinte blue."

Deleon looked at the two of them and felt the even tenor of his blood stumble. That brisk tug on a generous handful of hair was Calla's gesture to him. It appalled hm that he should be jealous that she used it on Aelim, who had almost certainly not welcomed the attention. It appalled him that he should still be jealous that Calla was paying this attention to somebody else, not that somebody was paying it to Aelim. Would he ever stop loving her? He had been living with Aelim for a year and a half. With no other person in all the world could he have shared those two rooms above the shop of Penamil the apothecary and his three black dogs, without going mad in a tenday. Aelim, with his long silences, his curious linguistic preoccupations, his glancing and intermittent humor, had made of his bodily presence a solitude, of his mental presence an embrace, and of his rare embraces an oblivion for Deleon. For someone whose heart had been starved for as long as he could remember not only of love but of privacy, Aelim was the only possible choice. And yet Deleon knew that if the chance were ever offered him, he would take Calla. Mercifully, she knew it too, and would never even seem to be giving him that chance.

He looked at them now in their Liavekan immunity, smooth and dark as deep water, full with the unthinking serenity of people who are living in their proper place. He thought of the snow he had never seen, the mountains he would never remember, the mad god he could not propitiate, the hot, intricate, friendly bustle of Liavek that had made his parents' failure permanent and their discontent a closed door he could neither break nor open.

Acrilat, he thought, thou art crueller to thy servants than to thine enemies. Those who hate thee prosper and those who love thee suffer entanglements of the spirit. I must love you, though I don't believe in you, because this is a supreme entanglement of the spirit. And on that thought, he felt Act Three tremble on the edge of his mind like a half-blown soap bubble on its hoop. He would have to balance it all the way home; if it burst he would never get it back and Acrilat would be his only refuge.

"Aelim?" he said. "Let's go."

Aelim drifted to his feet at once. Calla gave Deleon a look of rueful tolerance that was so wide of the mark that he laughed at her, kissed the top of her head, and snatched Aelim out the door. Behind them they heard Calla chortling. It was her delighted chortle, the way she laughed at people she was fond of, not the one she used when she thought something was absurd.

Aelim did not call Deleon a fool, or anything else, on the way home. He lit three lamps, which was an extravagance, and began to make kaf, which was a luxury reserved for death, illness, and inviting Malion and Thrae up for dinner. Deleon, writing frantically, let him do as he pleased. The entire family drama unfolded itself, perfectly and obediently, lavish with color and pure in form as a Tichenese silk fan. His only terror was that his mind was too small to hold it until he could consign it safely to paper. Grand, ringing phrases, homely jokes, terrible and simple accusations and denials, came to him in orderly procession like the lists of old words in Aelim's books. It was not yet dawn when he laid down the pen, shook his aching hand, and took a huge gulp of stone-cold kaf.

Two of the lamps had gone out. Aelim was asleep, flat on his back on the blue wool rug. He was one of those people who never slept with their mouths open. His breathing hardly stirred his striped linen shirt. He could pose for a statue of the young Acrilat, thought Deleon; and love and grief pierced him like arrows. He had not meant to wake Aelim up to read him the play; but he knelt on Penamil's worn tile floor and touched Aelim on the cheek.

Aelim was as dignified in waking as in sleeping; he opened his eyes and looked inquiring, as if he had been interrupted in contemplation.

"It's finished," said Deleon.

Aelim sat up and held out his hand, and Deleon put the inky pile of paper into it. He had meant to watch every expression on Aelim's face as he read it; in fact, he almost fell asleep, and jumped when Aelim spoke.

"This is splendid," Aelim said. "But where is Act One?"

Deleon thought for a moment that Aelim wasn't awake either; and then he understood. He had forgotten his royal court and its intrigues. And that wasn't all he had forgotten.

"I must be mad," he said. "This will require six extras, some of them with rather long parts."

"Wait," said Aelim. "Give me Act One."

Deleon fetched it.

"What have we, now? King, priest, their daughter, their son, their chamberlain, and their steward. Six, of course, a good fat part for everybody. Two messengers and a knife-maker. Where's Act Two? Thank you. Mother, father, two sons, two daughters. Six again. Deleon, what if you were to subsume the family drama into the court? Why shouldn't the priest's daughter be her chamberlain and her son the steward?"

Deleon stared at him. "I *will* make Thrae put your name on those posters," he said. "I'll run all over town with a paint pot and add it myself."

"Thank me after you've changed all the names and added at least two scenes to Act Three," said Aelim. "I'll make some more kaf." He looked at Deleon for a moment and added, "And some soup."

Despite a welter of minor criticisms and maddening observations of the most useless sort, everybody loved the play. Thrae emerged from her study into the hallway where they were all passing pages around and reading thrillingly from their chosen parts, and in two dozen words squashed everybody's spirits as flat as a piece of Ombayan bread. She gave her own part to Calla, Calla's to Lynno, Lynno's to herself, Aelim's to Malion, Malion's to Sinati, Deleon's to Aelim, and Sinati's part, the murderous blue priest with the will of a camel, to Deleon.

Everybody except Aelim and Deleon rose up shouting, swept Thrae back into the study, and settled in for a siege they all knew was doomed to failure, unless Malion took a truly violent aversion to Aelim's part. Deleon, whose eyes felt full of sand and his head of cotton, met Aelim's grave stare and suddenly began to laugh. "Do you like your part?" he said.

"It doesn't mean 'I might have been yellow,'" said Aelim.

"What does it mean?"

"'One who waits.'"

"Do you like it, Aelim?"

"I should like it better if I had a full month to fit into it."

"Aelim."

"I like it very much," said Aelim, thus fating himself to play a one-eyed young girl who loved cats and embroidered (badly) her own poetry (very good) on an endless series of cushions.

"Then the rest of them must live with it," said Deleon.

The rest of them did live with it, although with no very good grace. Calla was absentminded for two days, Lynno was obtuse for three, and Sinati sulked continuously. Malion and Aelim seemed to enjoy themselves from the start, but bemusedly; Thrae, who very often took no part at all, played the feckless brother intended for Lynno with an energy and a sense of comic timing that Deleon admired greatly, though he feared its ultimate effect on his tragedy.

Thrae, appealed to on this point by Calla, snorted and said

that all the best tragedies had a comic element. Just like a Liavekan, thought Deleon. But he held his tongue. The dark aspects of his play were beginning to alarm him; if Thrae wanted to light a few candles for the final turn of the plot to snuff out, he would trust to her judgement. He did wonder at her turning everybody's expectations, not least his as the playwright's, so completely upside down. Perhaps they had all been getting rather smug, and this was her way of beating the moths out of their brains.

His own part terrified him. He did not know where this woman Brinte had come from. She made for a complex and demanding part and had three of the best speeches in the entire play, speeches that he continued to be proud of long after many of his effusions had begun to make him wince. But he felt profoundly uneasy playing her. Or perhaps it was the playing out of her relations with the characters of Calla and Aelim that disconcerted him. Calla was the King, Brinte's husband, whom she scorned; Aelim was her dutiful daughter, the chamberlain, whom she pitied but did not value. Deleon, who had known better for years, found his true relations with the players colliding with the relations he was supposed to be playing out; he found hiself softening or clarifying his lines, adding bits of business to undercut them. This confused Calla, enraged Aelim, and, in the last week before opening, drew from Thrae a series of stinging rebukes that widened to include the entire company, when she saw that they were listening to her instead of conferring with Naril about the dispensation of the special effects.

Everybody improved miraculously after that, except for Sinati; but Thrae knew how to deal with Sinati. She did it through Naril, as usual. She was enabled to do it by the curious incidence that the first six performances of *When Lilacs Strew the Air* were already booked full and the first three not only reserved, but paid for. This had not happened since Thrae bought the theater, and probably had never happened in its history. Nobody reserved a seat because the theater was seldom full. Thrae took the money, paid everybody early (with exhortations against spending the money unthriftily, and specific instructions to Deleon to get a new shirt, Calla to buy a pair of boots instead of relying on Sinati's castoffs, which were too big for her, and Lynno to pay his bill at the Mug and Anchor before Daril put him into her pot-boil and ruined a recipe a hundred and fifty years in the making). She then tripled the order to Naril for special effects, and paid him for half of them on the spot. This cheered Sinati immediately; and when she saw how many of the additional effects would emanate from her character, she ceased to be any trouble except in rehearsal, and was no more trouble there than usual.

On the evening that Thrae paid them all, three days before the play opened, Deleon and Calla slipped up to the little front room with a lantern, dragged Malion's scribbled seating plan out of the drawer, and read all the names. Calla's family, of course, and Lynno's, and Sinati's. Verdialos, Calla's friend from the House of Responsible Life; he wanted four seats. Deleon thought of four short, green-robed people with untidy hair and hopeful expressions, sitting all in a row, and laughed. Calla pulled his hair, but said nothing. Deleon steadied his breathing, which was becoming easier after she did something like that than it had once been. Andri Terriot, who wrote for the Levar's Company. Aritoli ola Silba, a critic of painting who had recently shown a tendency to extend his endeavors to the patronage of other forms of art. Tenarel Ka'Riatha. Now *that* was an *old* Liavekan name. It might not, in fact, be Liavekan at all, but rather whatever it was that the original inhabitants had spoken before they were conquered by the nomads Tichen had driven out. Aelim would be interested. Dicemal Petrane, who wanted eight seats. That was an Acrivannish name, but the Petrane family was not in Liavek; it was gloating over its dominion of Acrivain. Perhaps it was a Zhir or Tichenese name that only looked Acrivannish. Transliteration was a tricky thing. He could ask Aelim.

"I wish ola Silba weren't coming," said Calla.

"He liked *Two Houses in Saltigos*."

"He hated *The White Dog*."

"Of course he did, it's an abominable—Calla!"

"Yes, of course I'm joking. You're coming along," said Calla. "Ola Silba should love your play; that's just the trouble. I fear this joy is prologue to some great amiss."

"You must, if you're quoting Mistress Oleander. What's the matter?"

"I've told you. Just walk warily. Let's not get too full of ourselves."

"Thrae will see to that," said Deleon; and when he saw that she still had three creases in the clear dark skin of her forehead, he patted her on the cheek. Over the sharp line of bone her skin felt like a velvet cushion a cat has been sleeping on. He thought of telling her so, but she would only laugh and ask if she should go for the clothes brush.

After Thrae's scolding, Deleon managed, not to banish his unease, but to disguise it. For the first two acts any hint of it that might show through would be all for the good; but if he could not manage to forget his private miseries by Act Three, he could single-handedly turn the play into a disaster. Perhaps that was what Calla had been trying to tell him.

Aelim, questioned about the linguistic oddities of their first-night audience, said that, yes, Ka'Riatha was a S'Rian word, and that he had thought it was a title, not a surname; but titles often became surnames. He wandered off into a list of examples. Dicemal Petrane, he said, did not sound like any reasonable transliteration from either Zhir or Tichenese; but there were at least two schools of unreasonable transliteration. Also it might be Ombayan; Aelim didn't know much about Ombaya. Deleon was greatly amused and somewhat comforted. Even if some unthinkable catastrophe had propelled the Petrane family from Acrivain to Liavek, they could hardly pose much of a danger to him or his family. It must have been a pleasant surprise for them, newly arrived in this barbaric community, to see that a civilized play was going to be performed. Deleon only hoped it was civilized enough. On reflection, he hoped the name was Ombayan and the entire matter irrelevant.

He was more worried about his own performance. He suspected Calla and Aelim of having conferred on the matter; Aelim became far less withdrawn than usual for the last three days before opening, and Calla's habitual friendliness lost its acerbic edge and became merely comfortable. He found his part easier for these dispensations, but not enough easier to keep him from being in a ferment the night they opened.

Mercifully, the first scene was Sinati and Calla's, and the second Sinati, Calla, and Malion's. Lurking behind the dusty green curtain, the other side of which Naril had made so potently a hedge of lilacs that Deleon could smell that bright, cool fragrance above the dust, Deleon realized that Sinati was being splendid tonight. Her lines contained a high proportion of poetry, much of it rhymed, because he had intended them for Malion, who could manage such things. Sinati had never been much good at poetic dialogue before, but it seemed that suddenly tonight, after a mere nine years of lectures from Thrae, the sense of what Thrae taught had finally found a place in Sinati's sharp, narrow, self-occupied mind. She was doing beautifully. Deleon could have kissed her. Besides getting her own part across just as she ought, she was setting the platform for his own entrance, as the mother to whom she owed what she was.

Calla was perfect as always; and Malion, as the young steward, was enough to break your heart. Malion was as gnarled as an apple tree and about as sympathetic as a worm in one of the apples. Naril, of course, had done most of the softening of Malion's appearance; but Malion himself was making that strong, young, diffident voice of the dutiful son who is despised, and cannot see why.

Deleon settled himself into the imperious, the impervious, the unimpressionable queen and priest, and, when his cue came, walked on platform with no trepidation in him anywhere.

It was not until very near the end of Act Two that he had leisure to examine the audience. There was an enormous bonfire of Naril's making taking up much of the platform; Naril had added a frieze of flames to the walls of the theatre and set a little blue fire dancing from the head of everybody in the audience. It made them all look ghastly, but Deleon could pick out the austere, moustached face of Aritoli ola Silba, the tired, thin, more sparsely moustached countenance of Andri Terriot; various strange faces wearing various expressions of absorption; an alarming visage with a thin scar on either cheek, framed in long dark ringlets, incongruous next to the alert, dubious face of a young girl; one very dark old woman who looked extremely grim. And there was Verdialos.

He had cut his hair. He was accompanied not by three other green-robed, untidy little men, but by a tall, dark, cheerful woman and two very tall, very pale, younger women. The flickering blue flames turned their golden hair a very pretty green. Behind them, all in a row indeed, were the pale faces and pretty green heads of a middle-aged man and woman, two men in their late twenties, two round young women in their early twenties, a more angular woman in her early thirties, and a man of about the same age who held her arm possessively. He, too, was pale-faced and green-headed, but his face did not bear the distinctive stamp of the others.

Deleon's family had come to his play. He knew that at once. Then bewilderment took him; he could not positively identify a one of them. The angular woman in her thirties, who was pregnant, was surely his mother; but that man who held her arm was a Casalena, not his father. The two young women with Verdialos must be Jehane and Marigand; but he could not imagine any set of circumstances that would bring them to the House of Responsible Life. And where was Nerissa?

Everything shifted suddenly, as if he had changed to the next leaf of a kaleidoscope. That was Nerissa in the row with Verdialos; she had grown. With her was not Marigand, but Jehane. His allies, with Verdialos. And the rest of them, his enemies, ranged behind him. The pregnant woman was Marigand, with her husband. The round ones were Livia and Isobel; the young men were his brothers. But that meant this placid middle-aged creature was his mother, and this hollow-eyed man who tapped his long, thin fingers on the bench beside her was his father. They looked like anybody's parents. They looked nothing like his. Deleon could hardly hear Calla's speech to Malion above the rattling of his heart. He wouldn't be able to utter a sound if he didn't calm down. Well, who would look familiar, in such a light? But what in the holy preservation of Acrilat were any of them doing here? Of course Verdialos had brought Nerissa and Jehane, probably with Calla's conniving. But to whose account should he lay the appearance of all the rest of them? Dicemal Petrane, indeed. That had Nerissa's handwriting all over it. What would make her do such a thing?

Calla, who was speaking lines to Malion that Brinte was not supposed to overhear, but was supposed to interrupt, repeated the beginning of the speech that was Deleon's cue, with a tinge of exasperation appropriate to her character's view of Brinte but intended to express her disapproval of Deleon. "Indeed, she's bloody, bold and resolute. I know not—"

Deleon turned his head with the majestic deliberation of some large reptile in Calla's direction, and began moving methodically but quietly towards where she and Malion sat in a bower of lilac. They would have to alter the undertones of this scene. It wouldn't hurt in the long run. Malion had wanted to do it this way in any case, and Thrae had overruled him. No doubt she would put Deleon's abstraction down to actual rebellion; which was in her mind the lesser sin. He moved faster, so that Calla would not have to improvise as much; she gave a guilty start and then flung her head up with the sort of defiance more suited to somebody's adolescent child than to her husband. Brinte bestowed on this creature, this smudged copy of a husband, a look of withering scorn, and began to speak.

Nerissa knew just when Deleon saw them. By then she wished he would not. Verdialos's face, when he met her and Jehane at the front door by arrangement, and saw behind them the tall, gold-crowned throng that had brought her to his keeping in the first place, had made her think as she ought to have thought sooner. He might indeed have known that her brother was working at this theater and had written this play; he might indeed have planned that she and Jehane should encounter him, and he them, unawares. But he knew her; through her he knew Jehane; in however small a degree, he knew Deleon. If he had thought it was time for the three of them to meet, he might have been right. His face as he looked from her to her family was not reproachful, but bore the sickened expression of somebody who has made a massive miscalculation and is going to have to pay for it. There was a class of things, thought Nerissa, that he had trusted her not to do; and she had done one of them. Through him she had betrayed Deleon not just to the sisters who loved him, but to the entire family he had fled from. She was glad Etriae was there. And she still wanted to deliver pain to the rest of her family more than she wanted to spare Deleon its sting.

Then the play began. Deleon was bright blue, with long black hair and judicious padding; she would never have recognized him without the list of characters and players someone had handed her on entering. But she knew his voice. It had changed since she knew him, though it was still rather light; and he had pitched it high, since he was playing a woman. But she knew it. She realized for the first time that all her family spoke with an accent. It was not in the pronunciation but in the rise and fall of the words that Deleon's origins proclaimed themselves. Surrounded by the bland, clear Liavekan of the rest of them, Brinte's slight oddity of speech set her off from the rest of her family very effectively.

She not only knew the voice; she knew Brinte. This was their mother, as she and Deleon had seen her in their childhood. The chamberlain and the steward were Nerissa and Deleon; not in their appearance or in many of their characteristics (although the chamberlain was dreadful at embroidery and liked cats), but in their alliance. The other son and daughter were far worse than any one of Nerissa's sisters or brothers, but, as the sum of Marigand, Gillo, Givanni, Livia, and Isobel's faults, they were very close to the mark. The King was kinder than she remembered her own father, but perhaps he had been so to Deleon. But with all its royal and religious trappings, all its deadly serious intrigue, this was the story of her family, and of her and Deleon's alliance, shorn of its ignoble aspects, faithfully retaining both its folly and its wisdom, and tending, she saw as the play progressed, not to its actual conclusion but to the one she and Deleon had desired in their darkest moments. And because of the royal and religious trappings, that conclusion was just and proper.

Nerissa's eyes filled up somewhere in the middle of Act One and continued to trouble her for the rest of the play. She was profoundly grateful that, as the top of the list of players proclaimed, in deference to the Acrivannish custom, there would be no interval. She did not dare look at Jehane, who, as far as Nerissa could tell, was not in this play at all but would certainly realize who was. She did not dare to look at Verdialos, either. Behind her her two sisters twittered softly together, her brothers made rather louder remarks until their mother silenced them, and her father, her married sister, and her brother-in-law made not a sound. Did Mama understand this play? Did any of them?

She saw something else, too, as Act Three proceeded. This was her brother's apology to her. The alliance, the awful discovery, the failure of the alliance. But because this was a play, there was a reconciliation and a final hideous plot. Nerissa felt that she could not watch the end and could not possibly look away.

Deleon had had doubts about omitting the interval, but as Act Two drew to its strung-up conclusion, he was grateful for this lack. A rest would not have helped. He wanted to finish this. Once Brinte had died as she richly deserved, perhaps he could go and be sick in peace.

Matters took their course. Sinati and Thrae, the wicked daughter and the feckless son, betrayed their mother's plot, which would not benefit them as much as they thought it should, to their father. The three of them then plotted to overthrow her plans; and their plot collided disastrously with a plot to the same end by Aelim and Malion. In a howling blizzard set about with lightnings, Sinati and Deleon had their final sorcerous battle. Naril was surpassing himself, perhaps even exceeding his commission. Deleon had perhaps not paid as much attention as he ought to the spectacle planned here, but he could not remember that the arcane motions he had practiced were supposed to result in quite so much light, music, howling winds, or damage to the set. His own lines frightened him; they seemed to take on sound and color and motion as they left him, to shape the air as a glassblower shapes the molten glass, to make themselves present. Naril was good, but Thrae was going to have his hide to patch the curtain.

Nor did things quiet down when they were supposed to;

Deleon and Sinati had to improvise for quite five minutes before the sudden hush that denoted a stalemate descended on the ravaged court of Brinte. Then the crossing and recrossing, the upsetting and the unintended effects of everybody's careful plans began, and swept the play and everybody in it to its woeful conclusion. Deleon spoke his last lines and died; everybody followed except Calla, who sat, the bewildered King bereft of his books and poetry, and pronounced a wistful and inadequate epitaph on the lot of them. The curtain dropped in a cloud of dust and lilac.

Everybody got up and brushed himself off; and Deleon remembered what, by immemorial custom, came next. The curtain would come up, they would all kneel to the audience; and then they would climb off the platform and mingle with the audience until they could conveniently sneak off to their dressing room and clean the paint from their faces and the dust from their souls.

"I can't do it," he said aloud.

"You have to," said Aelim's serene voice, and Aelim's cool, light hand closed with amazing force on his shoulder. "Are they all here, Leyo?"

"Every blessed one."

"I shall be pleased to have a look at them."

"Aelim," said Deleon, alarmed. "Don't make it worse."

"Only for them."

"That's worse for me, too."

Aelim's grip slackened, and through Thrae's skillful paint job and the fading glamour of Naril's arts, the brown eye not covered by a patch stared earnestly at Deleon. "That's a pity," said Aelim. "Don't worry, then, I'll be mute."

He wasn't the only one. Deleon stood oblivious in a chattering flurry of congratulation—smiling at Andri Terriot, and Aritoli ola Silba, and the dark, grim old woman in her gorgeously woven robe, and Calla's mother—waiting for the moment when the shifting crowd should show him his family. But most of them must have gone. What he finally found was Verdialos speaking with great force to a tearstained Nerissa, while Jehane towered in the background, looking as she had the day he brought an abandoned footcab home. She had grown even more than he had.

She felt him looking at her and met his eyes. Deleon grinned at her. Jehane pushed swiftly behind Nerissa and halted in front of him. "That," she said, "is the best revenge that ever I saw or heard tell of."

"It wasn't meant to be on you," said Deleon.

"I know," said Jehane.

"I think, in fact, that you deserve a mote of revenge on me." Deleon took her hands, which were even colder than Aelim's. But she had a nice firm grip.

"A whole dust pile," she said. "I'll forego it, Leyo, you look so miserable."

"I'm not, as a rule," said Deleon. "This is Aelim."

"You made a perfectly splendid chamberlain," said Jehane. "Some of Deleon's lines would have confounded a news-seller."

The two of them shook hands gravely, and Aelim said, as if he were suggesting they embark on some arduous, years-long plan of research. "You must come to supper soon."

"I will," said Jehane. She let go of his hands. "Leyo, you had better speak to Nerissa."

She said that, too, in exactly the tone she had used to explain that he would have to give the footcab to the City Guard, which would try to find its owner or deal with it properly if they could not. Deleon almost laughed, but now was not the time to say anything. She might have forgotten all about it. He would remind her when she came to supper.

Nerissa, mercifully, had stopped crying; she was pink in the face and regarding Verdialos furiously. Deleon, with the unnatural clarity that sometimes accompanied his understanding of a new part, realized what had happened. Calla had told Verdialos about the play; Verdialos had gotten seats for Nerissa and Jehane, certainly the only people it was at all reasonable to bring to see him; and Nerissa had decided to drag along the whole family. Acrilat alone knew why.

"Nissy," said Deleon.

Nerissa looked at him over Verdialos's shorn head. With her pink nose and red-rimmed eyes, she resembled a rabbit the

Casalenas had once had. Deleon had not seen her cry since she was three years old. His play had made her cry. He felt, for a moment, a pure pleasure; and then he felt guilty. He tried to look encouraging; she might just fling herself into his arms. She had used to do that when something had happened that she couldn't bear. Nerissa was always not being able to bear things; the problem with his family was that this normal childish reaction to being thwarted was caused in their case by things that really were unbearable.

Nerissa did not fling herself at him. She walked forward quite slowly and put her arms around him. She was as tall as he was and smelled of dust and paper and more pleasantly of limes. It did not seem necessary to say anything.

Jehane felt as if somebody had put her insides through a garlic press. Having supper with one's long-lost brother was all very well in its way; but that same lost brother had made her present dilemma desperate. She had to get out of that household. She had to find something to do. The awful clash of plots against their mother was going to happen, not in so clean and intricate and dramatic a manner, but it was going to happen, and she was going to be elsewhere when it did, with as many of her sisters as she could persuade to come with her. But where was she going?

"Jehane!" said a strong, dry voice, carrying easily over the hubbub of the audience. Jehane jumped, and looked around for Granny Carry. She was standing with Verdialos, of all people. What a dreadful combination those two would make, supposing they could ever have any goal in common. She negotiated the chattering little people of Liavek absently, gave poor duped Verdialos an eloquent grimace, and said, "Good day to you, Granny; did you enjoy the play?"

"It was extremely instructive," said Granny, dryly.

Jehane decided to keep her mouth shut, and promptly found herself saying, "That is a lovely cape. I particularly admire the subtle thread of green."

"It's a wall-hanging," said Granny, "and it's yours if you want it."

"What?" said Jehane.

"You heard me." Granny piled the material into her arms.

Jehane ran it through her hands. It was remarkably soft for something so rough-looking, remarkably resilient for something so light, remarkably pleasing to the eye when you really considered the threads and colors that made it up. "What a great deal of thought and toil something like this must take," she said. "But there's nothing like it, when you're finished."

"I can teach you to do it," said Granny, in the tone of somebody telling a cat to get down from that table this minute.

Jehane stared at her and wondered if the old woman really was as mad as her sisters thought. Whom did she think she was talking to?

"Well?" said Granny.

"Hana," said Nerissa's tear-drenched voice, "you've been saying you want some occupation. Some remunerative occupation. Do you know what you could sell that hanging for?"

"I couldn't sell it," said Jehane, clutching it.

Granny looked very pleased; all she said was, "We'd start you on something less imposing. Besides, you can't keep them all. They gather dust, and the cats have kittens on them."

"Well," said Jehane, collecting herself, "how could I possibly refuse such a prospect as that?"

Deleon passed with a kind of floating relief into the familiar dressing room, with its worn slate floor; its wavery green mirror; the six rickety tables each marked by its owner; the rough-plastered white walls covered with rejected sketches for costumes and characters, torn-off title pages of plays, and many of the costumes themselves, along with a quantity of brass lanterns, feathered fans, bronze bracelets, strings of Saltigan crystal and ropes of wooden beads. Thrae would install Andri Terriot in her study with a glass of wine, and then come and praise their performance to them. Tomorrow she would rip each of them in pieces like an old sheet fated to end its days as a collection of dust rags; but she never faulted anybody right after a performance. If she was too angry to say anything pleasant, she would fail to appear.

The room was rather crowded. Calla's mother had brought her a wreath of jasmine and firethorn, and stayed to watch her put it on. Deleon and Aelim's landlord lingered to give them a cream to take off the blue paint. The old woman in the beautifully woven dress was standing in a corner with Naril; she looked grimmer than ever, and Naril looked apprehensive. Deleon wondered if she had objected to his special effects.

He sat down at his own table and removed Brinte's cap, her hair, and her jewels. The door to the Lane of Olives creaked open. Deleon thought ola Silba must have thought up something especially cutting to say, and come back to let them hear it, since he had already, in a burst of uncharacteristic generosity, promised them a favorable review. He looked up. One by one, every member of his family except Jehane and Nerissa filed into the room. They stood in a clump, looking at him. Calla's mother and Penamil, as if by magic, melted out through the other door, the one that led back into the theater. Deleon devoutly hoped that they had gone to fetch Thrae. Malion, Lynno, and Sinati were still mingling gleefully with the audience. Calla and Aelim stood on either side of Deleon, like three rocks, thought Deleon, daring a flood to rush over them.

The old woman with Naril, whom Deleon had utterly forgotten, took three quick steps into the center of the room, her cane tapping on the tiles, and said, "How considerate of you, Mistress Benedicti, to save me the trouble of seeking you out."

Deleon saw that his mother and his sisters knew her, while his father and brothers and brother-at-law were bewildered.

"Granny Carry," said his mother. "If you knew where he was, why didn't you tell us?" She used the mild and reasonable tone that meant somebody was in for it. You're not twelve, thought Deleon to himself, you're twenty-one, and you've been earning your living as a player for nine years. There was something else about that tone, though. He couldn't think what; perhaps she would use it again and he would be able to remember.

The old woman his mother called Granny Carry took her time about answering his mother. When she did speak, she did so very softly, like somebody putting down one more glass lion on a crowded shelf of fragile ornaments. "Why should I punish him," she said, "for being the only one of all your children with the wit to run away from you?"

"You overstep your bounds," said Deleon's mother, in a truly terrible voice.

And Deleon knew both the tone and the words. Rikiki's three stripes, he had used them himself as Brinte. As if the sun had come from behind a cloud, the entire landscape of his mind lit up, and he understood his own play. Jehane and Nerissa had understood it before he did; Jehane, who had a right to be furious, had been mildly rebuking and Nerissa, who had a right to accuse him of callous desertion, had not been rebuking at all. He had killed, not his family, but their power over him. He wondered if the eight of them here knew it.

They certainly knew that tone. Livia blanched and Isobel hid behind Givanni, just as they always did when it came time to find out who had stolen the strawberries or broken cook's largest bowl. It occurred to Deleon that the rest of them might have had an alliance of a more normal kind, might have been more like real brothers and sisters. Not that it seemed to have done any of them much good, unless you thought that Larin Casalena was good for Marigand.

"I?" said Granny Carry, in a much stronger voice; Deleon, his imagination loosened by the play, could almost hear in her voice the glass breaking as she tipped the whole shelf of ornaments to the floor. "I overstepped my bounds? Oh, no; this is my city and my charge. It's you who have overstepped yours; and not even by intention, but by stupidity. You may be stupid in Acrivain if you like, but I won't have it here. Do you understand me?"

It was quite clear they didn't; neither did Deleon. They were all staring like stuck sheep. His mother was so angry she couldn't speak; but that wouldn't last long. His father was amused, his brothers irritated, and his sisters terrified, except for Marigand, who was almost as angry as her mother. It hurt his stomach to see how little, in ten years, they had changed. They moved in their respective orbits like the painted wooden figures in Penamil's Zhir clock.

It was Larin Casalena who actually spoke. "You'd better explain yourself, madam" he said.

"Bosh!" said the old woman, in a much more vigorous voice that carried a great deal less venom. "I live here; I don't need to explain anything."

"We live here also," said Deleon's mother, with extreme smoothness.

The old woman had wanted that reply. "You do not," she said. "Not in any way that matters. You don't live anywhere. You occupy a miserable space of the imagination halfway between Acrivain and Liavek. You can't live in Acrivain; you saw to that by staging an idiot revolution at an impossible time. And you won't live in Liavek. You make your children miserable by raising them to live in a culture they'll never see; you stuff them full of tales of food and flowers and weather they'll never know; you spit on Liavek as if it were a beggar in your path."

"If we do," said Deleon's father, to everybody's obvious amazement, "what's that to you?"

"Your wife has S'Rian blood. I am responsible for those of the Old Blood. And among you, you let in Acrilat," said the old woman.

Deleon burst out laughing. S'Rian blood! What a lovely irony. The old woman looked at him, and he stopped laughing. Beside him, Aelim said softly, "Granny Carry." Deleon looked at him. Tenarel Ka'Riatha. A S'Rian name that Aelim thought was a title.

"I am honored to let in Acrilat," said Deleon's father.

"I am not honored to have him!" said the Ka'Riatha. "He's a lunatic; not only that, he's a self-centered lunatic of the worst description, with less native wit on his best day than Irhan has on a bad one. I won't have him about; he's dangerous. Now listen to me. I'll give you a year. If at the end of that time any of you is cherishing any thought or action that Acrilat would find useful, I'll put you on the next ship out of here; and I won't trouble myself about which direction it's sailing or who's aboard. Do you understand me?"

They said nothing; the old woman smiled a chilling grim smile and added, "And if you don't think I can do it, try me. It would please me no end to rid Liavek of its ungrateful guests. You've got a powerful stink on you after twenty years."

She had not looked at Deleon except when he laughed; but he was a member of the family she was reviling. "Do you have any suggestions?" he said. "To remove the stink, I mean."

"You," she snapped, "make up your mind; and don't write any more plays about Acrilat. As for the rest of you: Livia! Your sister tells me you're engaged."

Livia nodded dumbly. Deleon, who was accustomed to thinking of her as a whining tyrant twice his weight who was constantly complaining of him to their older brothers, stared at her. What a round, quaking little mouse she was. She didn't have as much backbone as Nerissa, whom he had always regarded as a supreme, if justified, coward. How old was she? Twenty-four? Twenty-two? He supposed that living the last ten years in his parents' house, in a society where children could burst out on their own at fifteen, might have been wearing. And who was he to revile her for cowardice? He was the one who had run away; she, and all the rest of them, had stuck it out.

"To whom?" said Granny.

Livia gulped. Deleon's mother said, "She is betrothed to one Ebulli jhi Rovoq, the youngest son of a Hrothvekan family with seven children. He has his own fishing boat; she met him as a friend of Givanni's. They are to be married next year, possibly in the month of Reaping."

She had hated saying that. A fisherman, by all that was holy; a youngest son. But she said it in a tone of nicely modulated pleasure, implying that young people would do these foolish things, and parents must allow them to, if they were not actually bent on disaster. Deleon grinned to think of what Livia must have been up to that they had consented to this match. And yet, if they were in no hurry, it couldn't be all that desperate a case.

"The month of Meadows is better for weddings," said Granny.

"In Liavek, perhaps," said his mother, in automatic dismissal, and then shut her mouth hard. She always knew when not to make matters worse for herself.

The Ka'Riatha looked as if she were about to break another shelf of glass animals, and Livia said, quite loudly, "I want to be married in Wine."

"Meadows," said the old woman, very sharply. "Or Buds."

Livia gave her a betrayed look, and Deleon's mother said, "If you want Wine, my dear, Wine it shall be."

Calla made an abrupt movement; Deleon glanced at her. She was quivering with suppressed laughter.

"Isobel," said the old woman. "Did you marry Hanil Casalena?"

"No, madam," said Isobel, warily.

"Why not?"

"He's a toad," said Isobel, with her customary directness. "A *wooden* toad. He won't do anything. He reads poetry and weeps about Acrivain, day and night. And he won't argue." She looked sideways at her eldest sister and that sister's husband. "I'm sorry, Larin, but you know it's true."

Deleon's eyes stung. She was not talking about Hanil Casalena; she was talking about their father.

"Isobel?" said Livia. "Ebulli has a great many brothers."

Isobel flung her hair back from her face with a gesture that reminded Deleon of Sinati, and said distinctly, "I don't want to be married. I don't see how any of you could possibly wish to be married. It's nothing but misery. Nissy may be vulgar, with her notions about raising cats, but at least she knows the virtues of solitude." Deleon blinked hard, feeling Aelim's eyes on him. Isobel knew; maybe she had always known. He had thought her proud and secure in the center of their parents' esteem, the perfect Acrivannish maiden, except for a slight, deplorable tendency to be spiteful. She had a heart like granite and a mind like the map of a coal mine; and yet she knew, and had not been happy either.

"Isobel," said Marigand, in her soft voice, "must you always make a speech?"

Rikiki or Acrilat, Deleon was not sure which, laid hold of him. "Why shouldn't she?" he said. "The Levar's Company needs understudies."

Isobel looked shocked, not as if she thought this was an evil idea, but as if she wondered how Deleon had come upon it. She must be a superb player, and know it, to have behaved as she had all this time. Maybe nine years with somebody like Thrae would make Isobel no worse than Sinati.

"And when you have become a player, Issa," said their mother, in a perfectly steady voice, "will you write such a play as your brother's?"

Deleon, who would have stared into the bore of a cannon, the mouth of Acrilat's temple itself, before he looked at her, looked at her. She was completely serene, if a little white and strained about the mouth. What do you expect, thought Deleon. People don't change their natures in an instant. But she had noticed; she had understood.

Isobel stepped out from the clump of family so she could look their mother in the face, and said, not loudly at all, "Shall I need to?"

There was a perfect and hideous silence, as those two composed, pale, unyielding faces gazed at one another. Deleon would have run out of the room if he could have moved at all. His mother looked like a bad drawing of Isobel. It was entirely possible that, like Brinte, she had not enjoyed the last twenty years any more than the rest of them had.

The Ka'Riatha broke the silence. "You had better not write such a play as that," she said brusquely. "It's full of extremely potent summonings of Acrilat, and a great deal of sentimental poetry, too. I trust you can do better."

Deleon's desire to weep dried up abruptly in a scorching blast of injured pride, and was replaced almost at once by an insane desire to laugh. Calla was having trouble too. Aelim was unmoving.

The Ka'Riatha dealt briskly with Deleon's brothers, his remaining sister, and her hapless husband, most of whom were living more or less independent lives, or at least doing something un-Acrivannish. Deleon, who had briefly felt entertained, found unease overtaking him. He began to be rather sorry for his family; and if Granny thought she had silenced his mother, she was less clever than she might be. He also found that he very much did not want to hear what she had to say to his father. It had occurred to him that he might, after this was over, wish to speak to his parents again; and if he had heard whatever dreadful things Granny was likely to say to them, the meeting would be even more difficult. He caught Granny's eye.

"Go along with you," she said. "And mind what I said."

Deleon took Aelim by the hand, which he had never done even when he was a very lost twelve and Aelim had been assigned to look after him. He tried to collect Calla with his glance, but she had perched herself on Sinati's table. She looked as if she were watching a very good play, with an eye to playing the lead herself. The soft yellow of the jasmine in her black hair caught the yellow of her eyes. Deleon had a certain premonition that Granny would have something to say to her; and he wanted to hear that even less than he wanted to hear the rest of it.

He said in the general direction of his family, "I'll see you later; just ask for Thrae's study."

He and Aelim shut the door carefully, and discovered Sinati and Lynno in the hallway, mouths agape.

"Where's Thrae?" said Aelim.

"Getting Andri Terriot drunk," said Lynno. "I think she's pleased, Del, but she won't say a word without you and Aelim. Malion looks like a very cross parrot; she won't even tell him he did well. Come on."

"What's happening to Naril?" said Sinati.

"Nothing untoward," said Deleon. "Come and get drunk with Andri Terriot."

They walked down the clean-swept hall with its patchy pink-painted plaster, into Thrae's cool study, with the Tichenese carpet and the green glass jar of Worrynot and the vase of Ombayan tiger-flowers, to be praised for their playing.

The month of Fruit in Acrivain was very dusty; and yet there was a great deal of rain, and anything anybody dared to plant came up in a tremendous hurry and flourished. Not one soul came panting, or crawling, or mewling, or ranting to the door of the Tower of Acrilat, begging admission to the priesthood. This was unfortunate insofar as there was a great deal of work to do with everything growing the way it was; but as an indication of the health of the general population of Acrivain, it was a good sign to the few who considered such things. In the month of Wine they ate their strawberries the size of peaches, and wondered whom to thank.

Mad God

by Patricia C. Wrede

AN UNEASINESS HUNG in the air of Liavek. It manifested itself in small ways. The merchants in the Bazaar drove harder bargains and scowled as they pocketed their coins. A gem-cutter on the Levar's Way missed her stroke, ruining a thousand-levar jewel. The number of persons seeking advice from the Faith of the Twin Forces increased so sharply that half a dozen Red priests normally employed in the lower ranks of church bureaucracy had to be hastily reassigned. The Zhir snarled as they went about their business, but the Zhir usually snarled at Liavekans whenever they could, so no one noticed any difference. The Tichenese delivered elaborately veiled insults with exquisitely relentless politeness. No one noticed anything different about that, either.

Among magicians, particularly those of Wizard's Row, there was more awareness of the uncomfortable atmosphere. One or two even went so far as to attempt to identify the source of the miasma. Their efforts were noteworthy only for their uniform lack of success.

In a neat little house on the Street of Trees, the old woman known most commonly as Granny Carry sat glaring at a silver bowl of clear water. It had been gathered from Liavek Bay by moonlight on the eve of last year's summer solstice, then boiled with wormwood from Ombaya, juniper from the mountains of the Silverspine, and yarrow from the back garden. The steam had been painstakingly collected, a drop at a time, by holding a mirror over the boiling water.

And it had shown precisely nothing. Granny snorted. Gods were all alike—they'd pester you with omens for weeks when all you wanted was peace and quiet, but ask them a few questions of your own and they shut themselves up like so many clams.

Granny's frown deepened. She rose and went to her loom. It was empty, waiting for the next project; she had finished the last weaving only that morning. She shooed two of the cats away and chalked a circle on the floor around the loom. Then she stood in front of it, closed her eyes, and drew on the birth luck that provided the power for every wizard's spells. In her mind, she wove a pattern to begin the long ritual.

Eyes still closed, she let the magic guide her hands to the rack of threads behind the loom, choosing the colors for the weft. She paused and opened her eyes to examine the selection. A pale, smooth linen flecked with red; a thin, vibrant green silk with a tendency to break; a nubbly, wildly variegated wool in a hundred shades of blue and white and a constantly changing thickness.

Granny blinked in surprise. The choices seemed clear enough, but . . . "Acrilat?" she said skeptically. "I thought I'd gotten rid of It."

She glanced back over her shoulder. One of the cats had jumped onto the table and was sniffing experimentally at the silver bowl. "You'll probably end up seeing double," Granny warned it. The cat looked up, twitched its whiskers, and began lapping water out of the bowl. Granny shrugged and went back to work. She drew on her luck once more, picturing a second pattern as she began to wind the weft onto shuttles. Then would come selecting the warp, setting the threads on the loom, and, finally, the weaving that would complete the spell. The entire ritual would take several days to complete, but long rituals, done correctly, made more powerful spells. Granny was patient.

When the warp had been cut and she could take a rest from her spell-casting, she made a pot of tea and sat down to think. Some months ago, Granny had put an end to the subtle interference of Acrilat, the mad god of Acrivain, in the affairs of Liavek. She had thought that would be the end of the matter, but apparently the mad god had more persistence than she had given It credit for. It looked as if It was going to try again.

Normally, Granny did not particularly care which gods were or were not worshipped in Liavek. Her job was to care for the city, its rulers, and inhabitants, and those few gods who had come from the ancient city of S'Rian before the Liavekans conquered it. Even with all the power and skill bequeathed her by her predecessors, the job was a big one, and it kept her busy. She would not have worried about Acrilat any more than she worried about the horde of gods who had been brought to Liavek in recent centuries, except that Acrilat had aleady demonstrated that It was not satisfied with mere worship. For some mad reason of Its own, Acrilat wanted to have Liavek the way It had Acrivain, and whether Its plans succeeded or not It might well ruin the city trying.

But Acrilat was not one of the Great Gods; It needed something to use as a link with Liavek before It could act there. Until last spring, It had been using the Benedicti family as a tie to span the thousands of miles between Acrivain and the City of Luck. Granny had been particularly put out when Jehane Benedicti had brought this situation to her attention, for the Benedictis were related to her. The elder Mistress Marigand Benedicti was the granddaughter of Granny Carry's next-from-youngest grandson, who had emigrated to Acrivain some sixty or seventy years previously. The fact that their Liavekan blood made the Benedictis the perfect link for Acrilat had not lessened Granny's irritation in the least. She had been very short with Acrilat when she had cut the link and sent It packing.

Granny scowled at her tea, and two of the cats made discreet departures from nearby chairs. Perhaps she should have stopped to ask a few questions before throwing Acrilat out so peremptorily. Well, it was far too late for that now. Granny gave herself a mental shake and returned to pondering her present problem. No matter how many ways she looked at it, she came up with the same answers. Acrilat still needed a link to Liavek, and the Benedicti family was still Its best and most likely prospect. But the original link between Acrilat and the Benedictis had been cut, so Acrilat could no longer work through them unless they initiated the contact.

The conclusion was inescapable. One of the Benedictis was doing something remarkably stupid.

Granny snorted. In her opinion, saying that one of the Benedictis was doing something stupid was like saying fish swam. The question was, which of the family was it, and just what was he or she doing? After a moment's consideration, Granny went to get a sheet of paper, pen, and ink. She wrote a brief note and folded it, then drew on her luck to seal the letter. Jehane Benedicti had more sense than most of her family, and she owed Granny something. She would come. Granny paid the driver of a passing footcab to deliver the message.

Jehane Benedicti's arrival the following morning was heralded by four of the cats, who trotted through the open door ahead of her like an honor guard. Jehane herself paused in the doorway as if wondering whether she ought to knock when the door was already open. She was tall, with light yellow hair, troubled blue eyes, and pale skin that showed signs of recent sunburn.

"Are you coming in, or have you decided to have another try at burning yourself red as a cooked lobster?" Granny inquired.

"I thought it was mostly gone," Jehane said, reddening further.

"Your nose is peeling," Granny said. "When you get home, put some aloe and eucalyptus oil on it. In the meantime, sit down and tell me what your family is up to now."

Jehane, who had just started to seat herself, jerked upright. "How did you know?"

"If I knew, I wouldn't be asking." Granny gave Jehane a sharp look, then handed her a cup of tea and said more gently, "What is it?"

"Nerissa's joined the House of Responsible Life."

"Is that all?" Granny relaxed slightly. The House of Responsible Life was very nearly the last place in Liavek where Acrilat could find a foothold; the whole place was devoted to breaking ties, not making them. Jehane's younger sister, at least, was safe.

"All?" Jehane's voice was incredulous. "They're an order of *suicides*."

"The Green Priests are not an order of suicides," Granny said calmly. "If they were, they'd be all dead. They are an order of people who *plan* to commit suicide, which is an entirely different thing. I should think that was obvious."

"Nissy's done more than plan," Jehane said bitterly. "She's gotten her luck bound into that cat of hers, so when the cat dies, she will, too. And I used to like Floradazul."

Granny shook her head. "You Benedictis! Don't any of you ever think things through? Floradazul was a spanking-new cat when I gave her to Nerissa; she's got at least eight lives to go. Even if she wastes a few more getting kicked by camels, she has a good chance of lasting another seventy or eighty years. Nerissa will probably die of old age long before the cat does. Drink your tea."

Jehane sipped at her cup obediently. Her sharp-featured face wore an expression of doubtful concentration, as if she were trying to duplicate Granny's calculations without really believing that cats had more than one life. Granny waited. Jehane would feel better if she worked things out for herself.

"I still don't like it," Jehane said at last.

"Has it done Nerissa any harm?" Granny said irritably.

"No," Jehane said thoughtfully. "I don't think so. She's more sure of herself now, and I think she gets along better with the rest of the family. She's even found a theater that's doing an Acrivannish play, and we're all going."

"All of you?" Granny said. Her eyes narrowed. "What play is it?"

"When Lilacs Strew the Air," Jehane replied, surprised. "I don't know who wrote it."

"Hmmph. Well, who's performing it, then?"

"The company at The Desert Mouse," Jehane said. She hesitated, then added in a doubtful tone, "The first performance is next week, if you think you'd be interested."

"Oh, I'm interested," Granny said dryly. An Acrivannish play, with most of the Benedicti family in attendance, sounded like something Acrilat would find useful. Very useful. But there was no point in disturbing Jehane by explaining. "Tell me about the rest of your family," she said to Jehane.

Jehane did so, with the scrupulous and slightly wary politeness of someone who is waiting to be told the real reason for the peremptory summons she had received. Her brothers, Gillo and Givanni, had sold the winery her father had bought them and purchased a fishing boat. Her brother Deleon, who had run away nine years before, was still missing. Her sister Marigand was pregnant again; Isobel had (for the third time) refused to marry the suitable youth her parents had found for her; Livia was engaged to a thoroughly unsuitable Hrothvekan. Jehane herself was beginning to feel the need of some occupation, preferrably one that paid. She did not say that her parents had ceased receiving money from Acrivain and would therefore eventually run out of funds to live on. Granny, who had learned those facts and more through channels of her own, saw the worry in Jehane's eyes and did not press her.

"It's about time you decided to do something with yourself," Granny said instead. "What are you, twenty-six? Well, better late than never. Don't let me keep you."

Jehane left a few minutes later, her expression announcing to the world that all Liavekans were completely unaccountable, and Granny Carry was the most unaccountable of them all. Granny waited until she was well out of sight, then went out and hailed a footcab. "The Desert Mouse," she told the runner, and they set off.

The Desert Mouse was a shabby little theater in Sandy Way. Granny took one look at the signpost and knew her instinct had been right. *When Lilacs Strew the Air* the playbill announced in large black letters, "An Acrivannish Play by Deleon Benedicti." So this was what Jehane's missing brother had been doing for the past nine years. Granny thought for a moment, then drew on her luck and wove a small, subtle spell to make herself easily overlooked. Deleon Benedicti was unlikely to recognize her, for his mother had never bothered to bring any of the males of the family along on her duty visits to Granny, but there was no sense in taking chances.

The interior of the theater was just as shabby as the outside. There were perhaps a hundred seats, and even in the dim light it was clear that the cushions had seen better days. A rehearsal was in progress on the small stage, presumably of the upcoming Acrivannish play. Granny snorted softly and slipped into a chair at the back to watch.

The rehearsal was proceeding in fits and starts; every time it looked as if a scene was actually going to get going, a tall, elegant woman would stop everyone to change the emphasis on a line or move one of the players three feet backward. Deleon Benedicti was easy to pick out; his pale skin and yellow hair identified him instantly as a Farlander. He was a very pretty young man, Granny thought as she studied him, but troubled. And there were undercurrents between him and the rest of the players that she didn't like at all. Acrilat had had plenty of material to work with here, that was obvious. But was this just one of the god's mad whims, or did It have some specific purpose in mind?

The scene on stage was approaching some kind of climax. Deleon stepped forward and began to speak. "Acrilat, thou art crueller to thy servants than to thine enemies. Those who hate thee prosper, and those who love thee suffer entanglements of the spirit."

Granny stiffened. Deleon was declaiming, with considerable spirit, the chief and most effective of the invocations of Acrilat. Even in Acrivain, that particular invocation was almost never recited in entirety, though its beginning was used in several more common prayers. Deleon had not had the sense to stop with the opening lines; he had made the entire text into a speech in his play.

The enormity of this stupidity was appalling, but worse quickly followed. Deleon and a beautiful woman, with an overly theatrical air even for a player, began miming gestures for a sorcerous duel. Despite the frequent pauses for consultation with the director, Granny could see the pattern those gestures would make when they were performed in unbroken sequence. Summoning and hypnotism. And Acrilat did not need to work through trained wizards with invested birth-luck; all it needed was an opening. This would give it one.

Granny frowned thoughtfully through the remainder of the

rehearsal. She might be able to persuade Deleon or the director of the Desert Mouse to alter the play, but Acrilat would only try something else. She had better things to do with her time than to run about watching Acrilat like a sailor eyeing storm clouds. She rose from her seat and made her way slowly backstage, in search of information.

A dark young man with a wispy moustache was sititng on the floor behind the curtain, looking from the scene being enacted on the stage to a complicated chalk diagram on the floor in front of him. He appeared, Granny thought approvingly, to have a goodly share of S'Rian blood in him.

"Naril!" the deep voice of the director called. "I want to check the timing of the effects this time; watch your cues."

"Ready, Thrae," the moustached man called back. He looked worriedly from the diagram to the stage again and began muttering under his breath.

Granny watched for a few minutes, and her eyes narrowed as various aspects of the stage magician's spells unfolded before her. She waited patiently until the director stopped the action to explain, at some length, the importance to the scene of each player's making certain precise movements at certain specific times. As Naril stopped muttering and sat back with a sigh, Granny stepped forward and loosened the threads of the spell that made the players overlook her.

Naril started, then scrambled to his feet. "Who're you? What are you doing here? Thrae doesn't like visitors during rehearsals!"

"I'm not exactly a visitor," Granny replied absently, looking him over. "S'Rian, are you?"

The stage magician blinked and glanced uncertainly toward the stage. "Well, partly," he said politely. "My father's a Kellan."

"Would that be Farro Kellan?"

"He was my grandfather," Naril said, staring.

"Ah." Granny nodded in satisfaction. "Time flies."

"I'd be happy to talk to you about my grandfather, if you'd come back after the rehearsal's over," Naril said. "Or if you'd give me your name and directions, I could come and see you."

"You," said Granny, "are a refreshing change from most of

the idiots I've had to deal with lately. I do not wish to discuss your grandfather, but you are welcome to visit me if you wish. I live on the Street of Trees at the top of Mystery Hill. My name is Tenarel, but most people call me Granny Carry."

Naril's eyes went wide, and he swallowed hard. Then he pressed both palms to his forehead and bowed deeply. "How may I serve you, Ka'Riatha?"

"So you're well educated in addition to being unnaturally polite," Granny commented, but less acerbically than usual. "Very nice, but don't get carried away. I want to know whatever you can tell me about those people out there." She gestured with her cane toward the argument on the stage. "Who they are, what they're like, who is friendly with whom, who irritates whom, that sort of thing. In as few words as possible."

"I—" Naril glanced toward the stage as if hoping something would occur to give him a reprieve, then took a breath. "I'll try, Ka'Riatha."

He did better than she had expected, and Granny was hard-put to control her reaction. The relationships among members of the company of the Desert Mouse were nearly as complicated as those of the entire Benedicti family. Deleon was, naturally, one of the worst offenders. The boy was, Naril said, in love with one of the players, a black-haired girl named Calla, and had been for nearly two years (though he thought he had hidden it from the rest of the company). Instead of pursuing her, Deleon was living with a different member of the cast, a man of striking good looks in his mid-twenties named Aelim. They had made this arrangement the previous year, shortly after Calla had begun visiting the House of Responsible Life.

Granny listened to the remainder of Naril's dutiful recital with only half an ear. So one of these players had an interest in the House of Responsible Life, did she? And it was Nerissa Benedicti, who worked at the House of Responsible Life, who had found out about the play and told the rest of the family. Granny didn't like the smell of this at all. "What's this Calla person like?" Granny said abruptly.

"She's . . . very decided," Naril said cautiously. "And sure of herself. She doesn't like to see people do things she thinks are foolish."

"Likes to meddle, does she?" Granny said.

"Naril! What's the matter back there? You missed your cue." A long arm yanked the curtain back to reveal the strong-minded director. The woman took in Naril and Granny in one glance and said firmly, "No visitors backstage during rehearsals. You'll have to leave, mistress."

"I'm not a visitor," Granny said. "I'm a customer. I wish to buy a ticket to the first performance of this play."

"Of course, mistress," the director replied smoothly. "If you'll come up to the front, we can take care of it immediately."

Granny nodded a goodbye to Naril and went to purchase a ticket, specifying a seat in the center of the front row. Then she left the theater; there was nothing more for her to do at the Desert Mouse. She took a footcab back through the Canal District and Old Town to the Avenue of Five Mice. There she entered a large, square, three-story house, plastered a pale green and half-covered with ivy, which stood on the corner of Five Mice and Neglectful Street.

"A good death to you," said one of the green-clad youths seated at the table just inside the door.

"Not for another couple of centuries," Granny said. "Where does the Serenity of this order keep himself these days?"

"Second floor, third door on the right," the second youth said. "Ask for Verdialos, if you get lost."

Granny nodded her thanks and went briskly up the stairs. She turned in at the proper door and found herself in a large, untidy room that smelled of warm leather, soap, and old books. At one side of the room, a tall, pale-skinned, yellow-haired girl of about seventeen sat at a table, copying something from a crumbling piece of brownish parchment onto a clean sheet of white paper. A black cat was curled contentedly on a pile of papers near the edge of the table. "Nerissa Benedicti," Granny said. "I should have expected it."

Nerissa looked up. "Granny Carry!" she said in the tone of someone who did not know whether she was pleased or sorry to have been surprised in this particular fashion.

"I'm glad your memory hasn't failed you," Granny said to Nerissa. "Hello, Floradazul," she added, holding out a hand to the cat.

The cat sniffed politely at the hand, then began to purr. "Were you looking for me?" Nerissa asked cautiously.

"No," Granny said. "But you Benedictis turn up all over whether I'm looking for you or not. Has Verdialos changed rooms, or was I misdirected?"

"This is Verdialos's room," Nerissa said. Her expression had gone closed and wary. "I didn't know you knew each other."

"We don't," Granny said, and raised a mental eyebrow at the expression of relief that flashed quickly across Nerissa's face. "I've come to pay my respects to the new Serenity of this House."

"Verdialos has been Serenity for nearly six months."

"Then it's about time I came, isn't it? Where do I find him?"

Nerissa provided directions, looking slightly less wary. Granny nodded and turned to go. At the door, she paused and looked back. "You're doing better for yourself than I'd expected," she said. "When your parents give you trouble over joining a church of hopeful suicides, come to me, and I'll take care of it." She shut the door on Nerissa's astonished gape and went looking for Verdialos, the Serenity of the House of Responsible Life.

She tracked him down at last in a musty-smelling room, half-buried in account books. Verdialos proved to be a medium-sized man with brown eyes and a round, expectant face that was clearly misleading. He turned when he heard Granny's cane on the floor and came forward to welcome her.

"You're Verdialos?" Granny said before he could speak.

He gave her a quizzical look and nodded, obviously amused. "You were looking for me?"

"I was. I am the Ka'Riatha; I came to see what the new Serenity of this order was like."

"Have you come to a conclusion?" Verdialos said.

Granny noted that, though his expression had shown recognition and comprehension when she gave her title, he had not altered his manner. "You'll do, I think," she replied.

"I expect I'll have to, mistress," Verdialos said. "What else can I do for you?"

"You can call me Granny; most people do," Granny said. "And you can tell me which of your members is advising Nerissa Benedicti. There are some things he should know."

Verdialos laughed. "There are any number of things he should know, as I am all too well aware. Nerissa is one of my students."

"I should have guessed," Granny said. "Those dratted Benedictis have a knack for complicating everything."

"Nerissa is a very promising young woman."

"If I hadn't known that, I wouldn't have given her a cat," Granny snapped. "I suppose you're the one the player has been talking to, as well. The one named Calla."

"I know her." Verdialos looked at Granny. "Forgive me, but what is your interest in Nerissa? I understood that the Ka'Riatha concerned herself mainly with S'Rians."

"Quite true. The Benedictis are one of the exceptions, for a number of reasons. The chief one is that they're family."

"Family? Nerissa is related to you?"

"She's my great-great-great-granddaughter on her mother's side," Granny informed him. "Which is one of the things you ought to know about her."

Verdialos stared. After a moment, he began to laugh. "Are you sure it's the Benedictis who have a knack for complicating things?" he asked when he could control himself. "I seem to have done a remarkably good job of it myself."

"Oh, it's the Benedictis, all right," Granny said. "The Benedictis and their blithering maniac of a god, Acrilat. That's the other thing I came to tell you. You've gotten Nerissa out from under Acrilat's influence, which was better done than you may realize. See that she stays that way."

"I'd try in any case," Verdialos said. "But there's not much I can do about a god."

"Acrilat's not much of a god, to my way of thinking. One more thing: Whose idea was it to take Nerissa to her brother's play?"

"Is there anything you don't know?" Verdialos said, looking considerably startled.

"Quite a bit," Granny said, "or I wouldn't be standing here asking questions. Who thought of taking Nerissa to that play?"

Verdialos studied her for a moment with an air of innocent speculation that Granny was certain was not innocent at all. "Calla suggested it," he said finally. "But I'm the one who's taking her. Is there a problem?"

"In a way," Granny said absently. Of course it had been Calla; Calla, the player who was so sure of herself, who disliked watching people do things she thought were foolish, who liked to meddle. Calla was the last and cleverest link in the chain Acrilat had formed to connect Deleon and the Desert Mouse with Nerissa Benedicti and the rest of that troublesome family. And it would all come together on the opening night of Deleon's play. Granny contemplated the arrangement with horrified fascination. How had she missed seeing any of this six months ago, when she thought she had sent Acrilat packing for good?

"What kind of problem?' Verdialos said with an exasperated patience that drew Granny's attention back to him. Granny studied Verdialos for a moment, wondering whether to tell him that the rest of the Benedicti family would also be attending the play. She decided against it; she didn't know how he would react to the news and the Benedictis were more her business than his anyway. And she certainly wasn't going to warn him about Acrilat. She contented herself with saying, "The main problem's mine. But I think you'll want to keep a sharp eye on Nerissa; she may be in for something of a shock."

"Oh?"

"I've seen the rehearsals."

Verdialos looked thoughtful. "I see. Have you any other inflammable information to give me?"

Granny chuckled. "Not today. I'll look forward to seeing you and Nerissa and Jehane at that play. Good day to you, Serenity."

She left Verdialos pondering, and threaded her way back through the building to the street. From the House of Responsible Life, she returned home, to her cats, her weaving, and her preparations. She went first to her loom.

The hanging she had begun as part of her divination ritual was only half-finished. The crazed blue-and-white yarn, held in place by the pale linen, fanned out across a warp of alternating dark blue and shimmering gold, nearly hiding it from sight in some places. The thin green silk made attractive accents here and there, but if the pattern of the weaving kept on, it, too, would be buried under the blue-and-white wool. Granny studied the hanging with care, knowing that what she was contemplating was even riskier than facing Acrilat would be. Layering one spell over another was tricky enough when the first was complete; with the pattern only half-finished, the result could be disastrous. But she could not see a reasonable alternative.

Granny shooed the cats out of the cottage and closed and locked the door behind them. She set her cane aside and, for the second time in two weeks, chalked a diagram on the floor around her loom. In its center, immediately under the half-finished weaving, she drew a curving symbol, extending and re-shaping the lines of the partly-finished design above. Then she rose and went to the shelves where she stored her threads.

Weaving a pattern in her mind, she reached out for the spool she knew rested at the back of the top shelf, being careful not to touch any of the other threads. Her right hand groped for a moment, and a wave of heat swept over her; then her fingers closed around the one she wanted and drew it out into the light. It was a bicolored yarn, one strand of dark blue wool and one in an even darker crimson twining inextricably around each other. Granny had spun it herself, long ago when she was first made Ka'Riatha, mingling the crimson of S'Rian and the blue of Liavek the way the two peoples had mingled, to the benefit of both. She'd used the thread sparingly in the years since; she didn't like taking chances with it unless she had to.

As she lifted the spool, a strand of decorative purple fluff caught on the end of it. Granny frowned, then shrugged. She'd have to use it somewhere, now that she had it, but there wasn't enough of it to affect the pattern much. She crossed to the loom and began winding the purple thread and the bicolor onto bobbins.

The week that followed was a trying one. Granny spent much of her time at her loom, painstakingly coaxing the spell-driven shape of the hanging into the pattern she had chosen. In the brief intervals between work, she tried not to think about the possible consequences if her choice were wrong. But Acrilat had fooled her once already, and even now she had no way to be sure she had discovered all she needed to know.

Slowly, the tapestry neared completion. The block of blue-and-white-variegated wool broke apart in a swirl of dark blue and crimson. The decorative fluff had an unexpectedly strong core, and made a nice accent at the apex of the pattern. From there, the variegated wool vanished, leaving the other threads to interweave in a harmonious balance. On the afternoon of the day Deleon's play opened, Granny finished the last of the weaving and cut it free of the loom.

The overall effect of the woven pattern was startling, but not unpleasant. Grimly, Granny tied off all but the last few warp threads and rolled the hanging up. She had a map; now she would have to get Acrilat to follow it. And hope that she had not missed anything this time, that she had made her map complete . . . She shook her head to dismiss the doubts; they would only distract her, and she would need all her concentration tonight. Quickly but with care, she dressed in a caftan of deep crimson and gold she had made with her own hands. Then, with her cane in her hand and the rolled-up hanging under her arm, she set off for the Desert Mouse.

She arrived well before the play was scheduled to begin. She allowed the greeter to show her to her seat, but as soon as his back was turned she rose quietly and slipped backstage. There, as she had expected, she found the stage magician Naril, deep in preparations for the spells he would use in the evening's performance. He looked up at the rap of her cane.

"Ka'Riatha!" Naril said. He palmed his forehead in greeting and scrambled to his feet. "How may I serve you?" he asked in a harried tone.

"I want you to make some changes in the spells you're using in this play," Granny replied bluntly.

"I can't," the stage magician said with a touch of desperation. "I have an agreement with Thrae . . . She's very particular about how things should look."

"Don't panic, child, I don't want you to alter anything your director is likely to notice."

"What do you want, then?" Naril asked warily.

"Look here." Granny sketched a pattern in the air with the tip of her cane. Green light trailed behind the cane tip, leaving a brilliant afterimage that burned the eyes. "I want you to add that to this diagram of yours. Here." The cane stabbed down in the center of the smudged circle Naril had been occupied in drawing.

Naril bent forward, concentrating, and Granny noted with pleasure that his diffidence was gone. "A wave breaking?" he muttered to himself. "In that position . . ." He looked up in puzzlement. "I'll do it, if you like, but it doesn't *do* anything!"

"You let me worry about that," Granny said. "And mind you don't use it until the last act."

Naril nodded, bewildered but obedient, and Granny left. The theater was filling up now, and as she walked toward her seat in the front row, she scanned the audience. She recognized a number of them, but the only other wizard she spotted was Aritoli ola Silba. The self-styled Advisor to Patrons of the Arts was seated at one end of the first row and chatting comfortably with a thin, fluffy-haired man beside him; he'd apparently found a way around the little problem he'd had with his eyesight a few months previously. Granny snorted. She did not have a particularly high opinion of the foppish ola Silba.

Verdialos, Nerissa, and Jehane were already seated in the second row. The rest of the Benedictis were in the third row, their pale skin and yellow hair a startling contrast to the dark Liavekans around them. Verdialos had seen them; he gave Granny a reproachful look as she made her way to her seat in the center of the front row. She nodded to him and settled into her seat as the curtain opened.

The first two acts had little to do with the summoning of Acrilat Granny anticipated, but as the scenes flowed by her lips tightened. Deleon had drawn heavily on his experiences with his own family in writing the play, and the results were disturbing. Granny recognized the personalities of most of the characters at once, and she strongly suspected that many of the incidents were straightforward examples of the way Marigand Benedicti had been raising her children. Granny was appalled by the sheer misery the play implied had been the normal state of affairs in the Benedicti household. No wonder Deleon had run away; no wonder Nerissa had joined a church of suicides; no wonder Jehane's face had worry lines. And no wonder Acrilat had had so little difficulty in using the rest of the Benedictis for his own purposes.

The third act arrived at last. As Deleon began his invocation, Granny let the hanging she had woven unroll halfway across her lap. She drew on her birth-luck and waited. Then Deleon's speech ended. The fire and light of the sorcerous duel leaped into life around him. And with the eerie blue fire and the thundering snowstorm came the ominous, crackling power of Acrilat.

The flames on the stage rose and fell hypnotically, calling all who saw them to the strange and terrible delights that Acrilat offered. Suddenly the light emanating from the stage changed. Granny's eyes widened; some wizard in the audience must have spotted Acrilat's trick and was trying to alter the hypnotic patterns enough to eliminate their effect. The idea was a good one, but alone the wizard did not have enough power to defeat a god's spell.

Granny reached out with a corner of her mind and poured her own luck into the other wizard's spell. She reinforced and strengthened his efforts, then added her knowledge of Acrilat to the subtle spell-web. The compulsion in the flickering light withered, and Granny felt an instant of relief. At least she would not have to worry about untangling an audience of madmen when the play ended.

The illusionary flames became bluer as the blizzard reached its peak; Acrilat did not seem to have noticed that they had lost their power to command. Granny tensed. Then, as Acrilat attempted to manifest Itself, Granny reached out with her birth-luck, the source of all her wizardry. She caught the thread she had had Naril insert into the stage spells, the image of the design she had so painstakingly woven, and pulled. At the same time, she snapped the hanging with one hand. The thread of magic unrolled invisibly across the stage as the hanging unrolled across her lap, blocking Acrilat's materialization.

The stage exploded in light as Acrilat howled Its anger and frustration, but Granny's spell did not weaken. Acrilat could not come through, and It would not go back. All It could do was to increase the sound and fury of the illusionary blizzard on stage. Fortunately, the sorcerous duel was still going on, so the audience would think Acrilat's extravagances part of the play. Most of the audience, anyway; from the corner of her eye Granny saw Aritoli ola Silba frown and lean forward. Then she was distracted by an insidious whisper in the back of her mind.

"You don't need to keep me out," the mental voice murmured. "I am Acrilat; let me in. I can give you wonderful things, things beyond your strangest dreaming."

"I don't want strange things," Granny thought at the murmuring voice. "Therefore your offer is no use to me."

"I am Acrilat; I can give you whatever you want."

"True," Granny said. Her forefinger traced one of the swirls in the weaving, following it inexorably to the apex of the pattern. "I want you to stay out of Liavek; you are perfectly capable of doing so. Give me that."

Acrilat paused. "You are trying to confuse Us."

"Nonsense!" Granny replied. "You're in Liavek. Liavek is more logical than Acrivain; I'm simply being logical."

"Liavek is mine," the mad god said emphatically.

Granny winced, but her fingers continued moving along the ridges of the hanging in her lap, following one after another to the unavoidable peak where the variegated wool vanished from the pattern. "Acrivain is yours," she said steadily. "Liavek is nothing like Acrivain. You have no temple in Liavek, no servants here. Liavek is not yours."

"Liavek is Ours!" Acrilat cried. "As Acrivain is Ours!"

"Shouting won't make Liavek yours. You don't belong here. You might as well face it and go home."

Acrilat's mental voice turned suddenly smooth and reasonable. "You say that you do not want what I have to offer. What of others? You cannot keep Me out if they want Me."

"They don't," Granny contradicted. "But it makes more sense to show you than to sit here arguing all night." She threw her mind like a shuttle down the row of spectators, dragging Acrilat's attention with her like a strand of warp. She stopped at Aritoli ola Silba, Advisor to Patrons of the Arts. Sarcastic dandy though he was, Granny was reasonably sure that ola Silba would not allow even a god to dictate his opinions. "Look here," she thought to Acrilat, and pointed the mad god's attention at Aritoli ola Silba's mind.

She saw at once that she had chosen better than she realized; it was ola Silba who had tried to disrupt Acrilat's hypnotic compulsion earlier. The critic was methodically considering the strange attack with part of his mind; the rest was systematically analyzing the play. Acrilat recoiled from the neat chains of reasoning, and Aritoli started. "Who's there?" he thought at the two observers. "What do you want?"

"I want to give, and take, and mold to my liking all things that are mine," Acrilat said. "I will be and change and be changed, and you will metamorphose, and be metamorphosed."

"I beg your pardon?" Aritoli replied uneasily. "I'm afraid that didn't make much sense to me."

"Of course it didn't make sense," Granny put in. "It's the mad god of Acrivain. I told It that It wasn't wanted, but It required convincing."

"I've had a bit much of gods and madness lately," Aritoli replied with a touch of acid. "I don't suppose you could have picked someone else for the honor?"

"Honor it is, and honor it will be," Acrilat said wildly. "Honest honor, bent but not broken, winding to new heights of glory!"

"Frankly, I'd prefer a good philosophical discussion," Aritoli said carefully.

"Babble not of philosophy, but worship me!" Acrilat thundered, and a spectacular display of lightning and blue fire flared across the stage.

Aritoli remained prudently silent, but his distaste for Acrilat's whole performance was evident. Granny gave a mental sniff. "You can see that you don't belong here," she informed Acrilat. "You don't like us any better than we like you. Go back to Acrivain where you belong."

With a shriek and an explosion of blue light, Acrilat lunged madly against Its restraints. Granny released the binding spell an instant before Acrilat broke it. The effect was that of someone running to break down a door which is opened just before he reaches it. Acrilat overshot Its goal; It was out of Liavek and halfway across the sea to Acrivain before It realized what had happened. In the moment of Acrilat's distraction, Granny reached out once more for the thread that had blocked Acrilat's appearance, the thread that Naril had unknowingly woven through the very heart of Acrilat's own spells. She bound the insubstantial thread of magic into the material of her weaving, and with it she bound the mad god of Acrivain.

Immediately, with a quick twist and pull, she tied off the last ends of the weaving, finishing both it and the spell within it, barring Acrilat from Liavek for as long as the threads of the hanging held together. She gave the mad god a good shove with all the energy she had left, just to speed It on Its way. Finally, she said a quick mental farewell to Aritoli and settled wearily back to watch the end of the play.

The lightning and flames faded from the stage, and the players proceeded to their final speeches. Neither they nor the audience seemed to have noticed anything untoward. Granny rolled up her weaving and relaxed. Acrilat, at least, was taken care of. On stage, several bodies fell as the play reached its final bloodbath, and Granny frowned. There were still the Benedictis to be dealt with.

The curtain came down, then rose again as the players knelt to the audience in thanks. The players climbed down from the stage to mingle with the audience and receive congratulations. Granny made her way to Deleon, who was scanning the crowd with a dazed and rather apprehensive expression. Presumably he was expecting his family, and from the look of him he wouldn't hear more than a third of what was said to him until he found them. Granny limited her remarks to, "That was a singularly illuminating performance, young man."

As she turned away, she saw Aritoli ola Silba staring at her with a thunderstruck expression. Of course; he'd finally recognized her voice. Granny made her way over to him.

"I believe I owe you an apology, mistress," ola Silba said by way of greeting.

"It seems there's more to you than I'd thought, ola Silba," Granny said.

"Thank you. And there is more to you, also, than meets the eye," Aritoli replied. He hesitated, then said with studied casualness, "I trust you enjoyed the play?"

"Enormously," Granny replied, amused.

"A very . . . powerful performance, wouldn't you say?" Aritoli looked at her with a sort of worried inquiry.

"Powerful in a number of ways," Granny said dryly. "Some of which fortunately cannot be repeated. And that's all I'm going to say about it, so you needn't bother to keep fishing for information."

"You relieve my mind," Aritoli said. He made her an elegant bow and slipped away.

Deleon was talking to his sister, Jehane; Verdialos stood a little way away, apparently scolding Nerissa. Verdialos saw Granny, and a moment later, when Nerissa went to join Jehane and Deleon, he came over to her.

"You might have warned me," he said.

"About the Benedictis, or about Acrilat?"

"Acrilat?" Verdialos looked startled. "What does Acrilat have to do with this evening's—" He stopped short, his eyes widening even more, and he glanced in Nerissa's direction as if to make certain she and Jehane and Deleon were still there.

"Even the Benedictis couldn't make this much of a mess without help," Granny said. She bit back a stinging remark about Verdialos's lack of thoroughness in investigating his protegé's background.

"That still doesn't explain why you didn't warn me."

Granny snorted. "It's not my business to tell you where to set your fishing nets. Though I doubt that the Benedictis will cause quite as much trouble as you're worrying about."

"What's to keep them from it?"

"I've a few things to discuss with them," Granny told him dryly.

"All of them?" Verdialos said, looking toward Nerissa and Jehane again.

"All of them," Granny said, "but not necessarily all at once. Jehane!"

Jehane, who had moved tactfully away from the reunion between her missing brother and her youngest sister, turned at the sound of her name. When she saw Granny standing with Verdialos, she stared in surprise, then came back to join them. Granny studied her while she gave the appropriate greetings, then thoroughly startled the girl by offering her the wall-hanging. The binding that remained in the weaving would hold Acrilat outside Liavek as long as it remained intact. Jehane was careful; she'd keep it well. And the fact that the hanging was in the hands of a Benedicti would add to the effectiveness of the spell. Granny explained none of this to Jehane, but she was pleased enough by the girl's reaction to propose giving her weaving lessons.

Jehane was still too stunned by this offer to answer when Nerissa rejoined them. The younger girl gave Granny a speculative look and then reminded her sister that she had been looking for a remunerative occupation. Weaving of the sort Granny did was *very* remunerative. When Granny left them, Jehane had accepted and the following morning had been set for the first lesson.

Naril pounced on Granny as soon as she was free of Verdialos and his charges. He took her down to the players' dressing room and demanded, in the most polite and respectful terms he could manage, to know exactly what had been going on.

"I did less than half the effects in the third act," he said. "And there was more happening than an imitation blizzard and blue fire. What did you do?"

"Nothing whatever, as far as your special effects were concerned," Granny replied. "The enhancements were someone else's work, but it needn't concern you. It won't happen again."

Naril apparently did not find this entirely reassuring.

"Still, I think it would be better if you made a few changes in the spells you're using in the third act," Granny went on. "There's no sense in taking foolish chances."

"No sense at all," Naril agreed faintly. The dressing room door opened to admit a group of players and their friends, all of whom ignored the conversation in the corner as they set about removing their makeup.

"That's settled, then. I'll send you the alterations in the morning," Granny told Naril. "You'll probably find them easier than that elaborate jumble you've been using, and they won't affect the look of things at all."

"Thank you, Granny," Naril said. "I think—"

The outside door of the dressing room opened again, and a string of tall, pale-skinned, yellow-haired people filed into the room. They clumped together like butter separating from cream and stood staring at Deleon Benedicti, who had frozen in place with only half his blue makeup removed. Granny held up a hand to silence Naril, then crossed the room to tell the Benedictis what she thought of them.

The initial reactions of the family were more or less what Granny expected. The elder Marigand Benedicti was stiffly furious at being called to account by anyone. Her husband seemed to think he had done something meritorious by being weak-willed enough to be of use to Acrilat, while their children were stunned to see someone berate their mother with apparent impunity. And all of them were thoroughly taken aback by Granny's ultimatum—put their lives in order or leave Liavek within a year.

During most of this lecture, Deleon sat like a stone between Calla and Aelim, the graceful, finely-boned man Naril had said he was living with. When Granny informed the rest of his family that they had one year to pull themselves together, however, Deleon stirred and caught Granny's eye. "And do you have any suggestions?" he said.

He'd learned a lot about playing in nine years, Granny thought; that tone said plainly that, runaway or not, he was a member of this family and entitled to be abused with the rest of them. It was a pity he didn't realize how true that was; on the other hand, he'd been through more than enough penance already, if that play of his was anything to judge by. And Granny had made mistakes of her own regarding the Benedictis.

"Don't write any more plays about Acrilat," Granny told him briskly. She paused and looked pointedly from Calla to Aelim. "And make up your mind."

A look of surprised resentment crossed Deleon's face, as if he had not really expected the rebuke he had asked for. Granny suppressed a sudden smile. She would have to handle this irritating and intractable family the way she handled her shuttles and bobbins: pull too hard, even in the right direction, and the weaving would be ruined, but prod and poke correctly and the thread would slide into place perfectly. "Livia!" Granny said sharply to the first Benedicti who caught her eye. "Your sister tells me you're engaged."

Livia gave a frightened nod, and Mistress Benedicti's face grew stiffer than ever.

Granny eyed them both narrowly. "To whom?" she said, in a tone calculated to frighten Livia into silence and force Mistress Benedicti to answer for her daughter. Mistress Benedicti would hate admitting that she had allowed one of her children to become engaged to a Hrothvekan, but she was angry enough that she'd marry her daughter off tomorrow if she thought Granny disapproved.

Mistress Benedicti reacted with gratifying predictability. With very little additional effort Granny was able to prod most of the rest of the family into an intelligent discussion of their futures. She was pleased to find that the Benedictis junior seemed quite willing to be assimilated into Liavek if they were allowed, and for the most part she stayed out of their deliberations.

Near the end of these proceedings, Granny noticed that Deleon Benedicti was wearing an expression of suppressed alarm. Granny glanced over her shoulder and saw Mistress Benedicti coming toward them. She looked back at Deleon. "Go along with you. And mind what I said."

Deleon escaped with an expression of heartfelt relief, taking Aelim along. Granny turned to finish dealing with Mistress Benedicti and her husband.

"You take a great deal upon yourself, Granny Carry," Mistress Benedicti said coldly.

"That's my job," Granny replied. "And I do it well, which is more than can be said for you."

"You need not think you can blithely arrange the lives of my family to please yourself," Deleon's mother continued in the same tone of frigid anger. The rest of the family had fallen silent to listen apprehensively.

"I haven't the slightest intention of it," Granny said, and paused. "Nor will I allow you to continue doing so."

"Exactly what is that supposed to mean?"

"It means that your children are not children any longer," Granny said severely. "Not even according to the ridiculous Acrivannish standards you insist on living by. There's no reason whatever for them to be still tied to your fishline like a string of sinkers. They can make their own decisions; in fact, I shall require them to. From the sound of things a minute ago, I'd say they won't have much trouble adjusting once you've stopped stuffing them with foolishness."

"I will not allow—"

"Fiddlesticks," Granny interrupted. "You can't stop me, but if you choose to waste the next year trying, that's your affair. I'd advise against it."

"What have we done to deserve this?" Master Benedicti asked the air.

"By your standards or mine?" Granny said, skewering him with a look.

Master Benedicti, thoroughly taken aback, did not respond. Granny snorted. "Well, then. You've spent twenty years hankering after things you couldn't have and ignoring what you could; you've put custom, appearance, and convenience ahead of affection, substance, and industry; you've broken your own rules by living off your daughters' dowries when your funds stopped coming from Acrivain; you've taught your children so poorly that one of them knows no better than to use the summoning prayer for Acrilat in a player's speech. You've whined at the smallest inconveniences and sneered at the best fortune, and in the end you've made yourself and your family into a broad bridge for Acrilat to cross into Liavek. I've had enough of it. Settle down and make something of yourself, or leave Liavek altogether. I don't care which. You've a year to make up your mind, but I won't object if you decide to go sooner."

Master Benedicti stared at her as if she had just turned into a dog and bitten him. Granny snorted and turned to go. A brown-skinned hand on her arm stopped her; it was the player, Calla. "Don't you think you should stay until they've calmed down?" she said.

"No, I don't," Granny replied sharply. She saw an expression of annoyance flit across the girl's face, followed quickly by a measuring, speculative look that all her acting skills could not quite hide. "And you needn't try your tricks on me, young woman," Granny added.

Calla flushed. "What—I don't know what you mean."

"Don't you?" Granny looked directly at the girl. "Hmmph. You meddle in other people's affairs without considering that the results may be other than you expect," she said baldly. "If you aren't careful, you'll turn out like Mistress Benedicti here, arranging her children's lives to suit herself without worrying about what they want."

"I don't!" Calla said, genuinely shaken.

"Not yet." Granny studied the girl briefly. She nodded, satisfied that her message had gone home. "Mend your ways," she said to the room at large, and left by way of the outer door. Behind her, she heard a babble of discussion break out, and she smiled. She'd hear a great deal about this night's work, one way and another, but she rather thought the real trouble with the Benedictis was over. In a way, that was even more satisfying than her success with Acrilat. Still smiling, Granny marched down the Lane of Olives in search of a foot-cab.

The Tale of the Stuffed Levar

by Jane Yolen

OH, I WILL not bore you with the story of Andrazzi and her Shift Dreams, my lords, my ladies, she being the greatest ruler in living memory, always excepting our gracious Levar now on the throne. But every schoolchild knows of her: how she followed the awful Year of the Quick Levars in which a virtual alphabet chowder of Levars died one right after another, some of natural causes, some of unnatural causes, and some of magic.

The tale I would spin you now, my Excellencies, is not of Andrazzi but of the Levar who immediately preceded her, Zzzozza the Terrified, who collapsed of a surfeit of bad dates in the middle of ticklish negotiations with Ka Zhir, only to be revived within minutes by his loving wife, the redoubtable Zadir, a woman of somewhat dubious background and strange tastes. Strange, that is, for a Liavekan and the wife of a Levar. Zzzozza the Terrified, who even though he was habitually tongue-tied and full of a variety of incapacitating tics, still managed to keep us out of a fearful war with Ka Zhir before expiring at last at the feet of his successor Andrazzi some two days after eating the poisoned dates.

That, of course, is the story as we all know it, for it has been sung in such ballads as "Zzzozza and the Dates" and "When Levars Eat in Public." And no, my Magnificencies, you need not fear I shall sing them now. My tongue is for telling, not for warbling out of tune like some addlepated turtledove. Ballads have their place, and surely the ban on our Levars' public appearances at great feasts is as much due to the popularity of that latter ballad as Zzzozza's death itself. But the stories told in ballads are often changed to fit the meter. Poets have less regard for history than for rhyme.

What I will tell you now is the *real* tale. It has been handed down father to son, father to son in my family since that fateful day of the dates. Our tongues have kept the memory alive. We hold the truth in our mouths. We know that truth because one of my uncles, many times removed, was intimately connected with the tale. His name was Ovar the Tinmaker, not because he made tin but because he could make a loud noise or din, and one of his young nephews had christened him that before the child's mouth could properly pronounce the word.

Ovar was an entertainer of sorts, a professional din-maker as his sisters called him, a puppet master who could make wooden dolls speak, and a man who could balance oranges on his nose. A strange mixture of skills, but ones that would make him suitable for his role in the odd history I am about to relate. His ability as a performer left him little in demand, and because he had a wife and seventeen children—he had *some* talents a Levar might envy—all of whom desired to eat, he also owned a farm which lay in the shadow of the Silverspine. On that farm he grew dates. Yes, my Eminences, the very dates celebrated in song and story.

I see you are interested, my Graces. It is a small tale, but mine own. None can tell it save I, for it belongs to our family and I—alas—am the last of our line, since no one in our family but Ovar of the tainted Dates ever had more than a single child thereafter. It was Andrazzi's express wish. And as I am the last and I have no child to whom I can pass on the story, it shall die if it is not told. So I will tell it to you for a coin. A small coin. A copper in the palm. A copper in *each* palm will suffice. I will take no dates in payment. As you can imagine, no one in my family has eaten dates since that fateful day.

The story I tell happened during a fragile but interesting

moment in the magnificent history of our land. Due to the year of change and changing rulers, Liavek's hold on the Sea of Luck was daily threatened. You know it well. Need I rehearse for you the horrible incursions by the pirates of Ka Zhir? They raped and pillaged without thought to the age, sex, or religious inclinations of their victims. They swore—and the few pitiful survivors of their raids attested to this—that they were without official sanction. But I have it on good authority, since one of my aunts many times removed had been pillaged and pillowed by the swine, that each captain sailed under a letter of mark from their king.

So our Levar and their king negotiated a truce. But it was slow going, my Graciousnesses, for Levar after Levar had died in that terrible year and each time the ambassador had to be recalled and then returned to present his credentials in the proper way. By Zzzozza's turn, twenty-five such presentations had occurred in rapid succession, and the Zhir ambassador was exhausted.

Besides, Zzzozza spent so much of his time being terrified (it took him half a day just to be able to look at his own reflection in the mirror, in this much the ballads are correct) that the ambassador had even longer to wait. But Zzzozza was our Levar, and so I touch upon his frailties no more.

And so, the play of history unfolded. Zzzozza on his throne with his customary wide-eyed terrified look. His wife, the redoubtable Zadir, by his feet as she preferred not to watch his trembling lips and squinting eyes. His advisors on either side, urging action by wind or by war, depending upon their personal landholdings. The Zhir ambassador, a small man made even smaller by his large guard, on the floor making his obeisances, hands to forehead. And entering from the kitchen, my uncle many times removed Ovar, balancing a plate of dates on his head. In those days dates were the coin of negotiation and the only thing Zzzozza was not terrified of, they being small, sweet, and immobile.

Then Zzzozza held out his hand, Exultancies, a gesture fraught with fear. His hand trembled so that he spilled most of the dates upon the floor. Only a few landed in his hand. The rest he swept under the table with his foot, afraid, no doubt, that the ambassador might be offended by such clumsiness. However the dates were not the only thing under the Levar's table. His wife's three pet monkeys were there, she being a great collector of animals, both live and dead. The monkeys dined quickly upon the dates, in the manner of their kind, stuffing them into their mouths and swallowing in one swift motion. They subsequently went into loud convulsions, mercifully hidden from human sight by the vast white tablecloth and its intricate lace hem, and from hearing by the Levar's own distressed cries. He had, in his turn, eaten the few dates in his hand, turned the color of Tichenese mud, that strange brown shot through with veins of green and gold, uttered three sharp cries that were augmented by the monkeys' screams, and passed out.

Recognizing her pets' voices, the redoubtable Zadir crept under the tablecloth and wept, but quietly. She was a woman used to being neither seen nor heard in the jungles where she gathered animals for her study.

The ambassador still lay on the floor, being a stickler for proper procedure. Failures in protocol are punished severely in Ka Zhir. So when he heard strange sounds from the Levar's throne, the ambassador did not look up. Zzzozza was known to throw up at shadows, to blanch at whispers of wind. It would have been inappropriate in the extreme for the ambassador of Ka Zhir to watch the Liavekan Levar lose his lunch. All of this gave rise to the rumors later on that it was he who tried to poison Zzzozza. But—alas—it was just a case of bad dates.

So only the Levar's closest advisors and my uncle many times removed Ovar, my Supremacies, saw the rictus of death beginning to spread the Levar's smile.

Ringing the throne with their fevered presences, the advisors hurried him into his dressing room by the simple expedient of making a chair of their hands. They carried his body away with more hurry than honor. Stepping over the prostrate ambassador and his guards, the chief advisor said quickly. "His eminence Zzzozza is not happy with your obeisance. He will return in an hour to see if your limbs have been more *suitably* arranged."

This delighted the ambassador. Such was the usual way things were handled in the court of Ka Zhir. It meant he had been noticed and that negotiations could now go forth properly. He spent the next hour twitching and manipulating his limbs into that most uncomfortable pattern, known in Ka Zhir as the Position of Broken Twigs.

Now the redoubtable Zadir had not seen the retreat of her dying husband on the arms of his advisors for she was still busy under the table gathering up her rapidly stiffening pets. Crawling out from under the table with the monkeys in her arms, she stopped to wipe her eyes quickly with the lacy edge of the cloth. When she stood, she found herself in a hall deserted except for the groveling ambassador and his guards, all face down on the floor.

Now Zadir did not hesitate for a moment. She knew it would take the ambassador at least an hour to compose himself. The Zhir were famous for such self-torture. They even had manuals on limb arrangement. She counted on that time. Being from a minor branch of the royal family that had fended for itself on the border of the Great Waste where her great-grandfather had been sent in partial exile for some infraction of court etiquette, Zadir was at her best in difficult situations. That was one of the reasons she had chosen to marry the unmarriageable Levar Zzzozza. All the other young women of royal blood had preferred to wait upon his demise—or to plan it, whichever seemed safest. But the redoubtable Zadir had chosen the most direct method—marriage. With one stipulation, which she got in writing. (Her great-grandfather had never put anything in writing, which led to his downfall.) She asked only that she be allowed to establish a royal zoological park and fill it with exotic beasts. Since it was the best, indeed the *only* offer Zzzozza had, his advisors took it, even though there had been rumors of a Zhir taint in Zadir's bloodlines.

So what did the redoubtable Zadir do, my Pre-eminences? Well you may wonder. Shouldering her poor dead creatures, she strode from the room, thinking briefly about contacting a wizard to help her animate her pets and then deciding instead upon taxidermy, that being the latest of her obsessions.

But as she passed her husband's rooms, she heard a strange

hubbub. Knowing him to be quiet in the extreme—for he also had an advanced case of noise-aversion—she worried that he might be ill, thus affecting the passage of the treaty with Ka Zhir which she devoutly desired since some of the known world's most exotic animals roamed the Zhir hills: the Septillan Ape with its seven-fingered hands, the Blond Marmez which bore feathered young though it was a mammal, and the deadly but glorious Nightcaller or Ninjus whose whimsical song lured lizards and ladies to their deaths. So she hurried into his chamber to offer what assistance she could. And there she found him surrounded by his gabbling advisors and my uncle many times removed Ovar who was standing in the corner noisily wringing his hands for, in his consternation, he was throwing his voice into his fingertips as if they were tiny puppets.

Now it took Zadir a long minute to realize that Zzzozza had, indeed, died, for he sat with his usual terrified expression, eyes rolled up till the whites showed, and his mouth uncomfortably ajar. But in that long minute, as Zzzozza had neither a tic nor a tremor, the redoubtable Zadir began to suspect something was horribly amiss. And when she purposely dropped one of her stiffened monkeys onto his lap and he did not scream, she knew.

"The Levar is dead," she announced to the gesticulating advisors. Such was the authority in her voice, the men were silent at once. Even Ovar's wrangling hands were still.

"What have you done?" Zadir asked. "Have you done anything?" Those being the two questions royal children are taught to ask.

There were no answers from the advisors, only head shakes.

The redoubtable Zadir shook her own head. "Men," she muttered, adding in Tichenese, *"Zabidip na sta ne cazz, zabidip sta ne cazzua."* Which, as you know my Ascendencies, means "Men, even when they are possible, men they are impossible." It does not translate well. And then Zadir issued a series of instructions which only in retrospect made sense.

"Send for a doctor. Send for a wizard. Send for my filleting knife."

Well, what could the advisors do? Until the royal doctor pronounced the Levar truly and eternally dead, Zadir was still his wife, not his widow. The widow they could safely ignore; the wife they had to obey.

"The doctor," said the first advisor, hurrying out the door.

"A wizard," said another, hurrying after.

"Your *filleting* knife?" asked the third, knowing the redoubtable Zadir as a fisherwoman of great renown and puzzling over the significance of his task.

"I mean to stuff these while I wait," Zadir said, pointing to her erstwhile pets. "And if you do not bring me my knife at once, I shall consider stuffing you as well."

Remembering the reason Zadir's great-grandfather had been exiled to the border of the Waste, the advisor hurried from the room.

Ovar alone did not move.

The wizard arrived shortly after. He was an unprepossessing sort who lived on the very edge of Wizard's Row, and not for very long either. It being a holiday, his house had been the only one visible at the time and the advisor had had no choice but to enlist him, unprepossessing as he was, in the service of the Levar. Being a patriotic sort, he came at once but he shook his head dismally when he heard Zadir's request.

"Actually," he said, cracking his knuckles and chewing on the right side of his pencil-thin, drooping grey moustache, "re-animation is way beyond my skills." For a moment he stroked the left side of his moustache, but it was already in tatters. "I deal mostly in water spells. In fact, I deal entirely in water spells. Wine into water. Water into wine. That sort of thing."

"How are you at fishes?" asked Zadir suddenly.

"Pretty good, actually," the wizard said. "Tench, carp, pike, and trout are my specialties now, though I did my independent studies on the goby, which is the world's smallest fish, and . . ." He paused, sensing Zadir's disapproval.

"But no humans?"

"Sadly, no, your Eminence." He cracked a few more

knuckles and started in again on the moustache.

Just then the doctor arrived. It was not the royal doctor. He had been called away to attend a rather messy business with one of the Dashforths (whose heirs would carry the title Count Dashif for just such messy businesses in the years to come). This one was a minor doctor who moved in a competent bustling manner to disguise the fact that he was, actually, incompetent in all but the most ordinary of diagnoses. He held onto Zzzozza's wrist and examined his bulging white eyes.

"He does not look well," the doctor pronounced at last.

"He looks dead," said Zadir.

"Maybe not," said the doctor. "We shall have to test further. One does not pronounce a Levar dead without proof. If I were wrong, he would have my head."

The advisors began gabbling again and the wizard made himself disappear, or at least managed to make his right side disappear. The left side, including the tattered moustache, was still visible. He was not, as he himself stated, good with humans at all. And my uncle many times removed Ovar in his great agitation began to throw his voice all over the room: whimpering from the candle sconce, whining from the Tichen carpet, slobbering from the mouths of all three dead apes.

The redoubtable Zadir was the only one who noticed. "Who is doing that?" she asked.

"Doing what?" they all replied before lapsing into hysteria again.

However Zadir had noticed that Ovar had been the only one whose lips had not moved. *"You!"* she said, pointing her index finger.

Such was the authority of her voice that Ovar came and knelt before her and whispered, "Yes, Eminence," in a voice that seemed to spring out of his left pinkie, the one that is called the swear finger in Ka Zhir though he meant no disrespect by it at all.

"You are a player?" the redoubtable Zadir asked.

"A player, Eminence?" the finger asked.

"An actor, a mountebank."

"A puppeteer," the swear finger replied. It thought it impolitic to mention that Ovar also grew dates

"Can you throw your voice anywhere?" asked the redoubtable Zadir.

"Anywhere," said the candle sconce. "Anywhere," said the Tichenese carpet. "Anywhere," said the three dead monkeys one right after another.

Zadir turned to the advisors. "Do you agree that we must negotiate with Ka Zhir?"

Half of the advisors nodded yes, the other half no. Only one remained mute on the point. Zadir, who longed to collect those exotic Zhir beasts, cast the deciding vote.

"And it is the law that unless the royal doctor proclaims my husband dead, he is still alive?" Zadir asked.

On this point they all agreed.

"Then," said the redoubtable Zadir, "I can certainly help, though I must first extract from you a promise."

"Anything," said the advisors and Ovar's left pinkie.

"In writing," Zadir demanded.

They found paper in Zzzozza's bath room and proceeded to write down Zadir's request.

After that the redoubtable Zadir dismissed them all, all but my uncle many times removed Ovar, and set to work. She slipped the filleting knife into Zzzozza's belly with an expertness the royal doctor would have envied had he been there to watch. She filled the cavity with sweet-smelling herbs: pandonum, cardenix, reedwort, and the hazy, odorous fresh trefeelium which was, by the greatest of luck, strewn alongside the Levar's bed, suggesting a phobia that even Zadir did not understand. Then she sewed him up again with large, ungainly black stitches, crossed with green when the black thread ran out. Needlework had never been one of her finer skills, as she was quick to remark to Ovar. She had been brought up along the borders of the Great Waste, with a boy's knowledge in her hands. Besides, she had women to do such stitchery for her now, though, as usual, they were nowhere to be found when needed.

And while Ovar was quietly but quite efficiently sick behind the bath room door, she eviscerated and stuffed the monkeys as well.

• • •

It was then, my Benevolencies, but a long hour past the time the advisors had removed the Levar from his throne. They returned to find Zadir patting the still-rigid Zzzozza on the head.

"Welcome," said Zzzozza out of a mouth that never moved. But as he had never been much for articulation before, the advisors were not unduly disturbed. "I would go back and negotiate with Ka Zhir."

The advisors picked up the unbending Levar and carried him back to the throne, followed in swift succession by my uncle many times removed Ovar and the redoubtable Zadir.

"You may rise. I find your position—suitable," said the Levar, never altering for a moment his terrified expression, though no one commented upon it. Beside him Ovar smiled a strange stiff smile.

The ambassador from Ka Zhir arose. He seemed quite pleased with himself, though he now walked with a peculiar shuffle, his limbs having sustained the Position of Broken Twigs longer than any living soul. Bowing low, till his bald, blue-washed head touched the floor, the ambassador said something in his own language to the floor, a customary greeting. Then he unbent slowly and stared into Zzzozza's unblinking eyes, translating.

"I come from the court of the great king of Ka Zhir with greetings and hope of a satisfactory treaty."

At that very moment, the royal doctor returned from Dashforth's side, entered the throne room, and swore. He took one look at the Levar's blanched face and staring white eyes and began to pronounce the ritual words of a Levar's death, being well practiced as he had spoken them twenty-five times already that year.

At that very same moment, the wizard of the water spells reappeared, munching on both sides of his moustache at once, and enthusiastically chanting a spell he had found in one of his old study books.

However, what none of them knew was that that very day was my uncle many times removed Ovar's luck day. He had chosen that time to present a plate of his best dates to the Levar hoping the free-hold gift might change his bad luck. His mother had had a short but agonizing labor, dying at the moment she had given birth. Ovar had planned to leave the dates and scamper home. He had not counted on the Levar's death. He had not counted on the doctor and the wizard. He had not counted on the Zhir ambassador. He had not counted on the redoubtable Zadir.

No sooner had the ambassador mentioned the word "treaty" than the doctor spoke the syllable "dead." No sooner had the doctor said the expletive "dead" than the wizard spat out the sound "live."

And the time of my uncle many times removed Ovar's mother's expiration coincided with them all.

Luck magic was indeed loosed in that hall.

With a flicker of surprise, the eyes of all three dead monkeys popped open and they scrambled stiffly onto Zzzozza's lap. Zzzozza himself woke as if from a deep sleep to find the grinning apes peering up at him. They all screamed.

The screams shut up ambassador, doctor, and wizard at once, just at the anniversary of my uncle many times removed Ovar's actual birth.

The monkeys keeled over, dead once more.

So did Zzzozza.

But it was an hour before anyone but the redoubtable Zadir noticed. In that hour, she had guided the Levar's hand to sign a shaky name on the treaty. Then at his own request, Zzzozza was taken off to his room feeling—as he said through clenched teeth—somewhat unwell.

As for the redoubtable Zadir, she had what she wanted in writing. For the rest of her life she was in charge of the Levar's zoological park, with trapping rights in all of the treaty lands. Her cousin Andrazzi, because of one of her many Shift Dreams, also saw fit to gift Zadir with the ownership of six small rivers. The redoubtable Zadir used to meet the wizard and Ovar at one river or another on all the official holidays when the zoological park was closed. The bait they used on their lines were dates from Ovar's farm. But they never felt inclined to eat any of them. Of that, my Tremendousies, you can be sure.

An Act of Love

by Steven Brust, Gregory Frost, and Megan Lindholm

1 THE PLAYERS

ONCE THERE WAS a man called Imman Toriff Curihan Denbar ola Vedneigh, Vavasor of Heartstone and Bluesprings, Count of Dashif.

He was born in the main house of the Dashif estate. The household consisted of: A cheery-eyed wet nurse who was his first playmate, although he hardly remembered her later; a pretty dark-haired cook and maid who spoke only in whispers; a butler with huge sideburns, who wasn't fast enough to keep the child Tori out of things he ought not to have been in; a bald-headed, dark-skinned gardener who taught him hundreds of interesting things about weeds and willows; a mother who spoke less than the maid, but hummed a lot; and a father who sang him to sleep at night.

Some three hundred and fifty years earlier, the land had been given to the first Count Dashforth for services rendered to the Levar. For generations before that, the ola Vedneigh family had been sorcerers. Tori's father continued in the tradition—devoting most of his energies to the sorts of small magics that would make his farmlands more productive. That is, he wouldn't destroy the locusts, but he would make his lands less attractive to them. He wouldn't force defective seeds to germinate, but he would discover which seeds were defective. He wouldn't control the weather, but he would determine the best time to plant.

When Tori was fifteen, he invested his luck into a sterling silver belt buckle. When he was seventeen, he joined the Levar's Navy, where he learned something of the destructive ends of magic, and where he spent a brief stint in Tichen making reports on the size and composition of the Tichenese fleets.

When he was nineteen, stationed at Minnow Island, he fell in love with a local girl named Erina. His father didn't approve of the match, so they made plans to leave for Gold Harbor together. The Count of Dashif died then, so the plans were changed from elopement to a public wedding, with the announcement to occur as soon as a decent interval had passed.

Before the announcement could take place, the new Count of Dashif's heart—or at any rate his eye—was stolen by Neelya, daughter of the Margrave of Foxhead. Dashif left Erina and married Neelya. Dashif didn't understand the blood of the ancient S'Rian race that ran almost pure in Erina's veins. He also didn't know that Erina had stopped chewing Worrynot. Erina never told Dashif that she was with child, or, later, that she had borne him a daughter, whom she was unable to support.

Dashif and Neelya had two children. It was several months after the birth of the second, a boy, that Erina succeeded in stealing Dashif's silver belt buckle, and destroying it exactly six months from his luck time.

Dashif sickened, but did not die. When he recovered, no longer a sorcerer, Neelya had taken their children and left him. He made no effort to find them. Instead, he procured a pair of double-barreled flintlock pistols and used them to shoot Erina in broad daylight in a small market on Minnow Island.

He never understood the change that took place in him then. He knew he'd been hurt, but he didn't understand why he felt no pain. He knew he should be angry, but he felt no more than a cold rationality.

When he was arrested, a friend sent him a note wishing

him luck. This struck Dashif as odd, and, thinking about it, he realized that he had no luck—Erina had taken it. His only hope, then, was to attach himself to someone who had a great deal of luck, and could protect him. Who had more luck than the Regent for the Levar? With a brazenness that would become characteristic, Dashif showed those who arrested him his naval commission and discharge, and explained that he'd been working in secret for the Levar. The matter was referred to the Navy, where he had enough connections to achieve an interview with His Scarlet Eminence, the Regent, Resh. No one knows what took place during the interview, but at its end he was pardoned. He put his lands under the care of the gardener and moved into the Levar's Palace.

For the next several years, then, he worked as the secret left hand of His Scarlet Eminence. His activities involved such things as extorting cooperation from a Tichenese emissary, engineerng the massacre of several priests of a defunct faith and stealing documents from a very dedicated Zhir agent named Brajii.

And so things remained, until a certain Jolesha came across his path, and Dashif found himself briefly communing with the spirit of the departed Erina, and, shortly thereafter, found Kaloo, and knew her to be his daughter.

The Dashif who lived alone and cold, hiding from his pain, could no longer exist. There could have been some question as to what sort of Dashif would replace him, but Dashif was never one to ask such questions.

Kaloo put the finishing touches on cleaning her room, just in case.

Dashif—she still couldn't, wouldn't think of him as her father—was expected to call soon. He had never actually been in her room, but she had learned lately to plan for all possibilities. And so she cleaned her room, and kept it picked up. Daril, her foster mother, misunderstood the reasoning behind it, and so approved of it. Kaloo was beginning to think that Daril misunderstood most of her reasons, and probably had all her life.

Usually, Dashif saw her in his chambers in the Levar's

Palace. He would summon her, and she would go, up to the chambers that were as sterile and empty as Dashif's soul. The only objects there would be the few items he had set out for her magic instructions, and a small portrait of herself. The portrait embarrassed her and made her nervous. It was, she had decided, intended to have that effect upon her. Look about his chamber as she might, she could learn no more of her father or his past than this: that he knew she was his daughter and was determined to rule her as he ruled everything else that fell under his authority. And so he summoned her when he would, and taught her, not only magic, but the cultural things she had missed growing up as the daughter of an innkeeper: dance, music, drama, and the arts. As if she wasn't good enough for him the way she was.

She slammed her hairbrush down, looked once more about the room. A bed, made up with a clean spread. A small dresser, a square of mirror. A woven rug. A chest to hold her garments. Nothing else. No ornaments, no vase of flowers, no stuffed dancer or toucan doll, none of the silly pictures she had drawn for T'Nar that had so pleased him, back in the days when she had sat upon his knee and thought of him as her father. If Dashif ever did chance to view her room, he would see that she had already learned one thing from him. He would find no clue to her here, no inkling of what she was. All he would ever know of her was the careful Kaloo she presented to him. Just as all she would ever know of him was Count Dashif.

She heard footsteps coming up the stairs. Daril's. She knew that step, hitch, step, hitch stride of hers. Her children had been adults when T'Nar had brought Kaloo into her life. More of an age to be my grandmother than my mother, Kaloo thought. For an instant she wondered if it had been very hard for Daril to take on a squalling, sickly infant at that time of her life. But the thought made her feel indebted to Daril, so she stifled it. Daril had only done what she wanted to, taken in a girlchild to raise up to stir kettles and wait tables. No, Kaloo owed nothing to anyone.

If Daril was coming up, then Dashif must be waiting below. Kaloo tried to sigh out her tension, but it didn't work.

Her belly was knotted as it always was before one of their evenings together. Instead, she looked at herself in the glass. It was a small mirror, but still enough to see the difference Dashif had already wrought in her life. Her garments were no longer the loose, practical, long-wearing ones that Daril had once sewn for her. No, the silky flowered fabric had come from the Farlands, and been sewn by one of Liavek's better tailors. Styled and sewn to Dashif's specifications, while Kaloo stood and was turned and pinned and measured, as if she were a doll. Chosen by Dashif were the emerald clips that secured her dark hair, and the emerald at her throat had been in his family for many generations.

He was probably standing below right now just as he had stood in the tailor's chambers. Red cloak flung back over one shoulder, white ruffles foaming down his chest, ignoring the nervous patrons of the Mug and Anchor as he waited for Kaloo. Reeking of danger, commanding respect even from the shaven-headed captains drinking below. The respect was something she approved of—grudgingly.

"Kaloo, your—your guest is here."

Kaloo contrived to be busy with her hem. "Thank you, Daril." She tried to sound like an adult speaking to a servant, and knew that the effort was plain in her voice. She sighed again, and turned to find Daril standing in the door with her worried-mother-hen look on her face. It irritated Kaloo that Daril thought she still had a right to wear it, but she kept all feelings from her face.

Daril looked her up and down, plainly disapproving of the clinging fabric over her young body. "How can he dress you like that?" she muttered.

"He's my father. He can dress me any way he wants," Kaloo said.

"Then let him dress you like his daughter, not some highborn . . ." Daril swallowed whatever sneer she had intended to make about nobility in general. "Or let him tell people you're his daughter. Or you tell people. You know what they think below, what the sailors think when he comes in a carriage to take you off like this. How can he let people think that of his daughter?"

"I doubt that he's heard the rumors. Or would care if he had. Legally, I'm an adult, Daril. I could take any lover I wished. Besides, I know what truly scandalizes you. It isn't when the sailors say, 'Count Dashif has taken up with a girl a fraction of his age, some little tavern wench from the waterfront.' It's not what I might be doing at all, it's who folks say I'm doing it with, *that* bothers you."

Daril was silent. Kaloo smoothed her hair, stared back into the cold eyes in the mirror. "Where's T'Nar?" she demanded suddenly. "I've warned you, I won't have another scene with him." Easier, sometimes, to speak to Daril as if she and T'Nar were servants, as if they had never had any hold on her heart.

Daril reddened slightly. "Gone down to the docks with T'Fregan. Something about a boat T'Fregan wants to buy, and wants to know if she's as sound as she looks. T'Nar's been raving about that boat for days. I hope someone buys it soon. He should know better than to dream about—"

"Good." Kaloo dismissed T'Nar and the boat he longed for.

"Where—where are you going tonight?" Daril's question was cautious.

"An Acrivannish play. He thinks I should receive some cultural as well as magical education." There. Let her chew on that. Think of what else she kept from me besides my magic. Kaloo knew that the inn would be busy tonight and the tables full. Once Daril would have forbidden Kaloo to leave, would have told her plainly that there was work to be done this evening. Now she didn't dare to. Or didn't care to. Whatever. It all came out to the same thing, Kaloo told herself. They had ceded her to Dashif as easily as they'd sell a leaky rowboat.

So. She would be Dashif's daughter then. Daril stepped aside as Kaloo brushed past her and went tripping down the stairs to the common room, where one of the most feared men in Liavek would be taking her to the theater. She put her head up and a little smile on her face. He would be so charmed with her, this daughter he had found and re-made for himself. She would put her hand lightly on his arm as she stepped up into his carriage, she would smile and chatter with him about the play afterwards. And all the time she would keep him from knowing even one more thing about her. His game was to make her his daughter; hers was to keep from him the only thing she knew he wanted. She smiled as he turned his eyes to watch her come down the stairs, exulted in the indulgent smile that suddenly lit his scarred face.

She expected to have a lovely evening.

Brajii walked the hunter's path.
Justice the load, vengeance the road
    She's taken.
Memory of failure fueled her wrath.
Shame like a goad—the hunter's code
    Forsaken.

Saltigos Road is cold and dim
Crossbow strung, caution flung
    To the air.
Three times she's missed her chance at him.
Defeat has stung, schemes have run
    To despair.

But dream a dream of changes,
Chance meetings in the square.
Spin the wheel another time;
Perhaps the gods are fair.

The gods of vengeance grant new hope.
The circle turns, the fire burns
    In Brajii's eye.
He's made the noose and set the rope.
Before he learns what softness earns
    She'll see him die.

Resh faced the map without seeing it and wondered if Dashif had outlived his usefulness. Dashif had been growing gradually less dependable for some time, but this business with the wench, Jolesha, was too much. When Dashif had said, "It is taken care of," that should have been the end of it.

Jolesha was alive, and either in Liavek or on her way, according to the reports that sat on the Regent's desk. The White Priests were still determined to get that thrice-damned artifact to the Levar. Then the Levar would be able to speak to his deceased predecessor, and she would learn what her Regent had done, and that would be the end of a fine career.

"It's your own fault," he told himself. "You learned long ago that you could never count on anyone but yourself. He was a useful tool, so you depended on him too much, and now you may have to pay for it."

He rubbed his eyebrows. The worst aspect of this mess was that it was taking his attention away from his real duty—the safety of his city. It was clear that the Zhir wanted to incite a trade war between Liavek and Tichen, and it was clear that trade war today meant shooting war tomorrow. That was where his attention ought to be.

He sighed. No, he would give the Count another chance with that artifact; otherwise, it would take too much of his attention. A calculated gamble, and if Dashif survived it... well, he would see then.

He focused once more on the map and blinked. If he could find a way to get fish to the inland cities along the Blackmud before said fish spoiled, it would go a long way toward undercutting the Zhir tariff....

He was the first customer of the morning: dark, black-bearded, and definitely not Zhir. Jolesha stared at him through her old-woman disguise and bade him sit down. The tent door flapped shut. He did not sit. Instead he said, in a deep rasping voice, "I have not come for a consultation with departed ancestors, Jolesha."

She froze at the use of her real name, and her thoughts went back to the time Dashif had walked into her tent, on the Saltigos Road outside of Liavek, and come within a hair's breadth of killing her. She tried to keep her face expressionless.

He said, "You needn't fear me. I do not come from His Scarlet Eminence."

She licked her lips and wondered if there was any point in trying to deny what he said. His eyes were deep and hard. He continued, "I am from the Levar."

"The Levar?" she said, realizing that she had resumed her natural voice.

"Yes. She offers her protection."

"Protection? What would she protect me from?"

"She knows there are factions within our government who would harm you. She will defend you against them. I am the means. This is the proof." And he handed her the Levar's signet.

Jolesha held the seal, studying the profile etched in it before handing it back. "What does she want of me?"

"The artifact, of course. And she would prefer to have you with it."

"Yes, of course." She paused, looking for something to say. "This is rather sudden."

"I understand. You needn't fear. I can give you a little time to decide. If you say no, then no harm will come to you—at least, not from us. If you flee, I'll take that as your answer, and there the matter will end where I'm concerned. But you must know there are others looking for you, in other places. And of course, I won't be on hand to protect you from His Scarlet Eminence or his creatures." He paused, looked at her curiously. "But maybe one of my competitors would suit you better."

She shuddered as she thought of Dashif, then shook her head. "What is your name?"

"Arenride." He looked around the tent. "You don't seem to be very settled in Ka Zhir. Could it be that you've wondered if you'd be returning to your home?"

She allowed herself a smile. "This city is rather gray for someone acquainted with the colors of Liavek. How long may I have?"

"Not long. I'd give you a day to decide, but that would give any others that same day. The Levar's acted, and Resh certainly has heard of it by now. I can give you only a few hours."

"Then I never really could run away, could I?"

He smiled commiseratively as he withdrew, leaving her alone in the tent.

After giving him a few minutes to be gone, she removed the leather pouch from around her neck, and the gold-filigreed cylinder from within the pouch. She held it tightly and spoke softly. "Klefti, Urgelian."

She felt their presence almost at once. "Dear Jolesha," said Klefti. "What is it?"

"I've had a visit, from an agent of the Levar. The Levar wants me to return with the artifact. She'll keep it. I don't know what to do, Klefti."

"Make sure it's safe," interjected Urgelian, predictably.

"Oh, I know, yes, but how? It's so strange. How can she protect me against His Scarlet Eminence, which means she knows he's her enemy, and yet she keeps him next to her? I have to think—that seems so crazy."

"Politics is strange," said Klefti.

"Be careful," urged Urgelian.

"I will." She sensed his frustration. How unfair it was to ask them when they were powerless to assist her. This wasn't right. "I have to go," she said.

Jolesha put The Gate—as she had come to call the artifact—back into its pouch, and pondered until the next customer arrived.

At noon, Arenride returned. Joelsha indicated he should sit. "Well, Jolesha?" he asked. "Have you decided, or have you more questions to ask me?"

"I've given it much thought."

"And?"

"I'm frightened," she said honestly. "I need to know that I'll be protected from the Red Faith."

His features clouded with anger for a moment, then he said, "There's nothing to fear from them. It's Resh himself, not his church. With the Levar on your side, you'll be safe. He won't dare harm you once you've reached her. And I'm sworn to see that you reach her."

She nodded and thought of the bargain she had made with Dashif. Would that make any difference now? Arenride had found her, it seemed, with ease. She had never had a plan beyond reaching Ka Zhir, and to flee them all now she would have to lose herself in further deception, another identity to replace the fortune-teller. And if Ka Zhir proved to be too close, then where was there to venture to? Tichen? Where would they not find her? Then once the Levar had the artifact, no one would care what happened to Jolesha. She wondered, though, if she could part with it now. To give it away would be to bid farewell to her friends, this time forever. To bid farewell or, it seemed, to join them.

Arenride said, "We ought not to delay."

There would come a point where she would have to bargain with the Levar; and hadn't someone told her once that the Levar was mad? A mad girl or a mad priest; they waited for her like pillars of destiny that she must walk between. She had run away, escaped fate for a year; but the pillars and the path remained and would still be there to face a year from now or ten years from now. "All right," she said, but she did not know if she meant it. "All right, then. I'll go with you."

"You've chosen well. We sail this evening, on *The Pardoner*. The ship won't wait for either of us, and if I'm not there, you must board it all the same."

"But—"

"No, listen to me. Someone will meet you on the other side. He'll know you're coming."

"How can anyone know before the ship arrives?"

"Because I'm sending word on a boat that departs within the hour. That's why I couldn't wait any longer. I made you promises, and I'll see them kept one way or another, but that may mean I have to stay behind and ensure that no one boards who doesn't belong." When she started to protest, he stopped her. "It's my honor, what's called my 'standard.' I don't do this for a pouch of Worrynot, understand?"

"Now here is the Levar's seal. It's proof of who you are, and you may have to prove that before you're secure." He took her hands between his for a moment, enclosing the gold seal in the center. "Sometime, I hope I'll have the chance to see what lies beneath that veil and the crags you've drawn on your face."

She looked down. What did lie beneath her fortune-teller

disguise? What was she, other than what she'd been forced to be in order to survive? "A thief is all," she said, and realized that she'd said it aloud.

"What else is there for you to steal?" he asked enigmatically, then turned away in a hasty retreat. Jolesha allowed herself to exhale only after the tapestries had settled.

2 THE STAGE

"You are Brajii?"

"What if I am? Who are you?"

"It doesn't matter. I am a servant of the Levar. No, no, that won't be necessary. See, I'm making no effort to defend myself, much less attack you."

"What do you want?"

"To give you what you want."

"What makes you think you know what I want?"

"You want a chance to kill Dashif."

"Yes!"

"I can tell you where to be, and when to be there."

"How did you find me?"

"Dashif has been looking for you for most of a year. Not all of his agents are exclusively loyal to him. You were seen around here, by one who wasn't."

"What do you get out of this?"

"The safe arrival of a package."

"Tell me more."

"Very well."

Jolesha arrived at the quay late in the afternoon. Her shadow stretched across the dock and onto the side of the ship. Despite what she'd told Arenride, she was having second thoughts. She decided to go at least as far as watching the ship on which she was scheduled to leave. On a group of kegs she perched as an old woman basking in the last of the sun's heat, as if there only to enjoy the smell of the sea, the cries of gulls blending with the cries of hawkers peddling cuttlecrab and squid and monkfish; as if the ship before her was of no interest at all.

It did not take Jolesha long to spot the captain, with her distinctively-shaved head. The woman shouted orders to two men on the docks, who got to their feet lethargically, grabbed the crate they'd been sitting on by the ropes around it, and hoisted it up the gangplank, muttering all the while. They were dock crew, not shipmates; most of their kind were drunks or men without luck. They were the scum of the docks, and they were paid by the hour. Efficient ship's captains irritated them, forcing them to work quickly and take less pay. The captain of *The Pardoner* was not among their favorites, and that was a good sign for Jolesha.

Everything about the ship looked orderly. No one hung about as if waiting to pounce on an old fortune-teller; but neither did Arenride appear. By sunset, with the ship ready to sail, he had not shown up, and Jolesha agonized over what to do. If what he had implied were true, then to stay would most likely mean death. They might be searching for her even now. To go meant putting herself into unknown and untested hands, and she had long since learned to trust no one but herself and the dead.

Finally someone on board *The Pardoner* blew a shrill whistle and she knew that she must decide. Perhaps Arenride was dead, but either way—

She ran back along the dock, still trying to move like an old woman. She came to the stall where she had placed her satchel, handed the peddler a gold piece and pressed both hands to her forehead to show him how grateful she was, then turned and went back to the ship.

At the top of the gangplank, the captain stood with an armed mate. The mate did not draw his saw-handled snaphance, but his hand hung near it, and he kept a few paces back in order to have time to draw it if necessary.

Jolesha went straight up to the captain and pressed the gold seal into her palm.

The captain had pale brown eyes that almost glowed against her dark skin. She said, "I've been expecting you."

"Can I come aboard? I feel like a target perched here."

"Yes, come ahead." She waved the armed mate away. "It wouldn't matter if they shot you from the quay," she said.

"That is, it would matter to *you*, but your gift would still reach the Levar."

"So you know about that."

The captain smiled. "Nope," she said cheerfully. "I don't know a thing."

Jolesha smiled back. "What about my friend?"

"Arenride?"

"Yes."

"I'd be careful about calling him a friend."

"You mean he can't be trusted?"

"Oh, quite the contrary. But his friends often find themselves in the thick of it." She addressed another seaman. "Take our passenger back and show her where she's sleeping tonight."

The man bowed and led her along. He did not smile; no one smiled except the captain. They would, most of them, not know why she was important, but they would know that her presence on board presented a special danger. Nevertheless, she thought on her way across the deck, she had at least chosen the right path.

Dashif stood in the Levar's Park, and tried very hard to keep his mind on business, instead of straying to the delightful conversation he'd had with Kaloo after the strange play they'd seen. It had been appropriate, too—all about families . . . No, dammit, he had to think about what he was doing now. This was vital to his career, perhaps to his life; why was it so hard to concentrate on it? Why did his thoughts keep straying to the daughter he was teaching, training, trying to raise?

He shook his head impatiently.

"My Lord?" said the wizened little man with a face like a prune and almost no hair on his head.

"Yes," said Dashif. "Go on."

"It is called *The Pardoner,* the captain is—"

"I know the captain. Who has taken responsibility for her safety?"

"The ship's?"

"No, idiot. The fortune-teller's."

"Someone named Arenride. He is one of the Levar's personal—"

"I know him," said Dashif. Damn. Arenride was good. This might take a while, which would keep him away from Kaloo. Her lessons were progressing well, though. She'd be a fine sorcerer someday, if she could master her impatience, or, better yet, make it work for her. Perhaps the drill with the broken bottle would be—

He shook his head once more. "When will *The Pardoner* arrive?"

"Midday tomorrow, my Lord."

"Very well. That's all." He handed the little man some gold, careless of the amount, and went to visit a dancer at Cheeky's who also worked as one of his agents and had good connections in Wizard's Row. There was one obvious way to deal with this. Dashif would have preferred to give this one to The Magician, but he knew that particular wizard wouldn't consent to such a task. There were few others good enough to pull off the thing he had in mind, which meant it probably wouldn't work, but it was worth the attempt. And he had a man aboard *The Pardoner,* too, if his memory served, who would be able to answer some questions, and who would be no loss if the ship went down. It would be better if the problem were solved before he had to go up against Arenride—if the ship never made it to port.

"You came in awfully late last night, missy." T'Nar's eyes pinned Kaloo where she stood.

"And you're drinking awfully early." She copied his disapproving tone, went on wiping tables.

"Don't get snippy with me, girl! Where'd he take you?"

"How could it possibly concern you?"

She was baiting him. She enjoyed it, in a painful way. I thought of him as my father, she reminded herself as she met his wordless glare. You. With your grizzled beard and shaven head, with your waterfront ways and your net-scarred hands. I believed there wasn't a ship you couldn't steer or a crew you couldn't command. Then along comes Dashif and points to your child and says, "She's mine." And you let go, not just of your daughter but of everything. Drinking in the mornings, falling asleep with your head on the table by mid-afternoon, and Daril tries to pretend it's just age creeping up on you.

"Don't look at me that way, girl!" T'Nar growled, and Kaloo almost jumped, wondering how much he knew of her thoughts. Once he had known everything about her, more than she knew herself. Now she treated him as she did Dashif, telling him no more of herself than she could help. But despite her guard, she always had the uneasy feeling that he still knew too much about her. "Come over here," he continued. "I want to talk to you."

"I'm busy."

"Count Dashif's uppity daughter is busy wiping greasy tables in a second-rate waterfront tavern."

Her eyes suddenly blazed. "The Mug and Anchor. . ." she began hotly.

"Isn't a second-rate tavern," he finished for her. "Any more than you're Dashif's daughter." He belched loudly after the second part of his sentence, while Kaloo flinched, glad there was no one else in the tavern to hear his indiscreet words. His tone changed abruptly, startling her. "Come here, my little Kookaloo nestling. Come here, and find out who you really are."

Forgotten, the rag fell from her hands. She came a few steps closer, drawn by his words as if by a magnet. Closer. And those shrewd eyes weren't drunk at all; he had been watching her half the morning, pretending to be nearly stuporous, and thinking . . . What?

"Sit." He kicked out a chair for her, and she sat. He straightened himself on his chair, then hooked his heel on the rung and leaned forward, one elbow propped on his raised knee. She felt herself drawing back from him, forced herself to sit still. Who was he that she should fear his look? A captain too old to sail, just an old sailor helping out around a tavern, setting out mugs and telling lies to his friends and . . .

"I had a little girl once," he said, and his words stopped her thoughts. "Slim as a willow wand, hair black as tar, growing up all knees and legs, like a wave-wader bird. I had a little girl

I loved dear as life—and it wasn't you, Kaloo. No. Not then."

He paused, his eyes growing distant. "We lived on Minnow Island, and she was my father's daughter, my little half-sister. Younger than me in more than years, and in some ways, smarter. But not all. No. She wasn't careful where she loved, or how much. And it killed her."

He stopped. He lifted his mug slowly, took a swallow of his beer. "That's all," he said suddenly. "That's all I wanted to tell you. That you weren't the first skinny little brat to make my life miserable."

Kaloo didn't move. She stared at him, waiting. He stared right back. She should get up and turn her back and walk away from him. Who did he think he was, anyway, to play these rotten tricks on her? His gaze didn't waver. Hers suddenly found the tabletop. "I have to know about her."

"There isn't a lot to tell." There was suddenly gravel in his voice, and pain such as, well, such as only she had ever given him. Or so she had thought. "She loved a man who wasn't worthy of that kind of love. He left her. She had a child, and she couldn't care for it. She tried. But she had convinced herself that her love had turned to hate, and she couldn't look at her baby without seeing his face. And I couldn't look at her baby without seeing hers. So I took the child from her. Later, she . . . died."

"I was the baby," Kaloo whispered, as pieces of her life suddenly assumed new shapes. "Dashif was the man." For long moments she wondered. Suddenly she demanded, "Who was my mother?"

T'Nar stared at her, dumb with misery. "My baby sister. My pretty little shore-bird, my Erina."

Erina. She'd once heard Dashif utter that name. He'd been in horrible pain, pinned to a cart by a crossbow bolt through his knee. And he had called out to someone named Erina. She was suddenly shaking. "Why are you telling me this?" Kaloo felt her throat closing up. For the first time since that horrible day when she had invested her magic, the day T'Nar had fought Dashif for her, and lost, she felt close to tears. The careful layer of coldness she had wrapped around herself was thawing. It hurt.

T'Nar was staring at the tabletop. He traced the ancient outline of a wet mug bottom. "Should have told you a long time ago." He looked up at Kaloo suddenly. "I thought it would hurt you. I guess finding out the way you did hurt you a lot more."

"I have to know more," Kaloo began.

"No. Any more you have to know, you have to find out from him. No, stop pouting at me. Doesn't bother me a bit, brat. You listen to me. I've been thinking. Drinking, too, yes, a lot of that. Sometimes a man has to drink to think straight. Sometimes thinking straight hurts too much to do sober. But listen to me. No, shut up and listen. You look like her, Kaloo. Like Erina. It's her he sees in you, her he buys those dresses for, her he takes to those stupid, snooty plays. You know why? Well, I do. Finally. Because he loved her. He loved her, and he knew it too late, and he loves the child they made and he's terrified that it's too late for that, too. He loved Erina and hurt her, and she loved him and hurt him. Because they were so busy pretending they hated each other, pretending that everything was all spoiled, when all they had to do was to look at each other and say, 'I love you.'"

Kaloo sensed what was coming next and it terrified her. She rose suddenly, but T'Nar was fast, faster than any old man had a right to be. His grip was iron on her wrist, and his gaze was barbed, she couldn't tear free of it. He whispered the words that roared inside her head. "Don't be too much like her, Kaloo. Don't convince yourself you hate where you want to love. And, listen to me. I don't given a damn who it is you want to love. Even him. But don't you dare set yourself a course for the same rocks Erina foundered on. Don't you dare, girl! Don't think you're Dashif's daughter. Because you're not. You're Dashif and Erina's daughter. And love made you, not hate."

With a cry she pulled free of him. She fell twice running up the stairs to her room, and when the door was safely slammed behind her, she sat on the bed, and found she was sobbing. Because her scraped shins hurt her so very much, she thought, worse than anything she'd ever felt in her life.

The first squall struck after twilight. It came out of nowhere, a knot of clouds charging across the sea. *The Pardoner* was too large to be endangered by anything short of a typhoon—at least, providing the rigging was not tampered with. Doggedly, they rode out the attack of bad weather without a hitch.

The second squall struck from behind, forming out of nothing. A hammer of wind slammed across the deck, stretching the sails until the lanyards creaked from the strain. The sailors turned to see another mass of clouds, this one shot with lightning, bearing down upon them, and driving them fiercely toward the dark cliffs and dangerous shallows.

A rope securing the foresail snapped, and suddenly the sail was swinging wildly. Before they could react, it smashed into a sailor and threw him all the way against the gunwale. Quickly, two others snatched a new rope and ran it through the tackle, all the while dodging the sail that twisted like an eel around the mast. They hauled on the rope, other crewmen rushing in to help. Finally, they strapped the sail back into place; but one sailor was dead, victim of an unlikely storm. Sailors were superstitious by nature. Jolesha knew that well enough. She excused herself from the captain's company and went belowdecks to her cabin. She would be seen as the cause of his death, and she could not even satisfy herself that those who thought so weren't right.

Once more she drew The Gate from its pouch, and once more she called to her friends. The conversation with Klefti and Urgelian did nothing to ease her sense of guilt, but it did reveal that Arenride was not among the dead. Whatever had happened to delay him, he had not perished. She found herself unaccountably relieved to know it.

She huddled in her bunk and wished the voyage were over. Had the storms been natural? If the Regent knew she was aboard this ship, he had probably sent them. One who spoke with the dead presented a formidable threat to him, especially as she knew how much he had to hide. He might level Liavek if necessary to keep the artifact from reaching the girl who reigned above him. Jolesha wondered if there was someone in the Regent's pay aboard *The Pardoner*. Many of the sailors had been watching her, even before the disasters of the storms. How would she recognize one enemy among so many?

She decided to remain belowdecks for the rest of the voyage to Liavek.

As Dashif emerged from the Levar's Palace, at precisely twelve minutes after noon, a footcab drove up. Dashif signalled for it, and two priests who had been waiting for a cab for several minutes looked at him darkly, then looked away. Dashif climbed into the cab.

The runner said, "Yes, my Lord?"

"The Market," said Dashif.

"Yes, my Lord."

The runner set off with light, even strides. After a few minutes, they were well away from any pedestrians. At this point the runner, who seemed not at all winded, turned his head and said, "I'm sorry, Count Dashif. He failed."

"The ship survived?"

The runner turned back to make sure the road was still clear, then said, "Yes. The storms have delayed her arrival a few hours, but she survived."

"Very well. I hadn't expected it to work anyway. What about the other piece of information?"

"Our wizard was able to exchange messages with your man on *The Pardoner*. He said there was no sign of Arenride on board, and the fortune-teller was keeping out of sight. My Lord, he isn't the sort of man we could normally ask to do such things, but—"

"No. I'll take care of it myself when she docks. It was Arenride I was concerned with."

Dashif nodded. One thing the less to worry about, then. There had been no other ships from Ka Zhir; Arenride would not be able to arrive in time. Who would he have sent in his place? Dashif licked his lips and pondered, forcing his mind to stay away from thoughts of Kaloo and the dual problem of training her in sorcery and raising her as his daughter.

The runner said, "Should he try the storms again?"

"No," said Dashif. "That would be senseless. Do you know the new arrival time?"

"Tomorrow, before dawn."

"Very good. That will be all, then."

"Do you actually wish to go to the Market, Count Dashif?"

"No. Here will be fine."

The runner stopped and Dashif stepped out of the cab. He paid the runner, and sent him on his way. He looked around, then caught himself doing so. *I'm going to have to find that Zhir agent with the crossbow,* he said to himself. *Even if she doesn't kill me, she'll have me running into things, from looking over my shoulder too much.* He sighed to himself and began walking toward the docks, there to determine exactly where *The Pardoner* would arrive, and precisely how he would greet Jolesha, who had broken the bargain that had kept her breathing for the last year.

Wrapped in a heavy purple cloak, Jolesha stood on the deck and looked out at the city she had expected never to see again. *The Pardoner* had ridden out a series of nasty, shifting squalls most of the night. The pockets of storm battered them from different sides, taking turns like the offspring of the sea god shoving a new toy first this way then that. At one point they were driven perilously close to the rocky promontory south of Gold Harbor. That was when the trouble had come. But now, with the dawn creeping up, the sky ahead split into two layers of violet clouds sliced by a long vertical band of golden light, one could hardly believe that more peril might lie ahead, or even that last night's had been more than imagination.

The city dwelled in darkness; its buildings remained as shadows. Then the tips of the six towers ringing the Levar's Palace seemed to catch fire, and Jolesha remembered what a fabulous city she was approaching. She withdrew into the belly of the ship again.

Terror gripped her now that she had actually returned. She

wondered if anything was going to be as she'd been told.

There was a jar and a thud as the ship made contact with the dock, and Jolesha felt a collective sigh go up, as if everyone on board was relieved that they had landed safely. She waited patiently, studying the pre-dawn city, and tried to control the fear that threatened to turn into panic.

At last the captain approached her. "Come," she said, "it is time for you to disembark. There are those who await you." And she saw for the first time four red-clad guards waiting at the dock.

The captain smiled at her, as if seeing her fear and understanding it, then took her arm and gently pulled her away from the rail and escorted her down the gangplank. Then she was surrounded by the guardsmen. She heard one of them ask for a proof of who she was and felt herself showing him the Levar's seal, though she was more aware of her own fear than what was occurring around her.

Jolesha's first indication that something was wrong came when she felt a sudden tension in the captain's hand that held her arm. Then the captain stepped in front of her, and was flung backward into Jolesha, causing her to stumble backward, as Jolesha heard the crack of a pistol firing and a scream. The scream was her own.

It was no plan of hers that caused her to fall to the dock to escape danger; it was merely that her knees buckled as fear took over and her backward stumble turned into a fall. Yet it probably saved her life. She wanted to shut her eyes but couldn't, and so she saw the red-cloaked figure that emerged from the doorway of a nearby warehouse, a pair of pistols in his hands.

For an instant she held his eye, and even saw the twin scars running below his eyes. Then there was someone standing in front of her, and she saw shock on Dashif's face. She looked up to see who it was, and heard Arenride's voice. "Stay down, girl."

The rest of the scene was confused by panic. She thought Dashif fired again, and she heard a loud blast from a blunderbuss that Arenride carried. She saw Dashif roll backward into the darkness of the warehouse doorway while what seemed to be an arrow or a crossbow bolt embedded itself in the wall where his head had been. Then Arenride left her—to chase after Dashif. Through the doorway and into the warehouse, he was followed by a woman dressed in green with long, reddish hair, who was re-cocking a crossbow as she ran.

Then there was silence, and it seemed that everything had ended. The guards were gathering themselves up. Jolesha looked at the captain, lying face-up on the dock, and saw that there was a large, ugly wound in her chest. Her breathing came in ragged gasps. Then, as Jolesha watched, it stopped.

One of the guards said, "All right, girl, get up—"

"Look out!" called another, and Jolesha sobbed with fear. With a yelp, one of the soldiers fell back, and another pistol shot echoed across the wharf. Jolesha saw Dashif, now standing half out of a window on the second story of the warehouse, raised pistol smoking.

She knew then that Arenride could never protect her—that no one could. They only wanted The Gate. Arenride wanted it, and if Dashif killed her, what would that matter, as long as he could keep Dashif from getting it?

She had no memory of fleeing through the soldiers who were bringing blunderbusses to bear on Dashif; only dim memories of shots resounding as she reached the front ranks of the watching crowd. She recalled wriggling between the people, who drew back with repugnance from the hideous old woman they saw her as. And the one time she did dare to look back, she thought she saw, for a moment, the face of Dashif in pursuit.

Jolesha ran, and she didn't stop running until the press of the crowd around her told her that she had left the docks and attending danger behind. At that point she had no idea where she had come.

3 THE SCRIPT

Arenride caught two brief glimpses of Dashif as he hurried toward the Market area. At least, he thanked the gods, Jolesha had fled into a busy area. But no matter how Arenride struggled through the frightened crowd, nothing brought him closer to his adversary.

As the morning wore on, the crowds in the market thinned out. Arenride admitted to himself at last that he had lost both trails. He took scant satisfaction in having saved her life. It was hardly enough—he had given his word to her, and now she was alone as he had guaranteed she would not be. Whatever she was beneath that disguise, she had won a respect he paid few people, for having outwitted the Count of Dashif. This morning at least, he could not say the same for himself.

He made his way toward the palace to find one of his agents, a harmless-looking old lady who did charcoal painting in the Levar's park. He hoped that one old lady would spy out another. It occurred to him that this would be his first chance to test his forces directly against those of Dashif.

He was committed to bringing Jolesha safely to the Levar, and he would do so if it was humanly possible. He would also, if possible, determine what she looked like under her makeup.

The Stampede—the early morning rush at the market—was over now. The best of the fresh vegetables were haggled over and gone; the loudest of the customers were off cleaning, cutting, and cooking them. Jolesha sat in the shade of a large green tent. She didn't quite know what to do now that the crowds had thinned out.

She knew she was being sought. She felt the burden of The Gate in the pouch about her neck, and was once again taken with the notion of throwing it into the nearest body of water and bolting. But she didn't. The Levar wanted it, the Levar should have it—provided Jolesha could think of a way to get it to her without Dashif or his people catching her first.

She wondered if Arenride were still alive. He must have been aboard the entire trip, hiding, so Dashif wouldn't realize he was there. She wondered if Dashif were alive. Yes, he probably was. She suspected that The Gate would crack with the weight of his demise.

Jolesha studied the dwindling crowd in the market and

wondered if there were anyone out there who wanted to kill her.

They spotted each other at the same moment. She froze, not knowing whether she had found an enemy or a friend. The smile on the tall, red-haired woman's face indicated friendship, but—

On the other hand, she didn't really have anywhere to run to. She waited while the woman approached.

"I am Brajii," said the woman. It was a clear voice shaped by a strong Zhir accent. "I don't know your name, but we have a common enemy. Come with me—I've a safe place." When Jolesha hesitated, the woman said, "Don't you understand, old woman? Hurry. Give me your hand. He'll be nearby, looking for both of us. Had he found you before I did, you would be dead now."

Jolesha wanted to curl up in a safe, dark place and withdraw from the intrigue and the threats. Instead, she stood up and followed Brajii to a small, canopied wagon harnessed to a mule. Soon, like two peddlers, they were plodding through the fetid alleys and back streets of Liavek.

Kaloo looked at Dashif and wondered if his expression were the product of anger or weariness. Or something else. "Is something wrong?" she asked. Her voice was cool and level, only politely interested. Perfect.

"Yes," snapped Dashif. "You won't call me father."

It startled her out of her carefully-guarded reserve. She felt outrage flood her that he would dare demand this of her. Her carefully-constructed wall of artificial courtesy gave way. "I don't call you camel dung, either. We might say it's a fair trade."

For an instant, Dashif stared at her, his dark eyes going even darker. Kaloo braced herself. Then he laughed aloud, a sound she didn't think she had ever heard before. That it was directed at her brought a deep blush to her cheeks and flame to her eyes. Damn him, he had made her show herself to him, and the bastard knew it. Knew it, and delighted in it. He shook his head and wiped his eyes. "I'm sorry, Kaloo. No, you aren't what is upsetting me. Something else went badly today."

"What happened?" In her curiosity she forgot her embarrassment.

He shook his head again. "It is nothing, my dear. A run-in with enemies of the city. I really shouldn't be here at all, but I wanted to see you. Never mind that now. Let us return to your lessons. Come, try to repair the bottle."

Kaloo felt herself flushing. 'My dear,' was it? Without stopping to think, she pushed back. "Were they enemies of the city, or enemies of the Regent?"

Dashif looked up sharply. The indulgence had left his face. "Why are you so convinced there is a difference?"

She wanted to kick herself. "I have heard things of His Scarlet Eminence."

Dashif leaned back in his chair and crossed his legs. "What have you heard?" he asked quietly.

To the trolls with it, then. "That he is power-hungry, that he will destroy anyone who stands in the way of his goals, that he is cruel. Should I continue?"

"If you wish."

"Do you deny it?"

"No."

She stared. "And you work for him."

"Yes."

"Why?"

"My own reasons."

"But—"

"If you want justifications, Kaloo, I can supply them. Yes, all you say about the Regent is true. Yet Liavek is thriving as it hasn't in hundreds of years. We are not at war, although our perpetual enemies still sniff at us. Our trade markets continue to expand, and the people are fat and happy. If this is the result of being power-hungry, ruthless, and cruel, then we could use more leaders who are power-hungry, ruthless and cruel. And if we have completed today's lesson in politics, let us return to sorcery. Before you is a bottle with a crack in it. Repair the crack so it doesn't show."

Kaloo studied the man who was her father, wondering what

he was feeling. It was even stranger to wonder what she herself was feeling. Irritation, mostly, she decided, and tried to shelve the thought. Then she shrugged and, licking her lips, ran her finger over the fracture in the glass, trying to bring her power to bear on it. Nothing happened.

"No," said Dashif. "This is the point of the exercise. You aren't trying to join two things, you are restoring a thing that was whole. Levitation and similar things can be done quickly, just by joining your luck with your desire, but it you ever want to change an object, or repair it, you must first concentrate on understanding its unity. That requires patience. You must not be in a hurry to do it; let it take as much time as it wishes. Work slowly, attempt change to deepen understanding, use understanding to work change. Continue this process until the transformation has taken place."

She tried again. Nothing.

"No, dear. Patience. It isn't going to happen—"

"Can't you show me?"

"No."

"Why not? L'Fertti used to show me what he wanted me to do, and I could just hold onto him and feel how he used his luck and then—"

"No." He was adamant. The frustrated look on her face seemed to soften him. "Kaloo, much of what L'Fertti taught you was useless. Now you must learn to find the way your own luck flows, not just copy others. Be patient. Take your time."

"Useless? And fixing bottles is a useful skill, I suppose?" she asked sarcastically.

"Patience is a useful skill, one I won't have my daughter without," he replied evenly.

Something in her snapped. She swept the bottle to the floor, where it smashed into shards. Then she leaned back in her chair, staring at him, waiting for his reaction.

It surprised her. He glanced at the pieces on the floor. "You've only made it harder for yourself. But you seem to enjoy making things as hard as possible for yourself. The principle is still the same, Kaloo. Sense the unity, and apply yourself. With patience."

"I don't feel patient," she told him in as rude a tone as she could muster. "And I don't feel like any more lessons today." She stood up and began to walk toward the door.

"Kaloo," he said in a pleasant voice. "Are you still fond of that old sailor? The one who cut my ear off last time we met?"

She turned to stare at him.

"I think I've been very patient with him, don't you? Why don't you show me how patient you can be with me?"

He watched her come back, step by dragging step. Her eyes were very big. He watched her seat herself cross-legged on the floor, extend her hands toward the glittering shards of glass. "Don't cut yourself," he told her automatically. She glanced up at him, bit her lower lip, and then closed her eyes.

He sat very still and quiet, watching the bottle slowly draw itself together. Would he ever be able to get past her guard without evoking her anger? He knew how she shut him out with her coldness. If making her angry was the only way to reach her, he'd do it. Otherwise he'd never be able to teach her all she had to know before he could publicly acknowledge her. A grim smile crossed his lips. The heir of Count Dashif would have many enemies; he would not let her meet them unarmed. He would do whatever he had to do, to teach her what she had to know. And if she grew up hating him? Well, at least she would be able to hate as he had . . . with great patience.

"You live here?" asked Jolesha.

"For the moment," said the tall woman whose name Jolesha had forgotten.

They were in a tiny second-floor room in a boarded-up building between Old Town and Mystery Hill. There were no furnishings, nor, indeed, any sign of habitation except a set of neatly-folded blankets near the window. Jolesha noted that it seemed clean and free of dust, which couldn't be the natural state of an abandoned building.

The tall woman sat down against a wall. Jolesha sat cross-legged, facing her, and carefully peeled the makeup from her face, which had begun to itch. When she was finished, the woman said, "I had no idea."

"Good," said Jolesha. "I'm glad it fooled someone. Who are you, why did you bring me here, and do you have any water so I can wash my face?"

"My name, as I said, is Brajii. I'll get you some water, and I brought you here so you can help me find a way to kill Dashif before he kills us. And what is your name, by the way?"

"Jolesha." She digested Brajii's answers while Brajii got a dish of water. She washed her face as well as she could and dried it on her tattered coat. "Why is Dashif after you?" she asked.

"Because he knows I want to kill him?"

"Oh," said Jolesha. "Why do you want to kill him?"

"It is personal," said Brajii. "What about you?"

"I never wanted to kill him. But I need to be safe from him because of the Regent. If there were another way—"

"I doubt there is."

"Yes," Jolesha said with unease. "Well, have you a plan?"

"No. I have now missed four times. I am not a bad shot. He has acquired some protection. We must find out how to divest him of it, and then lure him into a place where—"

"Are you a magician?"

"No."

"Neither am I."

"Can you think of anything with which—" Jolesha stopped. She regarded her rescuer narrowly. "Am I your lure, then? Is that why—"

"No. Oh, you might be—but not without your agreement, and not if we can think of any other way. I came to you because he wants to kill you, and that makes you my ally. Since you've remained alive, a formidable ally, perhaps."

"I see."

"I need your help."

"What do you want me to do?"

"I told you. Help me kill Dashif."

"I don't know. What is your quarrel with him?"

Brajii looked away. "I was once in the employ of the government of Ka Zhir. He stole from me some documents I was responsible for."

Jolesha frowned. "But, well, that was his job. Is that a reason to hate him?"

"It is for me," snapped Brajii. Jolesha frowned. Brajii continued, "If we work together, and use his weaknesses, we can kill him before he kills you."

"Well, then, what weaknesses has he?"

"I know of one. A daughter he dotes on."

Jolesha's eyes widened. "A daughter? How old?"

"Fourteen or fifteen. Just a few years younger than you, I think."

"You've seen her?"

"Yes. She lives at the Mug and Anchor."

"There's your lure, then. You never needed me at all."

Brajii shook her head. "I'm not happy about using a child, even his child."

"Nor am I," Jolesha agreed, although she was thinking about Brajii's comparison of her to this daughter: *Not much younger than you*. Jolesha said, "But there's no reason why you'd have to harm her, is there?"

"That is true," Brajii agreed, her tone conveying that she had not considered that. So single-minded was she, the wider scope of reasoning seemed to elude her.

"What about that protection of his? How effective is it, do you know?"

"He still lives. I've hit him, but I haven't killed him."

"So you think it's magical," Jolesha said, and added, "He *is* reputed to be a powerful wizard. Still, you say you've hit him."

"Yes." She seemed lost in some deeper reflection.

"Ought the wounds to have been mortal?"

Brajii chewed her lip. "No."

"You're certain that it could not be your aim?" The question had been inevitable, she supposed. Brajii hardly reacted at all.

"Yes. Once, in Fortune Way, I—no, never mind the details. There is more to it than marksmanship."

They sat in silence for a while. Then Jolesha said, "I wish I could find Arenride."

"Who?"

"An agent of the Levar. He was supposed to guide me to the Palace."

Brajii snorted. "Didn't do much of a job of it, did he."

Jolesha felt a flash of anger, and wondered at it. Brajii noticed it as well. "I'm sorry. I didn't intend to—"

"No, it's all right."

"Do you think he would help us?"

"If he could find me, or I could find him, he'd guide me to the Levar. I don't think he'd help us kill someone. But to tell you the truth, Brajii, if I could get to the Levar, I wouldn't need to kill Dashif."

"You think he'd let you leave the city alive?"

"Why not?"

"Why did he want to kill you?"

Because I broke his agreement, and because I know about Erina. "You're right," she said. And she sighed. "We really are going to have to kill him."

"Yes," said Brajii. "But how? We don't know what sort of spells are protecting him."

"I'm not a sorcerer," said Jolesha. "But I know something about magic. If a sorcerer cast a spell to make a stick float in the air, a strong man could still push it down. If it was a powerful wizard, it might take several strong men, but it could still be pushed down."

"That is true, but how does it help us?"

"No matter how good his protection is, if our trap is good enough, and your aim is true enough, we can kill him."

Brajii was silent for a moment, then she nodded slowly. "Fine. Let's prepare a trap."

Very well, Jolesha thought, I will help you. But if I find a way to deliver myself safely to the Levar without harming Dashif or anyone, I'll do it. Whatever I am, assassin, I'm not your kind.

He was thin and lanky and dark and his name was Pitullio. When Dashif was in the field, Pitullio was in the office. He worked for Resh, and his job involved many duties. He handled the administrative details that the Regent couldn't be bothered with, and he served as a sounding board for the Regent's ideas. Few knew his name, and those who did didn't fear him, though he had killed more men by his pen than Dashif had with his pistols. He was usually cheerful.

"Your Eminence?"

"Come in, Pitullio. Well?"

"Dashif missed the woman." His Scarlet Eminence frowned at this, but said nothing. Pitullio continued, "There was shooting, but she escaped."

"I'm surprised."

"Arenride."

"Ah. We may need to dispose of that one."

"Very likely, Your Eminence. Shall I set someone on it?"

"No. Dashif ought to take care of him, if not during this affair, then after it. Is Dashif searching for the woman?"

Pitullio winced, started to speak, stopped, then said, "Not just at the moment, Your Eminence."

Resh's jaw muscles worked. "Indeed?"

"He is apparently engaged in some other pressing business."

"What business?" snapped the Regent.

Pitullio hesitated again. So far as he knew, he, Pitullio, was the only one who knew about Dashif's daughter, and it wasn't up to him to let the secret out. He said, "Something of a personal nature, Your Eminence."

Resh took a deep breath and let it out slowly. "I see." The Regent scowled. "Pitullio, keep an eye out for someone to replace Count Dashif, should he be expended."

Pitullio shifted uncomfortably. "Will that be necessary, Your Eminence?"

"I'm not yet certain, Pitullio. If it is, I want to be prepared. What about Arenride? Might he be open to an offer?"

"I'm not certain, Your Eminence. He is the Levar's creature, but I'm not sure if that is from loyalty or practicality."

"It may be time to find out. He is skilled and brave, and Dashif may have worn out his usefulness."

"Your Eminence, I—"

"That will be all, Pitullio."
"Yes, Your Eminence."

"Come in. Is that you, Aren?"
"I'm sorry, no, Your Magnificence."
"Where is he?"
"Your Magnificence, there was a fight at the docks."
"What? Is he—?"
"No, Your Magnificence. The Chancellor of Highgate is fine, but—"
"Then where is he?"
"During the fight, the woman, Jolesha, ran off, and—"
"Where is Arenride?"
"Searching for the woman, Your Magnificence."
"Why is he doing that when I want him here?"
"You sent him to bring the girl's artifact, so he's looking for—"
"I want Aren."
"Yes, Your Magnificence. I'll send someone to fetch him."
"Now."
"Yes, Your Magnificence."

4 THE ENTRANCE

Brajii, the hunter, knew she was being hunted. She couldn't have said how she knew, because there were no real signs of it as she and Jolesha made their way through the streets, but she didn't doubt it. She had changed from her usual green apparel to white trousers with a loose-fitting yellow top, she'd done her hair up in a knot, and she wasn't carrying her crossbow. Few of Dashif's agents would know what Jolesha looked like without her makeup. All these things helped, but she couldn't shake the feeling of pursuit, and she had learned to trust these feelings, so she was careful.

"That's it," said Brajii, pointing to the Mug and Anchor.

"She lives there?" asked Jolesha.

"Upstairs." Brajii led them into an alley across the street from the tavern, from which they could watch while remaining hidden.

"Have you been planning this for a long time?"

"Not exactly," Brajii replied. "We had a run-in some time ago. I thought it might be useful to find out who had saved Dashif's life, so I tracked her down. I was surprised when I found out who she was."

"I share your surprise. Well, what now?"

"Some time in the next hour or so, during the afternoon slack time, she'll be going out to run errands."

"Then what?"

"Then we take her."

"In broad daylight?"

"Why not? That's what the wagon is for. We'll have her away and hidden before anyone can follow us, and if they know she's been kidnapped it doesn't matter, since we're going to tell Dashif anyway. If you do your job well, we won't have to use violence. She's only a child."

"I suppose so," Jolesha said vaguely.

"Is something wrong?"

"I've never done anything like this before."

Brajii looked at her. She, Brajii, had kept herself going for the last year by looking at the world through veils of pain, hate, and vengeance. Now for a moment, she tried to see past them. "I hope you never have to again," she said abruptly. She returned to watching the Mug and Anchor.

"Who are you?"

"My name is Jolesha. Come along with me."

"Why?"

"You'll see. I don't have time to explain now."

"What's it about."

"It's about your father, Kaloo."

"My father? You don't know—"

"Yes, I do. Now hurry."

"But I can't—"

"Yes, you can. Come with me. I'll explain when we get there."

"Where?"

"You'll see. Dashif is in trouble. Now hurry."

• • •

Dashif approached a flower-vendor who worked at the edge of the Market. There was no one else around. He didn't bother to pretend to purchase flowers.

"Well?"

"No sign of the girl, Jolesha, but we have a good idea where Arenride is."

"Oh?"

"Yes. Old Town."

"Does that indicate that—"

"Maybe. We still haven't spotted them."

Dashif studied the flower-vendor. He didn't doubt that there were those who worked for him who also worked for others. Was this one? Could he find out? Could he take the chance?

No.

"Very well. I'll continue investigating. Stay in touch. Send messages to the bootblack who works on Threadbare Street."

"Very well, Count Dashif."

Kaloo looked around the room. Something was very wrong here. She tried to keep her sudden fear from her face, tried to slow her heart and breathing as Dashif had taught her. It almost worked. "Where's Dashif? Why do you have me here?"

The one who had called herself Jolesha turned away. The other, the tall, scary one, said, "You shouldn't be here long. We need you for—something we're doing. I'm sorry."

Kaloo felt a trembling begin within her. "I'm leaving."

"No. You're staying."

Kaloo studied her, felt her fear building up again. "I know you, don't I?"

"Yes. A year ago you shot me with your father's pistol."

A noise slipped out of Kaloo's mouth before she knew she was going to make it. She shut her jaws firmly for an instant. When she spoke again, her voice was too high. "Who are you?"

"My name is Brajii."

"You're going to kill Dashif, aren't you?"

"Yes," she said. "That is what we're going to do. I'm sorry."

"You can't," she said, and took strength from her certainty. But as she looked from one woman to the other, her confidence ebbed. "You can't," she repeated, and felt panic rise in her. Not now, she wanted to tell them, he can't die yet, there is too much between us that has to be settled first, too many things he hasn't told me, and he hasn't made me forgive him yet. Her own thought jolted her. For the first time, she knew that she would forgive him, that she had known all along it was only a matter of time. But he didn't know that yet, and these two were going to kill him before he did.

She had forgotten to control her face. She felt the two women looking at her, wished she could strike them dead where they stood. Brajii said, "All right. We don't need this," and walked into the next room.

"What are you going to do?" asked the other. But there was no answer except the sounds of moving and shuffling, until Brajii returned, and said, "Here, girl."

Kaloo looked up and saw Brajii holding a cup out to her. "Drink this," she said. "It will make you sleep. When you wake up, it will all be over."

Kaloo stared at her, but made no move to take the cup from her hand.

"Do it, girl," said Brajii.

Kaloo felt paralyzed. Sleep was the last thing she wanted and she didn't want to be poisoned at all. She didn't trust either of these two. Brajii cursed and set the cup down next to her and picked up her crossbow, set a bolt in it, and cocked it. The "click" echoed loudly in the room.

"No!" said the one called Jolesha. "Don't!"

But Brajii aimed the crossbow at Kaloo and said, "Drink."

Kaloo felt her heart pounding. The last time she had seen a crossbow bolt, it had been sticking out of Dashif's knee. When she had tried to pull it out, his blood had made it slippery. The fletching on it had matched the one on Brajii's bow now. She swallowed, sick. Almost in a dream, she saw herself pick up the cup and put it to her lips. It tasted like water, with a faint lemony flavor. When she had drained it, she set it down next to herself and curled up against the wall.

"Good," said Brajii. "You'll sleep soon."

Not if I can help it, thought Kaloo. She wanted to be away from here, to get up and run. Had it really been a sleeping draught, or something more deadly?

Poison?

It is impossible to poison a sorcerer, if the sorcerer is careful, Kaloo. The first thing you learn is to feel your body, inside and out. Some sorcerers can heal disease in others, but any trained sorcerer can heal himself. You learn to feel what is wrong, and you absorb it, or expel it, and make it harmless.

Without moving, Kaloo thought about, but didn't touch, the fan that contained her luck. They probably didn't know she was a sorcerer, she realized. Suddenly she felt a little less helpless. And yes, Dashif had been right. Now that she thought about it, she could feel the potion in her stomach, spreading to her blood stream. She pulled it back, pushed it down, through. It *was* easy. She felt as if she should have been able to do it before investing her luck. This was her body with a foreign object in it, it just had to go that way.

She lifted her head, tried to look dazed. "I need a toilet," she mumbled.

The two women looked at each other, and for a moment Kaloo feared she'd given herself away. But then Jolesha fetched her a slop-pot from the far end of the room. They watched her as she used it, which made her angry rather than embarrassed, but she kept the anger off her face. Her control was getting better.

She half-staggered to her spot by the wall and lay down. She let her breathing slow, become even and soft. Minutes passed as ponderously as hours. Patience, she reminded herself, and lay still. At last the one called Brajii said, "All right. I'm going to send the note. I'll be back soon."

"Be careful, Brajii."

"I will."

Kaloo remained still as Brajii's footsteps faded, and forced herself to think. What now? There was only the one called Jolesha, but she could overpower her. Was there magic she could perform that would aid her escape? But she couldn't seem to concentrate. A thought kept intruding; these women had been so confident that she would be bait enough to draw

Dashif out of cover. How could they be so certain that a threat to her would bring Dashif to them? An even stranger thought followed. Why had she come with them, so meekly? Because they had told her Dashif was in trouble. And so she had come, with no thought for herself. Would he come the same way? Certainty made her ill. He would. He'd walk right into their jaws.

Then Jolesha spoke, and this startled Kaloo so much that she opened her eyes. Jolesha was turned a little away, the hood up on her head. A bright violet light outlined her body against the dimness of the bare room. The source of the light seemed to be a cylindrical object in her hand. She repeated the word she had spoken: Klefti. It sounded like a name.

Suddenly there was another voice—a whispery voice—in the room. It seemed to emerge out of Jolesha, and it sent a chill through Kaloo. It said Jolesha's name.

"Yes, Klefti. I'm here. I'm in Liavek again. How are you?"

"As always, Jolesha. Urgelian, too."

"Klefti, Urgelian, I am . . . doing something."

"What?" asked a second strange voice. The light seemed to flicker, she saw, when they spoke. Kaloo gaped. Ghosts? Invisible spirits?

"I have found a—a friend." The word rang false to Kaloo. "Her name is Brajii. She has a plan to help me, but it's dangerous. I don't know if I want to do it, but they're looking for me, everyone's looking for me."

"Be careful, Jolesha," said Klefti.

"Yes, yes, of course. But it's all right, really, isn't it? If I fail, I'll die, and be reunited with you. If not, I'll still have—"

"Be careful," the other voice interrupted. "We must go, it's becoming painful. We love you."

"I'll speak with you again, when we're done," she said. She sniffled. Kaloo saw her slide something into a leather pouch, and hang that around her neck.

Kaloo closed her eyes again, and tried to understand what this meant, and what she should do about it. There had to be a way to use that thing, whatever it was. What was it? Her luck object? What had she said, "If I fail, I'll die, and be reunited with you." A device to speak with the dead! That had to be it. Could that be what her father had been looking for? And these two were going to kill him because he wanted to find it.

Kaloo lay there, feigning sleep, and wondered what to do. She didn't realize that for the first time she had thought of Dashif as her father.

She had come to no conclusion when she heard Brajii return, saying, "It is done. Help me carry the girl to the wagon. We must be there before him."

She felt herself being picked up and carried. Her mind raced, looking for a way to escape. She smiled to herself at her sudden confidence. They were clever, these two, but they didn't seem to realize what it meant to capture Dashif's daughter. Soon they would. Soon.

Pitullio studied the message and wondered what to do about it. It had been addressed to Dashif, but it wasn't sealed. Had that been an oversight, or was he meant to see it? Damn, there were too many forces at work. One could hardly tell which plots were one's own anymore. He should simply pass on the message to Dashif, but . . .

It was too clearly a trap. If Dashif wanted to see his daughter alive again, he was to come to the alley behind a tavern called the Catspaw, alone, in less than two hours. Not much time, for one thing. If he, Pitullio, chose wrong, and was responsible for the death of the girl, Dashif would kill him. But if he allowed Dashif to be killed, well, Resh wouldn't like it, and he, Pitullio, would be pretty unhappy, too.

He could show Resh the note, but what would Resh do? Probably ignore it, and have Dashif attend to business. He sighed. He hated making decisions in a hurry.

Finally, with some reluctance, he called in a messenger, gave him a terse message to pass on, and dispatched him. Then he settled back to wait, hoping he'd done the right thing.

Dashif moved through Old Town like a ghost, invisible, yet seeing everything. His agents would receive a tap on the shoulder and see him, answer his questions, and then he'd be gone.

It seemed slow to him, yet only half an hour after he'd arrived in Old Town, Dashif had found where Arenride was carefully searching, interrogating, and checking with his agents. Dashif was in no hurry, in any case. He waited for his opportunity.

Soon he saw Arenride, alone, begin a search through a small, winding street, where most of the houses were empty, and where Dashif knew there was a small cul-de-sac at the end.

He found three city guards in the area, and "requested" that they stand at one end of the street, to make sure no one wandered in. Then he checked the charges on his pistols once more, and began to follow. Arenride would never leave the cul-de-sac alive.

Then he heard his name called, and saw someone he recognized as a messenger of Resh's standing next to the guards, who wouldn't let her past. Dashif signaled to them, and she approached him.

She handed him a note, which he read quickly. "I was lucky to find you," she said. "I was directed by—"

"Quiet," said Dashif, reading the note again. He felt himself trembling. He crumpled it up and started to throw it to the ground, then stuffed it into his pouch instead. "Do you know any details that are not contained in this?"

"No, Count Dashif."

"Very well. That will be all."

"Yes, my Lord."

As he mounted his horse, he dismissed the city guards. He didn't know what was going on, but he knew they wouldn't be needed at the moment. Arenride—yes, and Jolesha, and His Scarlet Eminence—would all wait. His daughter had been kidnapped, and he was needed back at the Palace. Why the Palace, he didn't know; but if someone had done something to endanger his daughter, that someone would die.

5 BLOCKING

Kaloo peered out through her lashes. They had stuck her wide-brimmed sun hat on her head, "to disguise her," she'd heard Brajii say. It served Kaloo now by keeping her eyes in shadow. No one was looking at her. Jolesha was in the back of the cart with her, but she was staring at the sky. Whatever she was imagining was putting lines of tension around her mouth and eyes. Brajii was in front, guiding the mule. She knew by the tops of the buildings that they were still in Old Town. She wished she knew where they were going, but she didn't. The sooner she acted the better.

Dashif had taught her a great deal about the casting of spells and how to approach magic, but few spells of any practicality. She could just jump for it. Do it now, she told herself, up and over the side of the cart, hit the street running and get around the corner—before a yell from Jolesha and a crossbow bolt found her spine. No.

Think, she told herself. They believed she was asleep. Sleep. Perhaps—

She closed her eyes. Felt the fan on its loop of silk resting against her hip. Mentally she touched Jolesha, imagined stroking her temples. *Sleep,* she told her. *Sleep. The afternoon is warm, all is well. You have time to rest. You will awaken later, when it is time. Sleep.*

Nothing. No, it was growing, the spell was working, but she had to have patience. She needed to hurry, but the spell could not be hurried.

Sleep, Jolesha. Sleep. Rest. Close your eyes, the sky is so bright. Let the motion of the cart lull you. All is well, Brajii is taking care of everything, you are tired and you can sleep. The sun is so hot, it is time to sleep. Sleep, Jolesha. Sleep.

Kaloo peeked at her. Yes, her eyes were closed. Kaloo stood up carefully. She needed to make one jump and be gone, Brajii must not even feel a lurch as she left the cart, for the cocked crossbow was on the seat beside her.

Another thought struck her. She turned it over, considered it. Dashif wanted it, that was true. But if it did what she suspected it did, she had her own uses for it.

She didn't hesitate. She lifted the pouch over Jolesha's head, felt a sudden spasm of terror, and let it carry her over the side of the moving cart, out of the street, and between two buildings and down the alley behind them. Around corners and over fences and through one fancy garden, racing like a scalded cat. She never even heard Brajii's shout of anger and alarm.

The southwestern edge of Old Town was just that—an edge. A street called Meadowhill Road curved between Fog Way and Twanith Street and almost intersected Fairday Road several times. Fairday Road was proper residential Liavek. Meadowhill was filled with tall, leaning, grey houses, many of them empty, and all of them looking like they were either haunted or ought to be. The shops mostly didn't have signs.

The dark, bearded pedestrian walked past one of them and was accosted by a man who was probably younger than he looked, who should have quit drinking years before.

"Good sir, might I trouble you for some tobacco?"

Arenride stopped and looked at the derelict. "I don't know you."

"I'm a friend of Whitehair."

"Oh. What is it?"

"Have you spoken to our friend in the last hour?"

"No."

"You had no trouble in Ruckhoe Circle?"

"No. Should I have?"

"Someone who wears red was going to kill you there."

"He didn't."

"That is true. Whitehair tried to reach you, but I guess he didn't make it in time, or it proved unnecessary."

"What do you know?"

"That the one who wears red came by here, not long ago, on a white horse. He was in a hurry."

"Back toward the Palace?"

"Yes."

"I see. Anything else?"

"I didn't see this myself, but two people have been scurrying around here, searching for something or someone, in very obvious ways. One is young and pretty; I don't know her. The other had red hair, used to wear green, and I think she had a crossbow hidden under her cloak."

Arenride paused, considering. Dashif returning to the Palace, Brajii looking for someone—who?—with someone else—Jolesha? This was the second indication he had come across that the two of them had teamed up. Was it true? If so, why?

He paid the derelict and said, "Keep an eye out for them, and stay in touch with Whitehair. And my compliments on your disguise—you smell like offal."

"Thank you, Master Arenride."

"Who . . . ?"

"Can you hear me?"

"Who . . . ?"

"My name is Kaloo, I'm—"

"Who . . . am . . . I?"

"I don't—that is, Erina?"

" . . . "

"Erina."

"Yes. I was drifting. So peaceful. I am Erina. Who are you?"

"I think—I think I'm your daughter."

"Daughter."

"I am Count Dashif's daughter."

"Dashif. Tori."

"I—"

"Yes. Kaloo?"

"That's what they called me. Do you—"

"A pretty name. Kaloo. T'Nar always liked birds."

"What should I—"

"Are you happy, Kaloo?"

"Not really. I'm too confused."

"It will pass. Take care of your father, Kaloo. He's been confused, too. He needs to be happy again."

"What happened to you?"

"All in the past, my sweet Kaloo. You have a beautiful presence, here. Who has raised you?"

"Her name is Daril."

"Daril."

"But then Dashif found me again, he has been seeing me."

"Does Daril love you?"

". . . Yes. Yes, I supposed she does, Mother."

"No. Don't call me that. The woman who raised you is your mother."

"But—"

"You were conceived out of love, Kaloo. Daril raised you in love. Your father found you again to find love. Remember that."

"But—"

"I must go now. This is difficult."

"I—Erina? Are you there?"

"My Lord, wait!"

Dashif reined in his horse, and looked for the source of the call. It was the cab runner. There were people around. For the runner to be calling to him openly, it must be important. Dashif dismounted as the runner approached. Pedestrians looked at him and gave the pair of them a wide berth.

"You are looking for the little girl."

"I have a message—"

"From Pitullio."

"Yes. What of it?"

"He didn't give you all the information he had."

Several competing questions, all of them urgent, flashed through Dashif's mind. He settled on, "Why not?"

The runner worked his lips, then. "The man who cleans around His Scarlet Eminence's offices—"

"Bilthor, yes."

"He works for you."

"I know that."

"He found the message in your chambers, after having heard Pitullio give the message you were brought."

"Why wasn't I given all the details?"

"It was a trap, Count Dashif."

"Of course it was. So? Have you the actual details?"

"Yes, Count Dashif. You are to go, alone, to the alley behind the Catspaw tavern in order to get the girl back. You are to be there in an hour. My Lord, it is clearly an ambush."

"Yes. Anything more?"

"My Lord, everyone has been running around today like I've never seen. Arenride is out, and his people are looking for someone. We are looking for the girl, Jolesha, and, well, it is all very confusing. Things are happening that I don't understand, my Lord, and I suspect that things have gone wrong for everyone involved, until there is little but confusion left."

Dashif nodded. "Yes. I think you're right. All right, I don't suppose you ought to let the Eminent Pitullio know you've told me this. I'm going to go spring this trap, if it is one. After that, if I'm able, I'll return to the Palace."

"Yes, my Lord. Good luck to you."

Dashif mounted his horse again, muttering, too low for the runner to hear, that he had none, so skill would have to take its place.

Kaloo put the strange cylindrical object back in its pouch, and the pouch around her neck, then she held herself very still. She didn't want to think about what any of this meant. Everything she had believed in was now questionable. No one was behaving as he ought, everyone was saying unpredictable things, and there were people out there who had kidnapped her, and—

And she realized, suddenly, who she trusted in all of this. There was only one person with the strength to protect her, who *wanted* to protect her.

It was a hot midday in Heat. There were crowds to move through. Kaloo began to make her way to Levar's Palace, to Dashif's private entrance.

It took Dashif twenty minutes to determine that not only was there no ambush set up behind the Catspaw, but no one was there to meet him at all. This could mean many things. Any of a number of people could have lied to him, and any of a number of people could have been wrong, and any of a number of people could have changed their plans.

All he knew with certainty was that he wanted his daughter out of danger. That meant finding her, and he had no idea where to look.

He mounted his horse again, considering. Well, for lack of a better idea, perhaps he should return to the Palace and have things out with Pitullio. Or he could wait here. He was early, and it was possible those who had taken his daughter were foolish enough not to arrive early to kill him.

Then it occurred to him that his daughter was a magician. She *could* have escaped, and, if so, where would she have gone except to see him? If this had happened, she could walk into an ambush intended for him.

He dug his heels into his horse's flanks.

"I would never have recognized you," said Arenride. He had found them because someone in his employ had identified Brajii.

Jolesha stared pitiably up at him, trying to make sense of the relief on Arenride's face. Next to her, Brajii stood motionless, in the shadows of a tall deserted house on Meadowhill Road. Jolesha had drawn strength from the woman, but Brajii had accepted the blame for Kaloo's escape, and for the loss of the Gate: after all, had she not hatched the scheme to kill Dashif, Jolesha would still have had possession of it.

As the silence dragged on uncomfortably, Jolesha said, "Arenride, I've lost The Gate."

"The artifact?"

"Yes. Yes, it was stolen."

"We must get it back." He said it lightly, as if such things could be found anywhere. "Do you have any idea how lovely you are, without that hideous guise you wear?"

She lowered her head. "I'm not." No one had ever said that to her.

"Well, now. Do we have any idea at all what happened to it?"

"The girl has it. Kaloo."

"Who?"

"Dashif's daughter."

Arenride's eyes grew wide. "Dashif has a daughter?" He looked accusingly at Brajii, who looked away. "It seems there are things my ally neglected to tell me."

Jolesha said, "I thought the only way to be safe would be to . . . Well, we were going to kill Dashif. We kidnapped his daughter to bring him into a trap—"

Arenride began to laugh. "Everybody wants to kill the poor fellow."

There was a hiss of indrawn breath from Brajii. She said, "I do, for one."

"I know that," Arenride replied darkly.

"And your people were willing to give me a chance before."

"Not 'my people' in the sense you mean, but there you and I choose different ways to define our lives and our living. In any case, it was a chance you couldn't take advantage of, though you had ample opportunity."

"Something protects him."

"Yes," Arenride agreed. "It's called 'skill.'"

"No, there is more."

"I doubt that."

"Four times now—"

"I know, Brajii, all too well. But never mind. You wish another chance? Fine. I think that one more chance can be arranged, because we must retrieve that artifact."

"We can't find the girl."

"Where does she live?"

"She won't go back there," said Brajii. "It was near there that we took her."

"Then, where else?"

"I don't know. I don't know her well enough to know where she'd feel safe. But we have arranged for Dashif to meet us behind the Catspaw in half an hour. We can still be there, without his daughter, and—"

"And die," said Arenride. "He will be there already, waiting for you."

Brajii sighed, and for a moment she looked as if she would cry. "Of course. I know. We had intended to be there long ago," she said. "Now I don't know what to do. I'm not made for complexities. My skills are stealth and aim and reflex."

Arenride smiled. "I can think of one place she might go. To her father's."

Jolesha stared bitterly at Brajii, who took the weight of that glare as fit punishment. "If so," she said, "we are defeated."

"Not at all," said Arenride. "If Dashif is out waiting for your ambush, we can, perhaps, be at the Palace before him."

"What, in his chambers?" said Jolesha.

"Where better to catch him off guard? I've never done this, because it's the sort of option one uses only once, but I think circumstances justify the risk."

"Give me a chance at him," said Brajii. "Please."

"Happily," said Arenride. Shouldering his blunderbuss, he said, "Come, then, to the Levar's Palace." And he offered Jolesha his arm. It was not at all in keeping with the mood or the business at hand, yet somehow, she felt, it was right.

6 THE ACT

There were four guards at the main gate. One was a woman with very dark, very short hair who always smiled at Kaloo when she came with Dashif. The guard smiled even though Dashif wasn't with her, and Kaloo made her way around to the side and into his—her father's—private entrance. She unlocked the door with the key he'd given her months before, stepped inside, and fumbled with the lock for a while in the darkness of the stairwell before succeeding in locking the door behind her. She had no idea how many hidden observers might have watched her enter.

Climbing the long, narrow stairs was, somehow, different from when Dashif was with her—even more lonely, and frightening. She opened the door into his front room and didn't know if she was relieved or disappointed to find it empty. Hesitantly, she checked his bedchamber, and then the kitchen, but they were empty, too.

She clenched her hands, still frightened, then sat on the edge of a chair to wait for him. She noticed again how empty the room was, with nothing to look at except the portrait of herself, done months ago. She began to understand why he wanted it.

The minutes crawled on. What good had escaping done? She had no way of knowing where he was, no way of reaching him. He might have run his head into the noose anyway. Right now, this minute, he could be dead, could be bleeding in an alley, and she probably wouldn't even know it for hours.

Dead. She fingered the leather thong that held the pouch around her neck, and her thoughts returned once more to the woman who was—had been—her mother. What had passed between the two of them, Erina and Dashif? Dashif never spoke of it, T'Nar wouldn't. And Erina was, well, odd.

There was a thing Kaloo knew for certain, however: She was very glad that the strange cylindrical object had fallen into her hands. It was her connection to her ancestry in a way that Dashif could never be. Given time, she would understand all of it, who she was, why she had been raised in such strange circumstances. She wasn't going to part with it before then.

The door opened. Her head jerked up. For an instant, she saw him before he saw her. He was not guarding his thoughts. Something in his face brought Erina's words to her mind: *He needs to be happy again*. She was on her feet and moving, trying not to think about what she was doing or if it betrayed anyone. She wouldn't look at the astonishment on his face as she put her arms around him. For a second, all she could sense were the contrasts; his leanness compared to T'Nar's bulk, the immaculate white ruffles that folded under her cheek and smelled of sweet closet herbs instead of T'Nar's rough shirt and smell of oakum and pitch, the cautious way his hands settled on her shoulders instead of T'Nar's fierce hug. Then she recognized the thing that was the same. There was safety here, yes, and love. She thought of the shattered bottle that had been patiently drawn back together. Her love and her luck touched broken pieces, tried to sense the unity that should have been and draw them back together. Not yet, she knew, but in time she could do it. With patience. Carefully she tried the word upon her tongue, whispering it into the ruffles of his shirt, not yet ready for him to hear her say it aloud.

Dashif felt tears come to his eyes. "I thought you were taken," he said.

"I escaped," Kaloo said, her voice only a whisper.

He nodded. "I'm sorry you became involved in these things. It won't happen again." Well said, Dashif, he told himself. But how are you going to ensure that? He considered the matter while he sent someone to tell Pitullio that he was back.

She said, "Could they come after me here?"

Dashif shrugged. "I can't see why they would."

"I . . . I stole something from one of them."

"Oh? What?"

Trembling, she held up the leather pouch that she'd hung around her neck. "It is a thing that lets you talk with—"

Dashif, recovering from amazement, threw his head back and laughed. "Of all the—my dear, you are certainly my daughter. That little pouch contains exactly what everyone in Liavek and his troll are looking for. May I have it?"

"No!" said Kaloo.

Dashif frowned, and considered. "My dear, I don't think you know what you have there."

"I spoke to my mother," she said.

Dashif licked his lips. "Oh."

"I don't want to give it up."

Dashif sighed. "I won't take it from you, Kaloo. I promise. But you can't keep it. You'll have to see that. It is why people are following—"

He was interrupted by a knock at the door, which turned out to be a messenger announcing that His Scarlet Eminence would be pleased to see him at once. Dashif looked at Kaloo and frowned. He didn't like the idea of leaving Kaloo alone again—not even in the safety of his rooms.

"Come along, Kaloo. There are some people you should meet. We'll resolve this by and by."

"All right, Father," she said, and he stared at her, a lump in his throat and, yes, even a tear in his eye. Without another word, he led her toward the offices of His Scarlet Eminence.

Jolesha, behind the other two, glanced at every doorway, every window, every ledge as they approached Dashif's private entrance. This was a mad thing they were doing. At the small doorway, Brajii turned to her and said, "Stand back. We're going to have to break it down."

"Why?" Jolesha asked. Glad to do something other than fret, she stepped past them and studied the lock. It looked, from the keyhole, like a simple mechanism; she wouldn't even need special tools. Crouching, she borrowed one of Brajii's finer crossbow bolts and used the tip to wedge back the tumblers. Arenride offered her a small dagger no larger than his little finger, and with it she tricked the lock. All in all, it was distressingly easy and she said as much.

"The door isn't the danger," Arenride said. "We're under surveillance right now. My presence will confuse them, but that won't last long." He shrugged then, and unslung his wheel lock blunderbuss. Brajii, on the step below him, had her crossbow cocked and ready. Arenride pushed the door open.

They froze there for a moment, until Jolesha was ready to scream from frustration at not knowing what they saw. Then Arenride said, "It's empty. We were wrong."

"No," said Brajii, and led the way forward. Jolesha entered the room behind the other two, frightened, but reassured by their presence. It was as stark as a room at the Sri'dezj Inn in Ka Zhir. Brajii walked in and picked up a white sun hat from a chair. Jolesha recognized it at once as the one Kaloo had been wearing.

"She's here," said Brajii. Arenride nodded and carefully checked the adjoining rooms.

"What now," asked Jolesha.

Arenride stood next to a door and said, "This leads to a hallway, with a pair of guards stationed at the far end. Beyond them is another pair of guards. Beyond them are the offices of His Scarlet Eminence and his secretary. I suspect we'll find who we're looking for there. There are no other guards on duty within two-minutes' run of this area. We should be done with whatever we're going to do by the time they get here." He caught Brajii's eye. Jolesha trembled.

"Now," said Brajii, "you'll see that I can use this thing." She hefted her crossbow. Arenride wound the mechanism of his blunderbuss and put his left hand on the doorknob.

Pitullio studied Dashif and the girl, and smiled just a little. "I take it she's here for a reason, Count Dashif."

"You are correct," said Dashif. Pitullio nodded, walked over to Resh's door and called through it, "Your Eminence, Count Dashif is here."

"Very well," said the Regent from the other side. "Come

in, Dashif, and you, too, Pitullio." Pitullio opened the door, stepped through it, and stood aside. Resh, who seemed to be playing with model ships on a map but wasn't, nodded to him and said, "Very well, now—who is this, Dashif?"

Dashif looked down at Kaloo and smiled. He'd always enjoyed moments of drama, thought Pitullio. "Your Eminence, I'd like you to meet Kaloo, my daughter."

Resh stared at Dashif, and at the girl. His jaw worked. He said, "What is her connection to this affair?"

Dashif shrugged and said, "She is my daughter," as if that explained everything.

"Why is she here?"

"She was kidnapped by our enemies. They had hoped to kill me, using her as a lure."

Resh shrugged. "Very well. A pleasure, Kaloo. Now, Dashif, get her out of here. We need to resolve—"

"Our enemies have most likely followed her. I'll not leave her unprotected until she is safe." He smiled. "Besides, she has something you want."

"Indeed?"

"Yes. A certain pouch containing a certain artifact that—"

"*She* has it."

"Quite."

Pitullio stifled the laughter that came to his throat. "Well done, Dashif," he said under his breath.

Resh turned to the girl. Pitullio was surprised at the intensity of the Regent's stare. *He must be even more worried about it than he'd let on.*

"Give it to me," said Resh.

The girl shook her head and looked up at Dashif, as if for protection. Dashif sighed. "Kaloo, you must understand—"

"Forget the explanations," said Resh. "I want that thing. Dashif, take it from her."

The girl moved away from Dashif, until she was in a corner of the office, with the desk between her and Resh, and Dashif between her and Pitullio, who stood in the doorway.

"I think," said Dashif, "that she'll be willing to give it to us once we explain—"

"Girl," said the Regent, "I want that—"

Which was as far as he got before he was interrupted by shots, screams, and yells from outside. Dashif raised his eyebrows, Pitullio wished he had a weapon handy. "We're being invaded, it seems," said Dashif coolly.

Resh looked as if he were about to choke. He reached into his desk and drew out a large, ungainly wheellock pistol that, as far as Pitullio knew, he'd never used. But he seemed prepared to use it now. Dashif nodded, took his own pistols into his hands, and said, "I suggest, Pitullio, that you also find yourself a weap—"

Then he stopped, staring. The pistol in the Regent's hand was pointed at the child. "Give me the artifact, girl," said Resh. "Now."

The four of them stood there, frozen. Pitullio looking at Resh, Resh looking at Kaloo, Dashif looking at the pistol, Kaloo looking at Dashif.

Then the scuffling sounds became louder and closer, and Pitullio moved away from the door. Dashif turned his head toward the door as Arenride burst into Resh's office, a blunderbuss in his hands, followed immediately by a tall woman holding a cocked and loaded crossbow.

All Dashif could see were the blunderbuss and the crossbow swinging to point at him, to kill him. All he could think about was the pistol pointed at his daughter's head.

What had kept Dashif alive for all these years, as much as anything else, was the ability to think and act rationally when the moment for action came. He still had that ability. He knew, since he knew how fast he was, and had had the flintlocks on his pistols specially altered, that he had time to cock and aim both pistols before any weapon was discharged at him.

There was, in the strange half-world of split seconds, plenty of time to decide on precisely where he wanted each of his four bullets to strike. That he had to divide his attention and aim was no trouble to him, for he was a marksman. He knew precisely which targets he wanted, and why. Before anyone else in the room could do anything, then, he was able to bring both of his pistols to bear.

The thunder of his weapons filled the small room. The roar and echoes overwhelmed the sound of the crossbow spring releasing its bolt; the explosion as Arenride's blunderbuss fired seemed only to stretch the first blast into an endless reverberation. Somewhere nearby, Palace guards came running.

It didn't matter.

When it comes right down to it, a body is a body.

The most important characteristics of a person are those things that make him unique, interesting, and worth whatever special attention he merits from friends, enemies, lovers, and business acquaintances. But the things that make a corpse unique, interesting, and worth special attention matter to no one but embalmers.

And the transformation of a human being from one state to the other happens so quickly that the human mind can no more conceive of that space of time than it can truly conceive of the state of non-life.

Three bodies lie on the floor, each having found its own unique position from which to approach rigor mortis. There is little of interest there; let us turn to the living.

He stood motionless, unwilling to make the effort to understand what had just happened. He found himself staring hardest at the body of the woman with the crossbow, and wondered why, since he didn't know her. He licked his lips, shook his head, and, just in case it still mattered, moved over behind the desk to pick up the wheellock from the fingers of the corpse that had been the Regent. It made him feel better to hold the weapon. Then, only half-conscious of his actions, Pitullio moved around to where Dashif's daughter stood crying.

Jolesha looked from body to body to body. She saw the tall man step around the bolt embedded in the floor and take the unfired wheellock. She turned to Arenride and said, "I don't understand why he killed the Regent instead of you. I thought he—"

"Shhh," said Arenride. "Not now."

Jolesha watched as the tall man put his arm around Kaloo, who began sobbing into his chest. He spoke to her in whispers, then carefully removed a familiar pouch from her neck. He tossed it to Jolesha, who held it to herself and avoided looking down at Brajii, who had an ugly pair of holes in her forehead.

Arenride put his arms around her.

"I'll take you home," said Pitullio.

"My father—"

"I know, sweetheart." He was surprised at how close he was to crying tears he hadn't cried in thirty years. He wondered who they were for.

Six guards arrived, and stopped as they saw the bodies, as unsure as anyone else how to react. Pitullio straightened up suddenly and spoke to them, while pointing to Arenride and Jolesha. "These people need to see Her Magnificence, the Levar. Escort them. This girl is under my care. I'll take her home. See to transportation, one of you." He looked around and muttered, "I have no idea who's going to see to the future of Liavek."

He saw that Jolesha and Arenride were walking off, hand in hand and he thought that was good. He put his arms once more around Kaloo, who was still crying. All things considered, that was probably good, too.

7 THE CURTAIN CALL

She lifted her eyes from the red-edged documents stacked on the stained tabletop. "Is there a polite way to say I don't want it?"

Pitullio's brows gathered into a knot. "I beg your pardon?"

T'Nar's chair, which had been tipped on its back legs against the wall by the tavern's hearth, came down with a crash. The old sailor stood up. "She said she don't want it," he interpreted crankily. "You deaf or something?"

"T'Nar," Kaloo said gently. "I think this is something I have to handle myself."

"Then do it," he growled. "We're wasting a good tide. Tides and fish don't wait for you, doesn't matter if you're a Countess or a fisherman's brat. And Daril will sink us both if we're not back by evening with something fresh for the pot, and on time to help with the dinner rush. Don't leave much time for fishing."

"So go along, then. I'll meet you on the docks when we're done."

T'Nar growled something that might have been an assent and left the tavern noisily. Kaloo turned back to Pitullio. The man looked disoriented. She pitied him.

He cleared his throat, tapped the edges of the papers until they were even. "Count Dashif wanted you to inherit. It's not just the title, uh, Kaloo. There is land, and money, and certain other holdings. He chose you as his heir; he wanted you to have these things."

Kaloo was silent. The things he had left her meant nothing. The things she wanted most from him had gone with him when he died. So much she would never know, so much she would never say to him. She didn't need his land, or his title, or even his name. She'd had a little of his time, and a bit of his teaching, the chance to call him father. That was her share of the inheritance, the only share she wanted to keep. She wondered if Pitullio would understand that, decided not to even try. "He had other . . . children, didn't he?"

Pitullio smiled. The quality of the smile made her feel like His Scarlet Eminence must once have felt. This man could arrange anything to his liking. "The will is very clear. They will contest it, of course, and his, uh, wife will challenge it, but I have every confidence that—"

Kaloo was shaking her head. "No. The last thing I want now is some kind of legal scandal."

Pitullio pursed his lips. "It could be handled . . . discreetly. They could be made to understand there is more they could lose than the money. There is a certain man your father occasionally used for such . . ."

"No. Those . . . people have been raised to expect they would inherit what he left. Let them have it. I don't want any kind of a stir about this. They don't even need to know I exist," she added firmly. The man looked devastated. She reached across the table to pat his hand. "Count Dashif left me . . . other things. You don't need to feel you failed him."

Kaloo rose, signalling the discussion had ended. "And now I have to go, but you're more than welcome to stay, and have a mug of cold beer and a bowl of the Mug and Anchor pot-boil, if you wish. It's quite popular, here on the waterfront."

"You're going fishing?" Pitullio asked stupidly. Count Dashif's daughter was turning her back on a fortune, and going fishing. Liavek was headed for strange times indeed.

"Not really," Kaloo laughed. "We'll drop our hooks in the water, and then he'll tell me what a fool T'Fregan is for not buying that boat." She turned aside and called toward the kitchen door, "Daril, I'm leaving! But we'll be back before the dinner rush, and the fish will be fresh!"

Pitullio felt the conversation was leaving him behind. "It's a good boat, I take it?" he fumbled.

Kaloo nodded. "A very good boat, at a very good price. It's driving T'Nar crazy that he can't buy it for himself. And he's determined the rest of us will go along with him! Good day, Pitullio. And thank you for understanding."

So saying, she scooped up a greasy leather fishing pack and was gone. Pitullio slowly gathered his papers. It was not, he admitted to himself, as if he and Dashif had been what one would call friends. And now Dashif was gone, and Resh, too, and it looked as if his chance to be administrator for the Countess Dashif had just gone fishing. He'd be wise to find himself a new niche immediately, and give no more thought to unwilling heirs.

But . . . he weighed the papers in his hand. So easy to divert just a little of this. No more than a trickle, just a few of Dashif's enterprises that his heirs would know nothing of, and wouldn't have been interested in anyway. A brothel or two, maybe the money-changing stall in the Market, nothing major. Just enough to let him retire comfortably on his share, and still accomplish some of Dashif's intentions. The possibilities began to intrigue him. A bribe in the right place to keep the taxes on the Mug and Anchor down, a wealthy patron who would buy that boat and want to put an experienced captain in charge of it. Perhaps one of the better people on Wizard's Row would be seized with a sudden desire to give a likely newcomer some special instruction. Yes. It could be done.

Pitullio caught himself grinning as he pushed open the doors of the Mug and Anchor. Amazing. He'd never thought of applying his talents in this direction; he had a feeling it was going to be more interesting than anything he'd done before.

It has always been said in Liavek that to change a boat's name is to change her luck, and luck is a tricky thing to tamper with. But *The Dashforth* seemed to take on a new life with her new name, and only the best of luck with it. She was something of a legend even when the old captain was sailing her, but when his daughter took her over, she set speed records for the trading routes that weren't equalled by a ship of her size until steam came to the Sea of Luck.

The Dashforth was passed down for three generations, but always her sails were red and white, and a white stallion was her name flag. Some said it was wizardry that filled her sails with wind and her holds with a richer cargo than fish, but old captains will tell you, no, it was skill, which is all a sailor can ever rely on anyway. When she was too old for the trading runs anymore, a younger son took her adventuring, off beyond the Farlands, and no more is known of her than that. Some will tell you they've seen her, on the horizon off Minnow Island when the sun sets bloody and turns the waves to red, but the sailors of Liavek, like sailors anywhere, are a superstitious lot. They'd like to believe that boats, if not fisherfolk, can live forever.